RHEA, Nicholas

NORT

golden trough

The Curse of the Golden Trough

THE CURSE
OF THE
GOLDEN TROUGH

Nicholas Rhea

Constable • London

First published in Great Britain 2004
by Constable, an imprint of Constable & Robinson Ltd
3 The Lanchesters, 162 Fulham Palace Road
London W6 9ER
www.constablerobinson.com

ISBN 1–84119–876–5

Printed and bound in Great Britain

A CIP catalogue record for this book
is available from the British Library

Chapter One

Detective Inspector Montague Pluke was in the extra-ordinary Piazza del Campo in Siena. He felt very humbled by the experience, being just one insignificant person in the midst of a happy multitude enjoying this masterpiece of medieval Italian architecture. All around was the incessant murmur of countless international voices. They mingled to fill the air with a continuous amplified babble which echoed from the surrounding high and ancient buildings. It sounded like the buzz of millions of honey bees around millions of hives, yet it was a cheerful buzz, not the sound of threats or of impending social discord. It was the hum of complete happiness, contentment and international accord.

In Pluke's opinion, the ever-present noise was itself as impressive as this atmospheric setting. Thousands of people were wandering around in awe or merely sitting on the floor of sienna brown bricks which formed the sloping shell-shaped base of this world-renowned piazza. Many did not seem to want to move away; they were content merely to sit, chat and admire without any thought of the passing time. They wanted to slowly absorb the atmosphere which was preserved in the centuries-old features around them.

Several buildings were former medieval palaces. When they had been built, their windows had to match those of the even older Palazzo del Comune or Palazzo Pubblico, now called the Town Hall, which stands impressively at the foot of the piazza. Every building is the same colour, the distinctive and very warm sienna brown. That blending of buildings was one of the rules of the ancient city – in addition, there had to be no gaudy shop fronts or awnings, no colourful houses or cafés, although in recent years some brighter colours had sneaked in. Awnings on shops and restaurants should be sienna brown while the floor of the piazza and the encircling buildings are of that same warm colour – the overall effect is one of cheerful calm. It is not surprising that visitors find themselves so relaxed in this magical place.

In the piazza, a group of energetic small boys played football under the tuition of a diminutive nun; young children chased one other through the crowds; courting couples sat or lay on the ground enjoying a *gelato*, the local ice cream; outdoor restaurants and cafés beneath regulation sienna-coloured awnings were busy dispensing drinks and food while tourists of all ages, sizes, shapes and colours were taking photographs or just sitting quietly to absorb the atmosphere. There was so much to see and record – the open air theatre-shaped slope of the piazza itself with its incredible floor; the Town Hall with its tall and slender tower called the Torre del Mangia; the palaces of Sansedoni, Chigi-Zondadari and Piccolomini; the heights of the white marble cathedral peeping above the nearest buildings; and the Gaia Fountain with flowing waters, marble statues and ever-present pigeons.

In spite of the crowds today and every other day, there was not a spot of litter, and for all the youthfulness of many visitors, there were no signs of tension, no feelings of uncertainty as to whether or not a fight might break out. There were no drunks and no yobs, no stupidity or loud showing off. Just decent contented people from around the world enjoying themselves.

That prevailing aura of peace and contentment, however, was in direct contrast to this piazza's most famous events – the two bare-back horse races, each known as the

Palio. The races were centuries old. Ten horses with riders representing districts around Siena raced around the extremities of the piazza to the roar of the crowds who were packed like sardines in the sloping centre. For centuries, the horses had raced both for the honour of their contrada or ward and for the famous prize – a painted silk banner called the Palio.

Pluke knew the horses would be very thirsty indeed after each race – and after the hours of rehearsal and ceremonial which preceded it. And yet, in spite of its ancient and powerful association with horses, the piazza did not contain a single horse trough. There was only the Gaia Fountain, not the most accessible of places for thirsty horses with its high walls and barrier of spiked metal railings. Pluke found this rather disturbing – after all, horses had to drink, more so in such a warm climate and especially after a gruelling race. As if to remind him of the heat endured by the horses, the June sunshine was beating down upon his panama and highlighting his heavy black and yellow overcoat, a coat which would defy blizzards and frosts in Yorkshire and which seemed so out of place here.

His devoted wife, Millicent, stood at his side in more summery holiday clothes, a light short-sleeved pink blouse and pale blue skirt, with a wide-brimmed hat to ward off the sun and light sandals to give comfort to her feet. On a three-day trip to Italy, they were standing very close to the Gaia Fountain where pigeons adopted all manner of gymnastic postures as they tried to drink the waters which poured from the many carved outlets. They wanted to drink but did not like getting their feet wet and at times looked at risk of falling into the deeper parts. None did, however, for these pigeons were agile, careful and very experienced.

'According to a legend surrounding the earliest days of the Palio,' Pluke informed Millicent, 'the Golden Horse Trough was donated as a prize for the winner of the race, and by that I mean the horse itself, not its rider. The winning rider gets the Palio – that is a pennant bearing a picture of the Virgin Mary – but this award was for the victorious horse. It won the right to drink from the golden trough for the rest of its life. The award was in recognition that the horses themselves were very important. You see, Millicent, unlike English racehorses, those in the Palio could – and still can – win the race even if the rider falls off.'

Pluke had carefully researched his subject before leaving England.

'Fancy that,' said Millicent.

Pluke continued, 'The site of the golden trough was thought to have been very close to this fountain or indeed it might have been positioned at this very place. It might have stood exactly where this fountain now stands.'

'Fancy that,' cooed Millicent once more.

'In fact,' said Montague, now in full flow, 'if you examine the shape of this fountain, looking at the part which holds the water and ignoring the statues around it, it is nothing more than a gigantic horse trough. I do appreciate, however, that it is not very practical from the point of view of a horse wanting a drink, those iron railings and high walls would stop the most determined of thirsty horses.'

'It looks more like a swimming pool to me,' said Millicent sweetly. 'Perhaps the railings are to prevent people from jumping in for a swim?'

'It is a very ancient and famous fountain!' he retorted as he patted its marble walls. 'This is not a swimming pool, Millicent, and most certainly not a paddling pool or a goldfish pond.'

'Fancy!' smiled Millicent once more.

'This fountain was constructed between 1400 and 1419 by one of Siena's most important sculptors and it is supplied by an aqueduct which was built as long ago as 1344,' pronounced Pluke with some authority. 'The local people knew how to tap into underground water supplies; lots of minor waterways had, over centuries, found their way through the subterranean clay and the people were able to divert those channels into numerous fountains and private wells via a network of underground tunnels. That means that if the Golden Horse Trough occupied this site prior to the fountain's construction, it must have had one of those water sources to fill it. That was very important.'

'Or it could have been filled by people with buckets?' smiled Millicent.

'Many a true word is spoken in jest,' countered Pluke. 'But I doubt if such an important architectural feature would rely on people with buckets. I am sure it would draw its water from an inexhaustible underground source or from the aqueduct, a water source that might now be used to fill this very fountain. Unfortunately. though, in 1348 the Black Plague broke out with a vengeance and killed more than half the population of Siena. It was around that time – perhaps in the years that followed – that the golden trough disappeared. As an English detective of long experience, I suspect some person, or persons, obviously with the ability to transport such a large object, crept into the piazza at night and stole the famous trough while the residents remained indoors in fear of the plague. It has never been seen since and nothing further is known about it. It has, to all intents and purposes, vanished from the face of the earth. And I would like to find it.'

'That was more than six hundred and fifty years ago.' Millicent had made a swift mental calculation. 'There's not much chance of you finding it then, is there?'

'Trough lovers around the world would dearly love to find the Golden Horse Trough. Many have been searching ever since it disappeared,' said Pluke. 'Finding it would be akin to tracing the Holy Grail or the Ark of the Covenant. That had a gold lid, you know, the Ark I mean, and the rest of it was made of wood covered with gold. Just like those searchers of the lost Ark and the Holy Grail down the centuries, many have searched for the golden trough, but none has been successful.'

'Well, so long as you don't work too hard at it, Montague,' she smiled.

'As we are in Italy, in Siena itself, I do feel it is my responsibility to undertake at least a modest search. As an authority on horse troughs, *the* English expert no less even though I say it myself, I feel obliged to do something, to take some kind of positive action, however slight, with a view to tracing the golden trough. That will be my contribution to the worldwide hunt. After all, it is the most famous horse trough in history and this is where it used to stand.'

'If that's what you really want,' sighed Millicent.

'To find it, or to learn of its fate, would be a wonderful climax to my career,' he beamed. 'You realize there has not been a single authenticated sighting since 1348, not anywhere in the world. Imagine that! There have been false alarms, of course, confidence tricksters claiming to have found it in the desert, in Rome or in Greece, but all were fakes. I intend to find the genuine trough – and just suppose I achieved that? What a climax to my career! Consider the importance of such a success, Millicent. My name will go down in history.'

'Amazing,' she agreed.

'Truly amazing,' he nodded. 'Now, there is every reason to believe it may be hidden, perhaps unrecognized for what it really is. It might be lying in wait for the right person to come along and return it to its former glory. And I, as an English detective, can put my skills to good use in tracing it. And I have my rabbit's foot with me – that will ensure I enjoy the very best of fortune in my quest.'

'Perhaps the Nazis stole it during the war?' she suggested. 'They did plunder art treasures from all sorts of places in Europe.'

'Nothing is impossible, Millicent, but it vanished long before any of the modern world wars and it is most

10

definitely not the sort of thing that would turn up in a car boot sale. It is probably even now being used as a horse trough in some remote Italian village or on a farm, blackened with age and unrecognizable. It could be anywhere, Millicent my dear, anywhere at all. Anywhere in the world in fact, not necessarily in Italy. In a museum, art gallery, built into the wall of a monastery or palace or house, in use as an ornamental trough in some civic centre, buried below ground, placed on the side of a road for the use of passing horse traffic or even used in a garden as a container for flowers. Its fate could be anything anywhere, Millicent.'

'Or it might have been smashed into tiny pieces, Montague, six hundred years ago or more, and used to make roads or even a garden path.'

'No one would do that to the Golden Horse Trough! This was a treasure, a famous item, a true work of art, renowned throughout the world. *The* Golden Horse Trough, you must realize, almost certainly the only one in the world, a treasure beyond compare.'

'Yes, but golden does not necessarily mean it was made of gold,' she reminded him. 'There are paintings in these Siena churches showing angels with golden halos and so forth. Very clever gilt work, Montague. If artists or craftspeople could paint those sort of things to make them look like gold, they could paint the trough to look like gold too. Dress it in gold leaf, or something that looked like gold leaf. I doubt if it would be solid gold. You'd hardly expect a horse trough to be solid gold.'

'Well, the legend is not very clear on that, I must admit.' He smiled thinly. 'But the stories which have survived all suggest it was made of gold. It has always been known as the Golden Horse Trough, Millicent, always.'

'They were stories, Montague, legends no less. Not facts of history. I appreciate it is known everywhere as the Golden Horse Trough, but you must not rely on its name as proof of the material from which it is made. You must be very careful about all this, and not get carried away by your enthusiasm. You must understand that golden things are not necessarily manufactured from gold. Gold dust is not the same as golden dust, Montague, and a golden eagle is not a gold eagle. The distinction is very important, surely? I think it means the trough might not be so important or indeed as valuable as people have been led to believe.'

'Not important?' he almost shouted at her. This was near-heresy she was preaching. 'Of course it's important, it's the most important horse trough in the world, and I use the present tense quite deliberately. I cannot believe it has disappeared without trace; it must have survived and is probably hidden somewhere, either deliberately or more probably without the current owner's knowledge of its provenance.'

'I am not disputing that, Montague,' she smiled sweetly. 'I am just saying it might not be made of gold.'

'Well, we can agree to differ on that point. Now, Millicent, consider the question of this fountain. Consider the likelihood that the golden trough could be buried beneath it, almost below our feet as we speak. Is there any evidence to suggest the truth of that speculation? I think there is. The bricks which form the paving of the piazza were laid in herring-bone in 1347. They have been here ever since. That work was done just one year before the plague. We know there was a water supply before 1347 which adds to the possibility that the golden trough was actually in position whilst the bricks were being laid. There is no sign of the trough's presence in any other part of the piazza so I believe its original site cannot be in doubt, Millicent. Close to a water source, near the fountain. If records were kept or plans drawn before the piazza's construction, then the trough will feature in those records, or in drawings and paintings of that period of Siena's history. It was a very important period, you see, and the trough must have been an integral part of Siena's civic history.'

'Yes, but you can't get away from the fact that it has

12

disappeared completely, Montague. If it is buried under this fountain, you'll never find it. You should accept that and let the matter rest instead of worrying about such an ancient piece of foreign history. You are not at work, remember, we are on holiday and I have no wish to spend my days in Tuscany searching for an ancient and legendary horse trough which probably didn't exist anyway, and certainly doesn't now. It's a legend, Montague, you said so yourself. A very old legend too.'

'But we can conduct a subtle search during our tours of the art galleries and museums,' he said. 'If that trough stood where I think it stood, and if it was as important as I think it was, then artists of the time must surely have included it in their paintings of this piazza. It must also feature in the official records of the town's history. I know the Town Hall is full of paintings, it includes a museum, and there is also the chapel at the base of the Torre del Mangia, that's the tower which was built by the people of Siena in 1352 in gratitude for their escape from the plague. The whole of the Town Hall, various churches, museums and places elsewhere in the town contain paintings, then there is the Library of the Intronati full of ancient books, manuscripts and pamphlets, as well as sketchbooks and notebooks of famous artists who worked in Siena. If the trough was so important, Millicent, it must surely feature in some of those paintings and records. And if it is featured in such a way, that in itself might provide a clue to its present whereabouts. And remember, every legend has its base in real events. That is why I believe the trough did exist. It is the foundation of the famous legend, not the legend itself.'

'Then why have other people never found it? Or managed to trace it through those sources you mention?' she asked. 'Surely if it has links with the Palio, there will be records of it somewhere? Other people will have searched all the local paintings and town's civic records, you cannot be alone in this quest, Montague. You're probably five hundred years too late.'

'Certainly others have searched, Millicent, but perhaps they were not so diligent as I?' he smiled. 'Perhaps they are not professional detectives as I am? Few if any have been blessed with my unique skills and training. And, I believe, the key to my quest must lie somewhere here in Siena, in this very piazza perhaps. This must be my starting point. Now, while I plan my strategy, a long cool drink is called for. I find it quite hot in the sunshine.'

'With that coat on, I am not surprised. Why didn't you leave it at the hotel?'

'I never go anywhere without my family coat, Millicent. You know that. It is an important Pluke heirloom, far too valuable to be left behind in foreign places. And it is useful – like Arab garb, a coat of this all-embracing size and weight also keeps out the heat. Now, let us find a seat, my feet are killing me.'

'You should be wearing light clothes and sandals, not that heavy suit, the enormous coat or those brogue shoes. And spats . . . you should relax, Montague.'

'I am relaxed. I am on holiday . . . ah, there's a table,' and in a split second, he accelerated along the paving bricks as he zoomed in upon a table just vacated in a trattoria. He reached it before any of the other hovering tourists had realized it was available and sat down a few moments ahead of Millicent who was still struggling politely through the crowds. The table was out of doors, in front of a very old building which also housed a fine restaurant, but the trattoria was in the shade of the awning and therefore cool.

It was a fine choice, he congratulated himself. As he relaxed, his long coat tails reached the ground and more than a hint of sweat trickled down his face from beneath his hat. Seconds later, Millicent arrived at his side looking distinctly cooler than he, and after settling on her chair, began to study the menu.

'It's nearly twelve thirty,' she reminded him. 'I think we should have lunch here, not just a snack. Something light though. A salad perhaps, then we can eat later this evening in the hotel. And I might just try a glass of *vino bianco* as I am on holiday.'

'I would prefer apple juice and a bottle of still spring water, not the fizzy stuff – *aqua naturale* as they say here.' He wiped his brow without moving his hat and took the menu from her, her forefinger pointing to her recommendations. 'And yes, a salad – *insalata* – would be an excellent choice. *Insalata di pomodoro*, that's the one with tomatoes, isn't it?'

And so on that Wednesday in June, Montague Pluke began his quest to find *l'abbeveratoio del cavallo dorato di Siena*, the legendary Golden Horse Trough of Siena.

Chapter Two

After lunch, and following more discussions about the legend, Millicent made it perfectly clear she was on a very brief holiday overseas and had no desire to go trudging around in a hopeless search for a lost horse trough. It did not matter that the horse trough in question was the most famous in the world. She wanted to explore the churches and art galleries in Siena to view their collections of historic paintings and sculptures, many of which dated to medieval times. She expressed a particular desire to visit the Palazzo Pubblico or Town Hall as it was now known, which boasted its own unique collection of artistic treasures, and so Pluke announced she could do whatever she wished while he visited the Piccolomini Palace, only yards from where they were sitting. This housed the Municipal Archives and Record Office, a collection of invaluable documents relating to every aspect of the ancient history of Siena. He also wanted to visit the Library of the Intronati which contained a renowned collection of manuscripts and books. It was now one thirty – Pluke suggested they meet again at four thirty outside this very trattoria when they could settle down over a nice refreshing drink and exchange stories of their experiences.

Millicent, delighted to be granted such unrestricted freedom and with half a mind to find a shop or two, smiled her agreement and assured Montague that if she did notice the golden trough in any painting, she would make a note of the title of the work and its artist along with the date.

And she would make sure he was told about it. That was her modest way of supporting his quest.

Happy with these arrangements, they began their separate missions with Pluke checking that his rabbit's foot was still in his coat pocket to ensure the very best of good fortune. Undaunted by the fact that he did not speak Italian, Pluke began with the Library of the Intronati which was two or three minutes' walk away in Via della Sapienza. It was to the rear of the Piazza del Campo and close to the Church of San Domenico. He felt sure the officials would understand English if he spoke clearly and loudly; besides, the people of Siena were accustomed to the tongues of many nations. The Italian waiter who'd earlier served them spoke English, German, French and even Norwegian, not only quoting from the menu but also conducting a conversation in all those languages about topical events.

As he walked the short distance through narrow streets squeezed between tall brown buildings, the humming sound of voices in the Piazza del Campo began to fade and by the time he reached the library, the noise was no longer evident. Unlike the busy Piazza del Campo, the streets in this area were almost deserted and the shops were shut; as he walked in the afternoon heat he was perspiring heavily and then he realized that the Italians would be enjoying their siesta. Many shops and other places closed at lunchtime, so would the library be open?

Fortunately, it was. A notice said it was open from 9 a.m. until 8 p.m. except for Sundays and holidays when it was closed all day; it was also closed between 1st and 15th July and entrance was free. Cheered by this piece of good news, and anxious to enjoy the cool interior of this impressive building, he walked in to find a curious mixture of ancient and modern architecture.

There were oceans of modern glass among the old stones, lots of colour and atmosphere, all aided by a cool marble floor and air conditioning. In these fine surround-

17

ings, he felt surprisingly content and not in the least over-awed by the occasion. The only other visitor was a man sitting at a table; he was studying a thick volume and was clearly a priest. Pluke was surprised to see no one at the reception counter.

Then a young raven-haired Italian woman appeared behind a glass screen. *'Buon giorno, signore.* Can I help you?'

She smiled at the curiously dressed man in the huge thick overcoat with the big black-framed spectacles and long black hair poking at odd angles from beneath his panama. Judging from his eccentric appearance, he was clearly an Englishman.

'Ah, yes, you speak English?' he asked. *'Parla inglese*?'

'Very leetle,' and her smile would have made the most faithful man experience yearnings which were in conflict with his marriage vows. The priest seemed oblivious to her charms but the sight of her made Pluke feel cheerful. 'How may I help you?'

'I am seeking information about the Golden Horse Trough of Siena.' He remained dazzled and even hyp-notized by her smile, her immaculate white teeth, her shining black hair, the warmth of her welcome. Maybe the rabbit's foot was working, perhaps his luck was in? And he remembered to speak slowly and loudly.

'Ah, *l'abbeveratoio del cavallo dorato di Siena*.' She pro-duced another of her smiles and he began to feel weak at the knees. In spite of the air conditioning, he was sweating even more profusely and could not understand why. A rabbit's foot didn't normally have this effect. 'Eet does not exist, eet is only story. How you say? *Leggenda*. A myth.'

'A legend, yes, it is a famous legend. The Golden Horse Trough of Siena. You have a book about it? Some infor-mation?'

'No.' She shook that shining black hair and beamed at him. 'No information, there is nothing, *signore*. Nothing. Eet is *leggenda*. Myth. No true.'

18

'But even myths and legends are recorded in books, *signora*.'

'Not this one, there is nothing.'

'But I have heard the story in England so surely there must be something written here, in Italy, in Siena . . .'

'Perhaps in Inghilterra, *signore*, but not in Siena,' and she smiled that wonderful smile again.

As they were speaking, the priest rose from his table and approached them. Clad in the long black garb and clerical collar of a Catholic priest, he was a tall thin man in his mid-fifties with grey hair and striking blue eyes. His hat lay on the table beside his books.

'*Padre*,' the girl smiled at him.

'Piera.' He used her first name and then followed with a string of Italian which was incomprehensible to Pluke before turning to speak to him.

'I am Father O'Flynn.' He smiled as his Irish accent sounded so strange in this country. 'I live and work here, at the cathedral, with a special responsibility for visitors who come to Siena, especially those from Europe. To be sure, it makes a welcome change from Liverpool. Please forgive me for overhearing your conversation, but I can tell you about the legend and perhaps save you a lot of unnecessary leg-work. If you have the time, please sit down,' and he indicated the table where he had been working.

'*Mille grazie, signorina*, thank you, Father.' Pluke hoped he had selected the correct words and then followed Father O'Flynn to the table and seated himself opposite the priest. He even removed his panama and placed it beside the priest's biretta.

'As I said, I am Father Patrick O'Flynn on secondment to Siena. And you are?'

'Pluke. Montague Pluke from Crickledale in North Yorkshire, England,' but he did not reveal his profession at this point.

'Ah, Montague Pluke! You are surely not *the* Montague Pluke, are you? Author of *The Horse Troughs of Crickledale and District since the Sixteenth Century*, and didn't you also publish a volume about civic horse troughs?'

'Ahem, well, yes, I am indeed that Pluke.' Montague had never before experienced recognition overseas; he had no idea he was so famous. 'Horse troughs are my passion but my literary endeavours are very modest. I must say I am flattered that you know of my work.'

'I did a similar work when I lived in Ireland,' beamed Father O'Flynn. 'My pamphlet was called *Horse Troughs in Irish Churchyards*. Centuries ago, troughs were installed to refresh the horses after the long trek to Mass in rural areas but the motor car has rendered them almost obsolete. I thought they should be recorded before they vanished altogether and it was while reseaching the history of horse troughs that I came across your books. The drivers and riders of horses always made sure they got themselves well and truly refreshed in the local bars, so I thought I'd record the fact that the horses received similar treatment. I illustrated the pamphlet too, with my own photographs. I found a rare trough too, said to have been used by St Patrick's horse, and another used by St Bridget's mare. But all that's another story or two.'

'You must tell me sometime, Father.'

'Sure I will, Mr Pluke, but at this minute we've other things to discuss. Well, fancy all this, eh? Me meeting you here like this. I've seen your work in the reference section of Liverpool library . . . this is fate, Mr Pluke, it must have been pre-ordained by a higher authority.'

Pluke decided not to mention his rabbit's foot but felt it must have had some influence on this most fortuitous meeting. 'I don't know what to say, I am quite overwhelmed by this meeting,' and Pluke hauled out his grubby old handkerchief to wipe his brow. 'Of all the people to meet in Siena, a fellow trough expert . . .'

'We are a true brotherhood, Mr Pluke, a worldwide fellowship, kindred spirits on a special mission. Only a genuine trougher would want to pursue the legend of the

Golden Horse Trough,' smiled the priest. 'As indeed I did when I arrived. I have been here five years now, and in spite of all my contacts and research, I have not discovered any factual support for the legend. There seems nothing to discover, you see. That girl – Piera – is right, there is nothing in writing about this trough, Mr Pluke. Nothing at all. No illustrations, no records from ancient times, nothing. I have searched, truly I have, believe me.'

'But the legend must have started somehow,' countered Pluke. 'There is usually some factual basis behind every legend. I am aware that legends get embroidered, enhanced, distorted and altered with every telling until they are almost unrecognizable from the original but every one of them has to begin somewhere. My instinct tells me that the Golden Horse Trough is more than a mere legend, the whole story has a strong ring of truth to it.'

'So it has, Mr Pluke, so it has. That is why I have conducted some very careful research in this town, here in this very library, and at the Record Office in the Municipal Archives in the Piccolomini Palace, in old documents, in art galleries, from old folks' memories of family chatter. If there is anything at all about the Golden Horse Trough of Siena, then it should be here, in our local records. But as Piera says, there is nothing. I am telling you this so you need not waste any more time trying to get to the root of the story. The fact is there is no root, no trough.'

'I don't quite know how to respond,' said Pluke. 'I find that very difficult to believe, especially here in Siena.'

'Precisely my reasoning too, Mr Pluke, when I arrived. I have spent five years searching and have been helped by some very obliging parishioners and knowledgeable residents of Siena, but have found nothing. I have found nothing because there is nothing. It is rather like those so-called urban legends of England – weird stories with no foundation. So, if I might ask, where did you first learn of this legend?'

At that moment, Piera approached their table bearing a

bottle of iced water and two glasses which she placed before them.

'*Prego*,' she smiled.

'*Prego, grazie*,' returned the priest as she departed with a flourish of her skirt, then said, 'This is for us, Mr Pluke, with the compliments of the management.'

In England, of course, Detective Inspector Pluke would never accept an unsolicited gift, not even a glass of water or cup of tea; police officers' conduct had to be beyond reproach and acceptance of any kind of gift was always risky. Allegations of bribery might follow. And for each favour granted, Pluke knew, one or more would be expected in return. This kind of thing was very subtle bribery – but it never worked with officers of Pluke's experience and perspicacity. However, he reasoned with impressive speed, this girl had no idea he was a police officer and neither had the priest; besides, he was in a foreign country where he had no jurisdiction, he was not engaged upon a police enquiry and it seemed the gesture was part of the local culture. His rapid mental gymnastics told him he could accept the glass now being offered by Father O'Flynn. And so he did – and it was delicious, so cool and refreshing, so welcome on this hot afternoon.

'I am very well looked after here,' smiled the priest. 'So, Mr Pluke, how did you learn of *l'abbeveratoio del cavallo dorato*?'

'I cannot pinpoint my knowledge to a particular time or place,' he admitted. 'It is one of those things which has grown imperceptibly in my consciousness. Over many years of trough research, I have grown increasingly aware of the legend of the Golden Horse Trough without really knowing how my knowledge arose or where it came from. The odd reference on television, perhaps in travel programmes or documentaries, the occasional mention in a book or article but never an illustration, the occasional person talking about it at Trough Society conferences. It's rather like someone knowing the North Pole exists without ever seeing it or going there; everyone knows there is a North Pole even if few have actually seen it. I feel the same about the golden trough, Father O'Flynn. I've always known the story existed with its base here in Siena and deep at the back of my mind, I made a resolution to come here one day and find out more about it. That is my great ambition – like many others, I would dearly love to find the actual trough.'

'I could tell you a similar story, Mr Pluke, a very similar story. Your belief mirrors mine exactly. And I came here because God sent me . . .'

'But you have concluded there is no trough? And never has been?'

'That is the sad reality. Everywhere I go, I am told it is nothing but a myth. There is nothing in the town's history to prove its authenticity, I can assure you of that. The official stance is that the trough never existed and that the story of its links with the Palio is nothing but a myth.'

Pluke decided he must make a determined stand if only for the sake of the true history of troughs. 'Father O'Flynn,' he said, 'I cannot accept that. As a keen student of folklore, I am acutely aware that every myth, every legend, every fairy story or nursery rhyme has a factual origin, obscure though it may be. I believe the same applies to the Golden Horse Trough.'

'You echo my earlier thoughts, indeed you do, but rest assured I have done my best. It has taken a long time for me to be convinced, but now I am. I have come to accept there is no trough and never was, Mr Pluke. You have found your answer, your quest is complete.'

Pluke felt deflated. It was like visiting the Great Wall of China only to discover it was a plastic replica. It was like believing man had actually travelled to the moon only to find it had been an elaborate hoax. It was like discovering King Alfred hadn't really burnt the cakes or that Father Christmas didn't exist. If it was true, then it was a terrible let-down, but as he told himself while the priest sipped the

23

water with evident pleasure, there *had* to be a reason for the story. There *had* to be a foundation to the myth – after all, it had endured for six hundred years! You couldn't keep a fake story going for more than six hundred years without it having some strong basis in reality. It was just like the tale of Robin Hood. That legend was about the same age as the story of the golden trough and it wasn't all fabrication, was it?

'You are clearly disappointed, Mr Pluke?' the priest interrupted his musings. 'Like discovering some unwelcome secret about a friend or member of the family?'

'I cannot accept there is nothing behind the story,' said Pluke with as much authority as he could muster. 'There is too much detail for it to be pure fabrication. I will continue my quest.'

'Well spoken, Mr Pluke, spoken like a true trougher! So tell me, what makes you so determined to continue this work? What drives you ever onward?'

Pluke outlined his accumulated knowledge, stressing the trough's close links to the Palio. He had grown to believe the trough had been specially crafted and given to the people of Siena by the banking dynasty Monte dei Paschi di Siena. The family seat at the time, the fourteenth century, was the Palazzo Salimbeni, still to be seen in Piazza Salimbeni. According to ancient lore, the trough had been donated especially to refresh the winning horse after each Palio. While the horse's rider was awarded the prestigious Palio, a coveted painted silk banner depicting the Virgin Mary, every winning horse had the right to use the trough for the rest of its life. As time passed, the superstitious people of the period thought the trough bore magical qualities, and that by drinking from it, a horse was given the power to win any future race, not just the Palio; indeed some humans would drink from it in the belief its waters were healing, strengthening, pure and healthy.

Pluke knew that the early history of the Palio was very vague; it is known the race was run before 1310 but in that

24

year it was formalized in a document of the General Council of Siena which stipulated the race should be run on 16th August in honour of the Blessed Virgin Mary. In 1656, a second Palio was established to be run on 2nd July – the Palio of the Contrade – and this one was in honour of the Madonna di Provenzano. By that stage, it was known the Golden Horse Trough had disappeared. Its role, therefore, was in connection only with the first Palio, not both.

When the trough had been given to the city, it had been positioned in the upper section of the Piazza del Campo, very close to the site of the present Renaissance fountain, Fonte Gaia. That fountain had been sculpted by Jacopo della Quercia between 1409 and 1419 and had made use of water from an earlier aqueduct. It was clear, Pluke stressed, that the trough had disappeared before the creation of that fountain. Pluke expressed his own belief that the trough could have been removed during the laying of the bricks in the Piazza del Campo during 1347 – it could have been dislodged to make way for the new floor of the piazza and never replaced, whether through forgetfulness, incompetence or for some local political reason. But in spite of its importance in Siena's history and in particular its links with the Palio, there was no record of it since 1347. Perhaps the fountain made it surplus to requirements? However, the Black Plague broke out the following year and Pluke expressed the view that the trough could have been stolen or removed during the uncertainties of that dreadful period.

'You have a description of it?' asked the priest, very impressed by Pluke's accumulated knowledge – but of course, this was *the* Montague Pluke, the renowned authority on horse troughs. If he did not know the story of the Golden Horse Trough, who would?

'You will appreciate that my knowledge is far from complete and it has been gathered from dozens of tiny snippets I've read and recorded over the years. I've gleaned details from a variety of sources, some of which are probably very unreliable or even fiction,' he reminded Father O'Flynn. 'I have to admit, however, there is no real description of the trough. It is the legend which names it the Golden Horse Trough, but was it made from solid gold or merely crafted from some other material, wood, stone, marble, bronze? With or without a lining of, say, lead? The Siena people were known for their craftsmanship, Father, they could have carved it in wood or marble, or they could have covered it with gold leaf or gilt, and lined it with lead. It could have been decorated with gilt like some paintings in these local churches and it may be significant that it is known as the golden trough, not the gold trough. I doubt if it was made from solid gold and have no indication of its size or whether it was single-headed, double or triple.'

'If it was a true product of Siena,' said the priest, 'it could be made of marble with symbolic carvings around it, probably in bas-relief, something connected with the Palio perhaps, or with horses in general, or a landmark from the town or even the Virgin Mary because the race is run in her honour.'

'My views also,' nodded Pluke. 'Now, I believe that if the trough was so much a feature of those early Palio races, then it would have been depicted in at least some paintings of the period, or noted in old records. It might even appear in paintings of the Nativity, disguised as the manger. Links with the Virgin Mary were, and still are, very strong in this town.'

'I can assure you it does not feature in any such paintings,' smiled Father O'Flynn. 'I used to think exactly like you, Mr Pluke, I have studied Domenico Ghirlandaio's *Adoration of the Shepherds*, painted in 1485, Geertgen tot Sint Jans' *The Nativity* dating from 1490 and, of course, Titian's famous *Sacred and Profane Love* which he completed around 1515. Any of those could feature the golden trough in disguise either as a manger or, in the case of Titian, a large white marble receptacle which, you must note, bears the images of carved horses and human figures. Just as I would have imagined the Golden Horse Trough to be. But, I have to disappoint you – none of these wonderful works has Siena as a background, nor indeed do they feature the Palio, and Titian's trough is of white marble, not gold or golden. And, you must appreciate, all those were completed a long time after the date you believe the trough was removed – 1347 or thereabouts. The golden trough does not appear in any paintings or literature, Mr Pluke.'

'But if it was removed to a safe place while the piazza was under construction, or to a palace, house, town or city, then it might have inspired the great artists to feature it, as a matter of record. Even if it was stolen during the plague, you'd think there would be some kind of record of its existence.'

'But there isn't, Mr Pluke. There is nothing, I cannot over-emphasize that point. Surely that suggests the trough never existed?'

'I repeat I cannot accept that, Father. The story is too strong. If I can discover the trough in some work of art completed *after* 1347, or in written records, then it would prove the trough *did* exist and *that it survived*, even at a different location. And if it survived at that time, Father, it might still be in one piece now.'

'I admire your faith, Mr Pluke, indeed I do. Would that some of my flock had such faith in the Church, but yes, you could be right. I bow to your superior knowledge, even if I have become a disbeliever. How wonderful it would be if it was still out there somewhere, somewhere in the big wide and terrible world, unrecognized for what it truly is. It would be like discovering America, Mr Pluke, or landing a man on Mars.'

'If it has survived,' smiled Pluke, 'I want to be the person who finds it.'

'Well, there speaks a man in my own language. How I wish I could have been that person, Mr Pluke. Here am

27

I, in Siena, the home of the legendary Golden Horse Trough, and have not found one scrap of evidence to say it existed. If it did exist, it has done a vanishing trick of impressive finality. I should add that I am being absolutely honest with you, I am not concealing any privileged knowledge. I have ended my own search but would not wish to stop you conducting yours. If you do decide to continue, then of course, you have my blessing. If the trough does exist, then I would like you, of all the trough experts in the world, to be the one to find it.'

'Thank you. I shall continue my search, Father. I consider it to be rather like Rembrandt's *The Circumcision* which vanished before 1756. Or those paintings of Suleyman the Magnificent. They have vanished too, but will surely exist somewhere.'

'They could even be hanging unrecognized on the wall of some stately home in England,' suggested the priest.

'Just as the golden trough could be serving as a horse trough on a remote Tuscan farm, Father, or languishing in the grounds of an English country house in the guise of a plant holder. For that reason, I shall continue my search.'

'Spoken like a true trougher, Mr Pluke. So what are your plans now?'

'My wife is in the town, hoping to see pictures of it in the local galleries, in the Town Hall perhaps . . .'

'It is the time of the siesta, Mr Pluke, many places are shut, even if this library remains open. The Town Hall, for example, closes at 1.30 p.m. for the siesta and the National Picture Gallery closes at 1.45 p.m. I do hope her efforts have not been wasted.'

'I forgot about that,' admitted Pluke, adding swiftly, 'but so did she. Now, if I cannot find any reference to the trough in Siena, I will look elsewhere. One day, in some obscure place, I might come across something I recognize as *l'abbeveratoio del cavallo dorato di Siena*.'

'Then I do hope our paths will cross again, Mr Pluke.

You know where to find me if you need me,' and Father O'Flynn presented Montague with his business card. 'I am sorry to have been the bearer of bad news but I am sure you would want to know the real situation rather than waste time searching unnecessarily.'

'You have saved me a lot of unnecessary work, Father, and for that I am very grateful but at the same time you have made me more determined. I am here for just one more full day, then I must return to Crickledale on Friday but if I do discover anything in the future, I shall contact you.'

'And if you care to leave me a contact address or telephone number, either in England or at your hotel, then I shall be pleased to pass along any information that comes my way.'

And so, with the necessary pleasantries complete, Pluke took his leave. Father O'Flynn remained to complete his own research as Pluke emerged with time to spend before his planned reunion with Millicent. As he walked out of the library and replaced his panama, the hot air assailed him; it was like putting one's head into a heated oven and it almost took away his breath. He halted and took a deep lungful of the heated air, wiped his brow and turned towards the piazza. The increasing sound of that mass of human voices rose almost to thunderous proportions as he drew closer, and with more than an hour to wait for Millicent, he decided to find somewhere cool, somewhere sheltered. Like a church perhaps. Or a shop – some were open in spite of the siesta, the ones which catered for tourists.

He opted for the cathedral. Maybe it contained a picture or some other representation of a horse trough? It was stunning with its façade of white marble contrasted with pink Siena stone and the dark green Prato stone. It contained a wealth of artwork and sculptures, including the Siena coat of arms in the central aisle of its pavement and a tribute to St Catherine of Siena. He noticed a baptismal

29

font in the chapel of St John the Baptist as well as some water stoups on its internal façade but there was nothing remotely resembling a horse trough – except that the presbytery pavement depicted Moses causing water to gush from a rock. Now that's where a horse trough should have been, thought Pluke. But he was cheered by a modern find beneath the cathedral. As recently as the spring of 2003, evidence was found, in a well under the transept, which confirmed Siena's long association with horses. The remains of a ritual sacrifice were uncovered; they were the bones of one horse and three dogs, each of which had been slaughtered and cut into three pieces. They were found in a hollow which had been cut out of solid rock. The sacrifice had been the work of ancient Romans who were trying to ensure good fortune for early Siena. So surely, in a city with such a long affinity with horses, there must be some evidence of the famous trough?

He enjoyed his leisurely and educational visit to this mighty church and found himself cheered by the latest discovery, but it was time to meet Millicent. He found her standing outside the trattoria bearing several shopping bags and she smiled a welcome. She looked so cool and composed while sweat was pouring down his face and he was panting with the effort of fighting his way through the crowds. But there was a table beneath the awning and they settled down, deciding to have a *gelato* and a long cool fruit drink each.

'So, Montague,' she smiled, 'was the afternoon useful to you?'

'Yes and no,' he shrugged. 'Yes because it saved me carrying out a lot more fruitless searching, and no because this town and its people, in spite of their historic love of horses, continue to deny the existence of the Golden Horse Trough. The official stance, which is odd to say the least, is that the trough never existed.'

He told her of his chat with Father O'Flynn and his discovery in the cathedral. She listened intently and said she was pleased he had been spared so much footwork in such hot conditions, and agreed it was now time to end his search. Perhaps tomorrow they might visit Florence before leaving for home?

'Yes, perhaps that is a good idea,' he consented with some reluctance, then asked, 'And you, Millicent? What did you do?'

'The art galleries were all closed, Montague, it was the siesta, I forgot about that.'

'And so did I, my dear, so did I. I am losing my touch, getting forgetful in my old age . . .'

'You're not old, Montague! But look, the touristy shops were all open and so I bought something for home. Postcards too, for the ladies of the sewing circle and flower arranging class in Crickledale, a nice piece of local glassware for us, for the lounge. . . . oh, and this. For you.'

She handed him a small object wrapped in tissue paper and bade him open it. It was a small plastic object in a light cardboard box, oblong in shape but beyond doubt when viewed through the cellophane window, it was in the form of a miniature horse trough. And on the front panel it bore the embossed image of the Piazzo del Campo with the Virgin Mary standing proud on an elevated plinth in the centre as the Palio horses galloped around her. And it was coloured gold. Heart pounding, Pluke opened the fragile box to gain a better view of his present.

'Millicent!' he shouted when it was fully revealed; everyone looked at him. 'You know what this is?'

'Yes, dear,' she smiled. 'It's a model of the Golden Horse Trough of Siena.'

31

Chapter Three

'Where did you get this?' His excitement was palpable. 'I've just been told there is no record, no images, no drawings of the trough, yet you've found a cheap plastic model!'

'It was in a little shop along one of those narrow streets,' and she pointed vaguely over her head in the general direction of her mini-expedition. 'I thought you would like it, a nice memento of our visit.'

'You don't seem to appreciate the importance of this!' His voice had reached falsetto pitch if not quite shrieking point and it was quivering with his suppressed emotion. 'If this is a genuine reproduction of the trough, then the trough must have existed, or must exist even now in spite of all the denials! Can't you see how important this is?'

'Yes, dear,' she smiled. 'That is why I thought you would like it. It wasn't expensive, you know, just four euros fifty. Quite a bargain, I thought, even if it is only plastic.'

The waiter arrived to take their order and while Millicent dealt with him, Pluke studied the flimsy cardboard box with the cellophane window, noting that the writing upon it was in several languages. It was like those boxes which contain model cars but the title '*L'abbeveratoio del cavallo dorato di Siena*' was very evident indeed, along with the English translation. He tipped the contents into his shaking hand and found himself holding a miniature gold-coloured plastic horse trough complete with an inlet pipe in the shape of a horse's head with its mouth open.

The scene depicted in the mock-up of the bas-relief carving on the front panel was very well done indeed; beyond all doubt, the setting was the Piazza del Campo here in Siena. The buildings and square were instantly recognizable, although the actual illustration was, of course, pure fiction, the figment of some artist's imagination. But was this an accurate reproduction of what had appeared on the original trough? A large circular dais accessed by steps was shown and standing on top was the Virgin Mary with a halo around her head. Her hands were clasped before her and she was clutching a rosary; her robes came down to her feet and one foot was shown standing upon a serpent. She was gazing towards heaven, the prelude to her assumption; it was a familiar pose but in this case ten horses with riders were shown galloping around the square which surrounded her. Without doubt, the scene was that of the Palio along with a celebration of her feast day, the Assumption of the Blessed Virgin Mary on 15th August. The image was on the front only; the rear and both sides of the little trough were devoid of any illustration – just like a real trough.

When the waiter left to execute their order, Pluke said, 'Millicent, I must find out more about this. You must take me to that shop without delay.'

'I told the gentleman I thought you would be interested,' she smiled. 'He is English, by the way, he came here to start a small business, it's a shop catering for tourists.'

'So you spotted this among his display? In a tourist shop of all places?' queried Pluke, now realizing that his rabbit's foot was working really hard for his benefit.

'No, Montague, it was under the counter,' she smiled graciously. 'He asked if I was interested in the legend of the Golden Horse Trough. When I said I was, he pulled this from under his counter and offered it to me.'

'Under the counter?' puzzled Pluke. 'You mean it was illegal? It's not full of drugs, is it? Or obscene in some way? This is not a secret pornographic model of some kind, is it? Or a sex toy?'

'Good heavens, of course it's not. What a suspicious mind you've got! It's just a plastic souvenir with no hidden meaning, I'm sure of that. It is a very full shop, every space is occupied by touristy souvenirs and there's something for all nationalities. The man just thought I would be interested in the Golden Horse Trough.'

'Now why would he think you of all people, a total stranger, would be interested in this particular souvenir of a very Italian trough?'

'I don't know, Montague. If you want answers to those sort of questions, you'd better go and ask him.'

'And so I will, without delay!' he said. 'You must take me to this little shop, please, Millicent, immediately we have finished our snack.'

Several minutes later and walking at a brisk pace in spite of the heat, Millicent led the puffing Pluke though the dense crowd and out of the Piazza del Campo towards the cathedral. Instead of heading past the mighty church, she turned right just before reaching it and hurried along a narrow street. Clearly she had remembered the route for she turned down an even narrower alley without any name on the walls. There she showed him the tiny shop and led the way inside.

'Ah, you are back, just as you said.' The man had recognized Millicent.

He was a small round man with chubby cheeks, a neat black moustache and black hair clinging to the sides and back of his balding head. In his early fifties, he looked rather like a plump Italian tenor and his smile was welcoming.

'This is my husband, Mr Montague Pluke, he is an authority on horse troughs.' She introduced him with evident pride. 'He wants to meet you.'

'Ah, yes, I recognize the name, Mr Pluke, from my time in England. Your work on horse troughs is very well known and I am not surprised you are interested in the famous Golden Horse Trough. I have more under my counter, Mr Pluke, maybe I should export them to Britain?'

'Under the counter?' Pluke expressed his amazement at this practice. 'Is there something wrong with these troughs? Are they illegally imported? Do they breach European government regulations? Infringe some international law perhaps?'

'Nothing like that, I can assure you. It is just that the people of Siena want nothing to do with the golden trough, and so I do not antagonize them by having these replicas on display. Not that many locals come in here of course, most if not all my customers are tourists, but I do get some discerning visitors who know of the legend and so I draw attention to my supply. I am the only Golden Horse Trough supplier in Siena, I might add. Even in Italy, I suspect.'

'Then you are to be congratulated, sir,' acknowledged Pluke. 'There are not many suppliers of troughs in modern times, not even toy ones in plastic.'

'I realize that, it's a gap in the market and I am taking advantage of it. I find it quite amazing just how many people have heard the Golden Horse Trough legend, Mr Pluke. I get lots coming in here, from all over the world, to ask where they can see the real trough; they are not trough experts like yourself, they are merely tourists who want to see the sights having heard the story. Many would ask if I had anything connected with the legend, and so I decided to produce my replica. This sort of thing is quite enough for some people. All they want is a cheap souvenir to take home.'

'You are very perceptive,' Pluke said. 'But, Mr . . .'

'Green. Joseph Green, late of Batley in West Yorkshire, now living here and running my business in Siena. It was the best thing I ever did. Have one of my cards,' and he delved into a drawer below the counter and handed a card to Pluke. He glanced at it before slipping it into his wallet.

'So what is your special interest in this Golden Horse Trough, Mr Pluke? Siena is a long way from England.'

Pluke explained and Mr Green listened, occasionally nodding and smiling when some aspect of Pluke's quest confirmed his own researches. After his speech, Pluke concluded, 'So you see, Mr Green, I wanted to visit Siena to test the truth of the legend. Sadly, I have found nothing, and have even been told the story is complete fiction – and then my wife presented me with this trough.'

'You will not find anything about it in this town, Mr Pluke. No one in Siena is remotely interested in the legend of the Golden Horse Trough. The only interest comes from outsiders, people from overseas mainly. People with an interest in legends, folklore, local history, that sort of thing, ancient and modern. I can assure you the legend has a large following overseas, beyond Italian shores that is. It is particularly strong in Japan, New Zealand and Tobago.'

'It is a very ancient legend, Mr Green, and I am not surprised it has circumnavigated and enthralled the world. But here, they say it is all fiction, nothing but a legend! There is even an official denial of the story. So what am I to believe?'

'You should believe in yourself, Mr Pluke, have faith in what you truly believe.'

'It is nice to hear you say that, for it is precisely what I intend to do, Mr Green. I shall continue my search. So tell me, how did you know my wife would be interested?'

'I cheated, Mr Pluke. I had my lunch in the trattoria, I saw you and Mrs Pluke there. I was sitting at the next table and heard you chatting about the golden trough, with you saying you were going to undertake some local research. I did not wish to intrude of course, but when Mrs Pluke came into my shop, I recognized her instantly as the trough lady.'

'Ah, an observant man!' smiled Pluke, thinking he might have done likewise. This man had all the instincts of a good detective.

'I have a good memory for faces and people. And here you are, the famous Montague Pluke in my modest little shop in his quest to find *l'abbeveratoio del cavallo dorato di Siena*. And all I can do is offer you a plastic model which most buyers use on their desks to contain their paper clips.'

'Nonetheless, it interests me deeply,' said Pluke. 'I hope you'll tell me where you discovered the design? Is it authentic? Or merely the product of some artist's imagination? Can it really have come from the actual and original golden trough? Could this be evidence that it did exist, in spite of the denials?'

'I have asked people here in Siena, but all shake their heads and say the trough did not exist. I have even spoken to a priest called Father O'Flynn who is very knowledgeable –'

'We have met,' Pluke interrupted. 'In the library.'

'I am pleased you have met him. When I showed him my plastic replicas, he said the design could not be authenticated. Even though it looks genuine, he said, there is no proof the design is from the actual golden trough.'

'I believe your replica has a ring of truth about it, the background of the piazza, the role of the Virgin Mary, the Palio horses racing . . . it's all there in that single composite illustration,' mused Pluke.

'That could have been faked by any competent artist or sculptor. Anyone with a reasonable knowledge of the Palio and Siena could have produced that picture.'

'I accept that, Mr Green, but might I ask the source your design?'

Green laughed and looked slightly embarrassed. 'It is from a snuff box, Mr Pluke.'

'A snuff box?'

'Years ago, I obtained a brochure about snuff boxes – I collected them at that time, you see, I was interested in antiques of all kinds but small collectables in particular. I discovered the snuff box in a tiny museum which had a collection of them. I went along to have a look, and the museum had – and still has – a brochure containing their potted histories and some photographs. One of the photographs, along with a short history, depicted a particular snuff box, Mr Pluke. It bore the same bas-relief image as the one you see on my replicas. I'd kept those histories, and so I later copied that one for my trough models. I don't mind admitting that, it depicted a lovely scene in Siena although I did not reproduce the frieze which is around the original. That was far too indistinct. At the time I first saw the picture, it meant nothing to me but on coming to live here I felt that it represented such a wonderful aspect of Siena that it should not be locked away in a remote English museum. I hope I have made good use of it.'

Pluke could hardly believe his ears. 'I find this incredible, Mr Green. How on earth did such an image find its way into an obscure English museum? And you think the museum knew it depicted a scene in Siena?'

'That's what their literature said, Mr Pluke, it is known as the Siena snuff box and is still there, so far as I am aware.'

'This story gets more incredible with each new sentence, Mr Green!'

'Well, at least you can understand how I have come to use that image on my plastic troughs. In my very modest way, I am doing my bit to perpetuate the legend, even if the authorities do not support my activities. I must stress I am not an authority on the history of either the Palio or the golden trough, but I can assure you that is where my design came from.'

'And it was definitely a snuff box, not a miniature model of the trough?'

'It was a definitely snuff box, Mr Pluke, it had a tight-fitting lid. All snuff boxes have tight-fitting lids, they were necessary to retain the powdery contents when being carried around in their owners' pockets.'

'Ah, yes, of course, and looking at your trough, it would

be a simple matter to accommodate a shallow, tight-fitting lid on this trough, and so convert it into a snuff box?'

'It would not be difficult, Mr Pluke, but my creation is a trough, a trough which is not a snuff box under any circumstances. I have no intention of marketing it as a snuff box. I have these plastic replicas made in England to that design and shipped out to me.'

'And the frieze? You mentioned a frieze, Mr Green. Can you tell me what it represented?'

'Sorry, no. It was illegible on the photograph I used as my model. It looked like lettering but it could be leaves or even a floral design. It ran down both sides of the front of the snuff box and along the bottom.'

'You say it might have been lettering?'

'I did not try to decipher it, all I can say is that in the photograph it looked very old and worn. I would add, Mr Pluke, that I am the only person making replicas of the golden trough and my work is as close as possible to what I believe is the original design – minus that frieze.'

'All this is fascinating, Mr Green, and it concerns me greatly. I must make enquiries at that English museum, it is my first priority upon my return to England. Do you remember which museum it is?'

'Yes indeed, it is at Pebblewick, that's a village in the North York Moors not far from Crickledale. It's a folk museum. Or it was. I think there was some suggestion it was struggling to survive after the effects of the foot-and-mouth disease outbreak although I would think it is sufficiently well established to survive a temporary problem. Some friends told me just a few months ago when they paid me a visit.'

'News travels fast and far, Mr Green. But Pebblewick? That is amazing, I know it well, it is close to where I live. I have been in that very museum many times, but I must admit I have never examined any snuff boxes. My interests were the witch posts and folklore exhibits, not fashion accessories like snuff boxes!'

'Well, there we are. All you have to do now is find out from where the snuff box manufacturer obtained that design – and you might be on the trail of the legendary Golden Horse Trough of Siena – via an English moorland village!'

In his own quiet way, Joseph Green was doing his best to keep alive the legend – and had now provided Pluke with another line of enquiry, almost on his very own doorstep. The rabbit's foot was definitely working in his favour.

'That will be my priority when I return to England,' said Pluke. 'And thank you for all your help, Mr Green.'

'Let me know what you discover. One day, you and I might be able to join forces to produce models of more famous horse troughs . . .'

'Let us get this matter settled first,' smiled Pluke. 'And I promise I will let you know the outcome of my enquiries. Now come along, Millicent, we have work to do in England.'

The Plukes returned to England late on Friday evening after a rapid visit to Florence. As Montague was not due to return to work until Monday morning, it meant he had the weekend free to pursue his quest for the truth about the Golden Horse Trough. To do so in a small rural community tucked away in the North York Moors seemed highly improbable although, as he told himself, it had required a journey to Siena in Italy to produce this kind of impressive result. And so it was, with Millicent driving the family car due to Pluke's inability to control a motor vehicle of any kind (he was known as a danger even when driving a mechanized lawnmower), that they sallied forth across the moors to Pebblewick and its famous folk museum.

Pluke still had the rabbit's foot in his pocket, he had made sure to rise from his bed by putting his right foot first on to the bedroom floor, and when he had opened the bedroom curtains he had frightened away two magpies which were exploring his vegetable patch. All good omens, he believed. The sighting of two magpies was bound to bring good fortune, he told himself, and just to make sure, when he left the house he ensured that his right foot was first across the threshold. With this kind of bountiful start to the day, success was sure to come his way although, he had to admit, Saturday was not generally regarded as fortuitous when starting a new project. But this was not a new project, it was the continuation of a project started earlier.

Fortified by his enthusiasm and good luck charms, he found himself in a cheerful mood as Millicent drove across the moors. They arrived at Pebblewick just before eleven, parked in the public car park and enjoyed coffee and biscuits in a coffee shop before Pluke strode majestically towards the museum. En route, he passed the village inn, the Marble Trough, with its famous inn sign depicting a pure white marble horse trough. He smiled – at least it was not golden, so there could not be any connection with Siena. Or could there? His earlier researches had never proved the sign was based on a genuine trough, the indications being that it was purely from the imagination of the artist. It was not known, however, what had inspired that artist although there had been a horse trough near the inn in days gone by; it had been removed during a road-widening scheme and its fate was unknown. It was thought the pub name was in memory of that trough.

Millicent, meanwhile, decided she would prefer a stroll around the village and perhaps a look in that rather good craft shop with its woollens and rugs. Pluke had no objection – he preferred to be on his own because it meant he could take whatever time was necessary to complete his studies. At this stage, he did not wish to announce his presence or attract the attention of any of the museum staff; all he wanted was the opportunity to quietly view the collection of snuff boxes and to find out as much as he could about the one bearing the scene from Siena. He hoped the supportive leaflet with its photograph was still available.

Entrance to the museum was via what looked like a lych-gate, the sort usually found standing before a village church. It was an old wooden structure with a tiled roof and at either side of the pathway through it were stone seats; some old men were sitting there, chatting as no doubt they had for decades. Pluke passed before them, bidding each man a rustic 'Now then' before heading for the main door, and noticed the distinct whiff of beer emanting from them.

'Are you that famous detective?' called out one of them, a man with a black and white cur at his feet.

'I am Detective Inspector Pluke,' he replied with more than a hint of haughtiness.

'Then are you going to ask me about them snuff boxes?' demanded the other.

'What snuff boxes?' asked Pluke, wondering how on earth this man knew of his interest.

'What snuff boxes!' The man poked fun at Pluke while smiling broadly at his fellow conspirators. 'Listen to that, lads! What snuff boxes, he asks. They don't know what they're doing, these policemen. They'll never catch anybody, this lot, not in a month of Sundays.'

Pluke tried to ignore the taunts as he strode up the tarmac path which ran across a patch of greenery as it rose slightly from the village street. The main door of the museum, a large glass one, was standing open and the wall beside it bore a large sign saying 'Entrance'.

When he entered the lobby, however, the woman behind the ticket desk recognized him and said, 'Ah, Detective Inspector Pluke, how good of you to come. You'll have come about the snuff boxes?'

'Er, well, yes,' he had to admit, wondering how on earth she knew that. How did everyone know he was here to discuss snuff boxes?

'I will get Mr Porter, he will come and see you,' she assured him.

'Er, well, no, it won't be necessary, really I have no wish to trouble him, I will be quite happy on my own . . .'

'But surely you will want to interview Mr Porter? He is expecting, they said you were on leave when we rang, Mr Pluke, but Detective Sergeant Wain said he would inform you immediately upon your return and that you would come and see us at the first opportunity.'

Pluke paused. Clearly, they were talking at cross-purposes.

'Mrs Collins –' he had spotted the name plate on her desk – 'I think we are not talking about the same thing. Yes, I am back from my holiday, I got back last evening and thought I would come here today to look at the snuff boxes, but I have not been in touch with my office and they have not been in touch with me. Clearly, there is something I should know.'

'Oh dear, yes, there is. I know Mr Porter is so very anxious to talk it over with you, Mr Pluke, but you should be prepared for some very bad news. It's about the snuff boxes, our collection, our famous collection . . .'

'Yes?' He could see she was distressed.

'They were stolen last week, Mr Pluke, all of them.'

Chapter Four

'Stolen?' Pluke could hardly believe his ears. Why would anyone steal his precious golden horse trough pattern? 'How on earth could they be stolen?'

'I think you'd better speak to Mr Porter. If you wait just a moment, I'll call him.' Without waiting for a response from Pluke, Mrs Collins pressed an intercom button and said, 'Detective Inspector Pluke is in reception, Mr Porter.' After a pause she said, 'Yes, right away,' and ended her conversation.

'If you go along the corridor behind you, Mr Pluke, you will see his office, the last door on the left. It is marked "Curator".'

Pluke was holding out the money for his entrance fee but Mrs Collins said, 'Oh good heavens, Mr Pluke, you don't have to pay when you are here to investigate a crime. Please go ahead.'

It seemed he had been unavoidably returned to duty in rather unexpected circumstances. As Pluke made his way along the corridor between shelves of Stone Age exhibits in this spacious former country house with its seemingly endless rooms and corridors, a door opened ahead of him and a cheerful man poked his head out to greet his approach with, 'Ah, there you are, Mr Pluke. Do come in.'

They knew each other fairly well, Pluke being a regular patron of the museum in his quest for information about folklore and rural customs. Neil Porter was a very tall slim man with a head of dark wavy hair, dark bushy eyebrows and a permanent smile. He never appeared to be miserable and his happy appearance endeared him to all; it was perhaps for this reason that his staff were always happy. They went about their duties with a reassuring cheerfulness and this atmosphere permeated through to the visitors who toured the museum. With smiles on their faces and a general air of well-being, they explored the former mansion and its extensive grounds. It was a massive house with large airy rooms, high decorated ceilings, an entrance hall the size of a barn, a wonderful curved staircase and long wide corridors which now housed exhibits. The grounds were extensive too, much of them behind the premises and now put down to well-tended lawns, but there was a large goldfish pond with a fountain shaped like a nymph who stood on a solid plinth, a copse of woodland, plus gardens and borders all beautifully maintained. One of the rustic features was a patch of wild flowers and weeds, all carefully tended but known as the Wild Garden. The range of outdoor exhibits included a former medieval manor house, three rebuilt thatched cottages, the most recent being completed only a few months ago, several shops and a village garage. There was an icehouse too and a pets' burial ground complete with stone memorials to several dogs and cats, and even a gravestone commemorating a much-loved peacock. These were relics of the time when this was a busy family home. Now, as a museum, it was known for its superb exhibits and grand style; everyone who came to visit the exhibits and house did so with a smile on their faces, usually thanks to Neil Porter. At this point, however, Pluke was far from happy and smiling. The cheerful atmosphere had not restored his happiness; the news he'd just received was almost like a bereavement.

'Sit down, Mr Pluke, how good of you to call. Coffee?' and Mr Porter indicated a percolator on a sideboard behind him. 'I was about to have a cup.'

Pluke, still reeling from shock, cast aside all thoughts of

bribes and unsolicited gifts and decided a coffee was just what he needed to stimulate him. He required something to launch him back into explosive and positive action because he was still in holiday mode, or had been until Mrs Collins had broken the news. And so he accepted a cup of black coffee with no sugar. That would help, he decided.

'It was a shock, Mr Pluke, a dreadful shock . . .' Porter was standing at his sideboard now, attending to the coffee.

'Mr Porter, you must forgive me for appearing dazed and out of touch with events, but I knew nothing of this dreadful crime until a few moments ago. Even now, I am not familiar with the details. I have been away you see, in Italy, and arrived here moments ago, merely to look at the snuff boxes – some research I am undertaking . . .'

'Oh dear, what a shock. So you've not been told about our break-in?'

'I'm afraid not, I have not been in touch with my office. I am not due back on duty until Monday, you see, and there were no messages awaiting me at home. But the shock is severe, more severe than you can possibly realize because there was one snuff box in which I am particularly interested.'

'You know we always try to help you in your researches, Mr Pluke.'

'I do indeed, but I had overlooked this item, snuff boxes never being of particular interest to me. However, I understand this one was among your exhibits, it depicts a scene in the Piazza del Campo in Siena with the Palio horse race being staged around the Virgin Mary . . .'

'Ah, yes, the Siena snuff box as it is known, a true masterpiece, Mr Pluke, and one of our most valuable . . . but yes, before you ask, it has gone with the rest of them.' Porter placed the coffees on the desk and invited Pluke to help himself to sugar if he required any. Pluke declined. He felt numbed by this development.

46

As he sat before the curator in this comfortable office which itself was full of curios, most of which seemed to be fashioned from stone, Montague Pluke was utterly deflated and in a state of mild shock. But he was made of strong stuff; he told himself he must be resilient, he must not allow personal feelings to interfere with his professional role and he must steel himself to react with the sheer professionalism for which he was renowned. In those few moments, he decided he must revert to his role of officer in charge of Crickledale Sub-Divisional Criminal Investigation Department, even if he was not officially on duty. It would not be easy because he did not have his official notebook upon him, nor did he have any idea of what had transpired since the break-in.

He felt sure, however, that members of his staff would have dealt with this crime in a highly efficient manner and they would, even now, be in pursuit of the culprits. Fortified by those thoughts, he took a deep breath, remembered the rabbit's foot in his pocket and said:

'Perhaps it would be wise, Mr Porter, if you told me everything that has happened, right from the very beginning. When I return to my office I will then be fully informed and more able to take command of this investigation.' He hoped that speech sounded very positive and took a sip from his coffee.

Neil Porter began his story by saying it could not have happened at a worse time. The museum had spent a lot of money on re-erecting a thatched cottage in the grounds, one transported stone by stone from the local moors, and they were now struggling to attract visitors following a disastrous two years in the aftermath of the foot-and-mouth outbreak. Porter felt that news suggesting criminals were actively interested in the museum's exhibits would deter visitors at the very time extra ones were needed to boost income. Porter admitted he'd had to lay off two part-time staff members and forgo the annual painting of the building's exterior.

'So you can see, Mr Pluke, this was the last thing we wanted. Anyway, you don't want to know our domestic situation, you want to know about the crime.'

He went on to say the museum had been very busy on Tuesday last with visitors being very well behaved and clearly interested in what they saw around them. There had been no sign of trouble, no indication that anyone was examining the building or its contents with a view to stealing them. In other words, it was a perfectly normal day and the museum had closed at its usual time of 5.30 p.m. Porter himself had been last to leave the premises along with Mrs Collins; her last duty was to safeguard the day's takings and his last duty was to tour the building before the doors closed. That was to ensure no one was locked in the toilets, hiding behind any of the displays or lurking in the spacious grounds. The other members of staff – groundsman-cum-caretaker, gardener, several attendants and one secretary – had all left moments before, as normal. Porter explained that members of the public, not necessarily patrons of the museum, tended to use those toilets for there were no public conveniences in the village. They were sited just inside the main entrance and the museum authorities did not object because, on many occasions, users bought memorabilia from the museum shop and some also decided to tour the exhibits. However, it meant the toilets had to be carefully searched at closing time.

'And the staff are to be trusted, I suppose?' Pluke felt he ought to make this point for it was always possible that such a crime might be, in crude terms, 'an inside job'.

'I have never had cause to doubt any of my staff, Mr Pluke. Some are long-serving and utterly dedicated to the musuem. Others may have been with us only for a while – there does tend to be a quick turnover with some of those staff, it can be quite boring, sitting on a chair all day outside a room full of exhibits – but even so, I've never had any reason to doubt their honesty. I doubt whether any of

48

them would reveal our procedures to outsiders, or explain to visitors how our alarm system works. They are bright enough not to discuss internal matters with anyone, certainly not with strangers.'

'It is always gratifying to have dedicated and honest staff, Mr Porter. But those who have left – could they have done this out of revenge?'

'I would very much doubt it. They include an elderly lady who came to us part-time, and a former university student, a girl who has since moved to Chichester to work. Your sergeant did ask me about them; I believe all our volunteers, past and present, are totally trustworthy.'

'I am pleased to hear my sergeant is doing a thorough job, Mr Porter. One must delve into all kinds of murky corners on an enquiry of this kind.'

'I must stress we could not function without reliable and honest staff, Mr Pluke, and that includes our unpaid volunteers. However, I do know that members of your team, those who came last week, are looking into all their backgrounds, their contacts, their relationships and so forth, just to ascertain whether any could have unwittingly revealed our security arrangements.'

'Those kind of background checks are a matter of routine for my officers,' said Pluke with some pride. 'So, Mr Porter, please continue.'

'The thieves broke in sometime during Tuesday night. We had no idea there had been a raid until the museum staff arrived at eight thirty on the Wednesday morning; the staff arrive half an hour before we open the doors to the public. I discovered the raid. I went into the room in which the snuff boxes were on display, saw the display cabinet had been attacked and emptied, and at the same time noticed a gaping hole in the roof. It is an upstairs room, Mr Pluke, a former bedroom in the loft of the original house. The thieves had found a way through the roof by removing some tiles and underfelt, and they, or he, or she, had come down through the ceiling, probably with a rope

49

ladder or a lightweight collapsible aluminium ladder, as one of your officers suggested. In gaining entry that way, they had bypassed the alarm which reacts to unauthorized opening of all external windows and doors. They left via the same route. Up into the loft and out through the roof.'

'Suggesting someone fairly agile?'

'That is the general opinion, Mr Pluke, both of your staff and those of us working here. We do not know with any certainty, however, how they got on to the roof, or down from it. Such a feat cannot have been easy. It does seem, though, that they gained access from the rear of the building, from the grounds that is, well away from public view.'

'My officers examined all those likely points of ascent and descent?'

'They did, Mr Pluke, with infinite care but there is a lot of space up there with many points of access from the grounds. These former country houses have roofs of immense size and complexity, often on different levels with plenty of hiding places and with access to the roof from inside the building, for routine maintenance. This is such a roof, very spacious and very solid with lots of peaks and troughs. But no one had heard a thing, Mr Pluke, or noticed anything untoward. We have people living either side of the museum, and none of them heard or saw anything, not a sound, not a motor vehicle, no voices, no alarms, no lights. Nothing. It was an expert raid, comparable with highly skilled raids on other museums both in this country and overseas. You know there was a similar raid in the Lake District?'

'I'm afraid not, I have been away, you see . . .'

'Of course, forgive me. A museum at Keswick in the Lake District was attacked in an almost identical way, a few days before ours. Down through the roof to avoid the alarms. It lost a collection of miniature oil paintings. It was in all the papers.'

50

'A series raider, perhaps? Stealing small but portable objects which can be disposed of with comparative ease. Do you know if my officers are aware of that raid?'

'They are, Mr Pluke, and told me they were making comparisons. I believe there are similarities, access through the roof being the most obvious.'

'Good, then let us hope we can gain some useful evidence from our combined efforts. Now, back to your case. Was the display cabinet containing the snuff boxes itself fitted with an alarm?'

'Sadly, no. A terrible omission in hindsight. None of our exhibits is fitted with an individual alarm system but the more valuable ones, like the snuff boxes, are in locked display cabinets. Experts told us that security of the means of entry and egress is usually sufficient, that's the main door, all other ground-floor doors and every window.'

'There are bars on some windows too, I note.'

'Yes, the window of the snuff box room is fitted with bars, Mr Pluke.'

'So we are saying that whoever did this knew exactly which room contained the snuff boxes, and how to effect entry directly through the roof?'

'Yes, Mr Pluke. It reveals a very intimate knowledge of the layout of the premises. Someone must have done a lot of research before executing this raid. We had the roof examined from a security point of view when we had the alarms fitted, but the assessors felt that access to the roof was highly dangerous and very unlikely without the proper equipment.'

'So unauthorized access via the roof *was* considered during the security assessment?'

'It was, but it was felt to be extremely unlikely. The roof is very high from the ground, almost impossible to reach without special extending ladders. Every time we have to work up there, our staff gain access through the house itself. No one would ever countenance using a ladder, Mr Pluke. In spite of the difficulties, that is how they got in

51

because the alarm was not activated and none of the doors or windows were attacked. And, I might add, that is how they left the premises, via the roof. It was a most carefully planned and very skilfully executed crime, Mr Pluke, with our collection of snuff boxes being the target.'

'Forgive my ignorance, but why would anyone want to steal a collection of snuff boxes?'

'For their value, Mr Pluke. They are worth a lot of money. As a collection, ours were worth a minimum of £285,000. That's a conservative estimate. We'd had them valued only six months earlier for insurance purposes. I might add that the insurance assessors expressed their satisfaction with our security measures and accepted that valuation.'

'Two hundred and eighty-five thousand pounds?' cried Pluke. 'That's incredible . . .'

'Some fourteen years ago, Mr Pluke, a porcelain snuff box by Meissen dated around 1730 was valued at £200,000; a few years before that, another Meissen snuff box brought almost £170,000 at auction. And in 1991, snuff boxes worth £50,000 were stolen from a museum on Teesside – for the second time! Snuff boxes are big business, Mr Pluke, and our collection, even if the museum itself is of modest proportions with a rural reputation, was one of the finest in the North of England. Having said that, there are many snuff boxes in the lower price range – £40 or £50, or even less.'

'The sort one might find in antique shops or car boot sales?'

'Yes, but in the case of the high prices, I am speaking of the upper range of the very best, the elite of the world of snuff boxes.'

'So yours were almost at that elevated level? Quite remarkable! If I may be so bold, how did you come to have such a prestigious collection when your usual exhibits are things like tradesmen's tools, Stone Age relics or artefacts from peasants' cottages?'

'The collection was left to us by the de Kowscott-Hawke family, owners of this house before it became a museum. Sir Joshua, who lived here until 1952, felt a museum was the best place for the collection, and he chose us because the boxes would remain in this house, his former home. We have informed the descendants of the family about the theft, by the way, and our insurers.'

'So how many snuff boxes have disappeared?'

'All of them, Mr Pluke, all twenty-five.'

'Of different styles?'

'Yes, and made from a variety of materials – ceramic, silver, enamel, agate, tortoiseshell, ivory, various metals, a range of woods some with hand-carvings . . . a wonderful variety, Mr Pluke, and such a sad, sad loss. They were collected by an ancestor of Sir Joshua de Kowscott-Hawke while travelling around the world. It was not a large collection by any means, but one of great variety and interest. I have supplied a full list to your officers and fortunately we have photographs of them too. Your officers now have copies of those photographs.'

'It was very wise of you to photograph them, ideal in helping us deal with a tragedy of this kind.'

'We found it a most useful record to have, and we could use the photographs for publicity purposes and brochures. Your officers assured me they would reproduce the photographs and circulate details to every police force, all antique dealers, Crimestoppers, the internet and so forth. I added I had no objection to the press being informed, press coverage being very useful in this instance.'

'And has there been any publicity? I must admit I saw none in Italy.'

'Yes, articles have appeared in several newspapers, and our loss was featured on television, with illustrations. I was very pleased with that coverage, and the way your scientific officers examined the scene. You would like to see the scene, I expect?'

'Indeed I would.'

'I'll take you in a moment. We have not used the room since, it is just as it was following the raid. I have kept it locked upon the advice of your Detective Sergeant Wain, he said his teams might want to return for a second search for clues, DNA evidence even. He is liaising with the police in Cumbria to try and establish whether there are any scientific links between the two crimes. Now follow me.'

Porter stopped to collect a set of keys from reception then led the way up the main staircase, the route used by members of the public and identified by arrows and signs. They climbed to the second flight and then the third, avoiding the exhibition rooms where members of the public were already viewing the contents. In all cases, the doors of the exhibition rooms were opened flat against the corridor wall to allow sight into each of the rooms; an attendant sat on a chair at the end of each corridor. A stout door at the top of the final stairs stood open to allow them entry and Pluke followed his leader along what had clearly been a corridor in the servants' quarters in the loft of the original house, shut off from the residential quarters of the house owners. The former loft-bedroom space, which had clearly allowed the domestic staff a degree of privacy, now contained nine small exhibition rooms, all of which were open today with the exception of No.1. Its door bore a notice saying, 'Closed for redecoration.'

'We felt it better to say that than to admit to a serious crime,' smiled Porter. 'We do not want our customers to be alarmed by the possibility of criminals being among them as they browse.'

Pluke made no comment as Porter unlocked the door and opened it wide; like the others, it opened outwards to come to rest flat against the passage wall and clicked home on a catch. The attendant was an elderly lady who acknowledged her boss and Pluke with a smile of welcome. The wide-open door allowed a broad view of the interior and permitted Pluke to step inside to a distance of

54

only a few inches as Porter switched on the lights. Pluke found he had a view of the entire room and so went no further. If the crooks had descended from the ceiling where the hole was, then there would be no risk of contaminating evidence in the doorway. The room had clearly been the bedroom of a former maid; it was small, only about six feet wide by ten feet long. The window, of the sash type, was on his left, barred and closed; the glass display cabinet occupied the outer wall to the right of that window. It stood on wooden legs so that its surface was slightly above waist level. It was about four feet six inches long by three feet wide by ten inches deep, and the glass had been smashed in two places where he could see the remains of bright metal locks.

In the far corner on the right was the hole in the ceiling; clearly, a saw had been used to cut the laths above. Pieces lay on the floor along with sawdust and plaster. No daylight was showing through the hole, he noted, but there was more dust, debris and plaster on the floor, temporarily undisturbed at the request of the police. Around the room were printed posters and notices, aided by colourful pictures; these told the story of the use of snuff and the importance of fashionable and ornamental snuff boxes.

This room had been devoted entirely to the history of snuff and snuff boxes. There were two dining-style chairs against one wall, but nothing else. The floor was carpeted, noted Pluke; it might contain more evidence if it was searched anew. Dust from outside, personal hairs, fibres from clothing, DNA – all such debris would have to be separated from that deposited unwittingly by visitors but he knew the carpet could be a rich source of evidence. His officers would have examined it very thoroughly.

'I am surprised that such valuable objects were kept in glass display cabinets with nothing more to protect them than two simple locks,' said Pluke. 'I would have thought they were extremely vulnerable during your opening hours, especially at the top of the building like this, away from the centres of activity.'

'The glass is toughened, Mr Pluke, and the metal of the locks will defy all but the most powerful tools. You will see we leave the doors wide open during the time our visitors are on the premises, and there is always an attendant on this corridor. If we are short-staffed, then quite simply we do not open this landing. I can assure you we do take care, Mr Pluke. Our measures mean that while the public have access to this corridor, there is always someone in attendance, but if an attack was made on any of the displays while the attendant was there, he or she would close that upper door; it locks automatically. It means the culprit would be locked in, Mr Pluke.'

'Unless he escaped through the roof, or took hostages,' smiled Pluke. 'But yes, I can see there is some element of deterrence here.'

'Clearly not enough!' sighed Porter.

'Let us say that if I had been your Crime Prevention Officer, I would perhaps have given different advice about the security of high value exhibits – not that you keep many on the premises. But let us not worry about closing the stable door now that the horse has bolted. I presume, however, that the hole in the roof has been repaired even if the ceiling remains untouched?'

'Yes, we had to effect that repair immediately to keep out the weather and other intruders – wildlife as well as burglars! Our groundsman-cum-caretaker did it.'

'Naturally I shall ask at my own office to determine how the criminals got on to the roof, there will be photographs of the scene in our crime file and I shall personally compare it with the Cumbrian file. I do hope my officers have found some evidence of these criminals' presence. Everyone leaves some evidence of their presence wherever they go. DNA evidence as a rule. Well, Mr Porter, I think I have seen enough for the time being. I may decide to have another look at this room after consulting my officers.'

56

'You are welcome at any time, Mr Pluke, and we shall not do anything in that room until you give us the go-ahead.'

'And now I would like to see the roof,' said Pluke.

'I have the key,' smiled Porter.

He led Pluke up to the top storey and then they climbed a short ladder which took them into the huge loft. Porter switched on the lights at which Pluke could see the large water tanks, electrical cables and an assortment of cast-off furnishings. The floor was covered with stout boarding and Porter led Pluke across it, and up a short flight of wooden steps to a heavy wooden door. It bore two massive bolts and a stout mortice lock. The experts were right – no one could break in here – but they had clearly omitted to consider the removal of tiles. Porter opened the door, allowing an eye-blinking light to enter the loft, then he led Pluke out on to the huge roof. Between the peaks of tiles and chimney stacks, the lead-lined path led rather like a maze and soon Pluke was staring down to the ground as visitors enjoyed the gardens, old buildings and fish pond totally unaware of his presence above them.

'This is where he got in,' said Porter eventually. 'If it was at night, no one would see him up here, that chimney stack would have hidden him anyway, but you can see how he could have reached the roof from those grounds down there and worked unseen by anyone.'

'It's a very long way down,' was all Pluke could think of saying. 'I should not wish to climb a ladder on to this roof!'

'Let's hope you never have to, Mr Pluke. Now, this is where the tiles were removed,' and he showed Pluke a sloping area where the tiles had clearly been resited because the stains of nature upon them no longer matched their surrounds. Pluke studied the area for a minute or two, and then thanked Mr Porter. It was time to return to the house below.

'Before I leave,' said Pluke as they made their way

downstairs, 'I would like information about that snuff box I mentioned earlier, the Siena – which is the real reason for my presence today.'

'I have details in my office, Mr Pluke.'

'I can get information about them all from my officers, I know they will have abstracted as much as possible from you, but from a private point of view I am particularly interested in the Siena snuff box.'

Back in his office, Neil Porter buzzed his secretary on the intercom and asked, 'Dorothy, get Mr Pluke one of those leaflets about the Siena snuff box, will you? And a photograph if we have one. And copies of that brochure about the entire collection of boxes.'

As they waited, Porter explained that the entire collection comprised all twenty-five snuff boxes which had been on display until this unfortunate incident; none had been added or removed. The de Kowscott-Hawke family had never asked to view them privately although it was thought members had come from time to time to view the collection as members of the public, without announcing their presence. At the time of the donation, the museum had managed to extract brief notes about each of the boxes, giving, where possible, its age, measurements, country of origin, material from which it was manufactured and notes of any previous owners or matters of historic interest. And photographs had been taken, first in black and white and later in colour. No value had been placed upon the donation at the time of its receipt although in later years the museum had had the collection valued for insurance purposes.

Dorothy arrived with the leaflets and a fistful of photographs which she passed to Porter. He thanked her, looked at them briefly, and then passed the entire file to Pluke.

'There you are, Mr Pluke, notes about all our snuff boxes including the Siena. If it's not in those notes, then we don't know it!'

'So the Siena box came to you with all the others from

the de Kowscott-Hawke family,' Pluke said. 'And since that time, nothing untoward has happened to it?'

'Nothing, Mr Pluke, it has been sitting in that little collection since 1952, with no dramas until this week. I have no personal knowledge of its previous history, other than what is on that piece of paper. I had better add that I know of no reason why the collection should have been stolen, apart from its obvious monetary value – which would be known to any expert or collector who saw it – but I do not think the Siena box was especially targeted, if that is what you are thinking. I have no reason to believe it has any special relevance; so far as we are concerned, it is just part of the collection.'

'It has special relevance, Mr Porter, but only from the point of view of my personal researches. Well, thanks for all your help. Now, one final question – do you have the address of the de Kowscott-Hawke family? I would like to talk to them both about the theft but also to test their knowledge about the Siena box.'

'No problem, they've always been most helpful and interested in our museum; in fact, Sir Eustace is one of our patrons. He is the grandson of Sir Joshua, the man who donated the collection. He lives at Kowscott-Hawke House, Crickledale.'

'I know it well – I did not realize until now that the family had any association with your museum,' smiled Pluke. 'I will pay him a visit in the very near future.'

And so Montague Pluke emerged from the museum clutching some snippets of information about the Siena snuff box but without seeing the object in question. Who on earth would want to steal it? he asked himself. And would the thief have any idea of its vital importance in the long and thrilling history of horse troughs?

With the feeling of dejection returning and threatening to overwhelm him, it was time to rejoin Millicent.

Chapter Five

Burdened by extreme misery at this outrage against the snuff boxes and the Siena box in particular, Pluke located Millicent in the craft shop where she was examining a long woollen scarf which looked as commodious and dazzling as Joseph's coat of many colours. She was holding it up against the light in an attempt to gauge its usefulness in width, length and warmth when Montague arrived. A most useful garment for the depths of winter upon these moors, it was in the summer sale at a bargain price.

'Montague!' She was horrified at the paleness of his face and the sadness which clouded his eyes. 'What's happened? You look dreadful.'

'It's the snuff box.' He sounded hoarse as the full realization of the crime made its dreadful impact upon him. During his visit to the museum, he had managed to maintain his traditional decorum in spite of the appalling situation but now he found himself unable to continue the pretence any longer. He felt like weeping, and looked like it. This was surely the worst day of his life.

'It's been stolen,' he whispered and with no further ado regaled Millicent with an unexpurgated rendering of the entire story. Standing in the shop with the scarf danging from her hands, she listened with complete sympathy as he unfolded his story. She listened in open-mouthed astonishment as the full import of the crime struck her, then said, 'I think you need a cup of good strong tea, Montague.'

She replaced the scarf on the sales shelf with a smile of appreciation at the hovering assistant who had clearly been hoping to find it a good home, but now abandoned all thoughts of making a purchase as she led the grieving Montague outside. She took him along the street to the tea shop where she fussed over him as if he had just suffered the bereavement of a favourite kitten.

'Now, Montague, you must talk about it,' she pleaded with him after ordering tea and cream scones. 'You must not dwell upon this matter, you must not bottle up any of your frustrations, emotions or anger. Get it all out in the open. So what are the full circumstances of this appalling tragedy?'

He told her everything he had learned from Mr Porter and pulled the literature from his capacious coat pocket, spreading it on the table before Millicent and indicating the pieces about the Siena snuff box. In fact, he had not yet read the notes about it but a glance at the photograph, in colour, showed that Mr Green in the Siena shop had accurately recaptured the design on his plastic paper-clip tray or miniature trough, albeit without the frieze. As the waiter arrived with the crockery prior to delivering the order, Millicent pored over the picture caption.

'That frieze is very indistinct, Montague, I can't see it very well but it might be flowers or it could even be words. I can't read them though. There's not very much here about its history, is there? It says the snuff box was made from wood, probably maple, and finished with bas-relief hand carvings on the face panel. The carving is generally accepted as a portrayal of Siena and its role in the Palio.'

'An unmistakable scene, Millicent, as we know.'

'Instantly recognizable, Montague. Now, it says the box measures four inches long by two and a quarter inches wide and one and a half inches deep; it has a tight-fitting lid, also of wood, but the whole of the interior is lined with tin while the exterior is gilt which makes it look like gold.'

'Gilt to look like gold?'

'Yes. The date of manufacture is uncertain, although it is thought to be around 1790. It is almost certainly the work of an unknown craftsman in Siena, one who specialized in miniatures; this was a regular feature of Sienese craftman-ship. Making miniatures, I mean.'

'Is there anything which confirms it was a miniature replica of the Golden Horse Trough?' he asked.

'Yes, yes indeed,' she smiled. 'It was folded under the bit I was reading . . . just another line or two. It says it is widely accepted that the box's workmanship is typical of the craftsmen of Siena during the late eighteenth century, although there is no guarantee it is an Italian work of art. It is just the opinion of someone who examined the box. It does say, however, that the snuff box is a miniature version of the long-lost Golden Horse Trough of Siena including the inscription on its face, and it adds that the inscription is difficult to read, due to age and fair wear and tear. There is nothing about the material from which the original trough was made, Montague. It would hardly be wood, would it, even if the snuff box was wood. These notes point out that ornamentation of snuff boxes was usually upon the lids but as this is a replica of a trough, the ornamentation is on the front panel as troughs do not have lids.'

'Well, there we are! The long-lost golden trough, eh? A snippet of evidence has arisen virtually on my own door-step, and unrecognized for its true worth. And now that evidence has been stolen!' Pluke issued a long sigh of utter misery. 'Is this a mere coincidence, or is there some sinister anti-trough motive behind the crime? Did someone know I was engaged in that research in Siena? And what about that inscription, Millicent? What does it say? I must find a way of determining those words, they could be most important.'

'It might be a frieze of flowers, remember, or some other ornamentation.'

'Yes, yes, I know, but I must look on the positive side, Millicent, I must look forward with hope.'

'Well spoken, Montague, this is the real you. Now, let's start again. You say the trough has been missing since 1347?'

'Perhaps a little later, after the plague. 1348 or so. A year or two is of little consequence, for it has been missing for a very very long time. That was long before that snuff box was made. Does it mean, Millicent, that the trough was still intact at the time the snuff box was made? If not, how was the copy achieved? And who wrote the words on that frieze? Indeed, who wrote the words on that piece of paper? Who knew his history well enough to realize that this was indeed a genuine replica? Surely, it means the trough *must* have survived somewhere after being removed, legally or otherwise, after the resurfacing of the Piazza del Campo! It must have been recognized for what it was, otherwise how could anyone reproduce this miniature copy and have it recorded in these pamphlets?'

'That is a very good point, Montague. You are most observant.'

'It means I must speak to the de Kowscott-Hawke family, Millicent, I must find out just how much they knew about the snuff boxes, and this one in particular.'

'Yes, but it is not all that urgent, Montague. I saw a nice woolly sweater in that shop just before you came in, and I thought how nice you would look in it . . .'

'Sweater, Millicent? In the height of summer? I do not wear sweaters anyway, so how can I be interested in one at such a devastating moment of my life? No, thank you. Now I must leave. I must speak to Sir Eustace de Kowscott-Hawke without delay, he lives in Crickledale, you know.'

Before leaving the table, he studied the illegible frieze, now concluding that it appeared to be more like writing than flowers or mere adornment, but he could not decipher it.

'Come along, Millicent, we must go.'

And so the Plukes finished their snack and left immediately.

Sir Eustace de Kowscott-Hawke was a man of military appearance whose impeccable bearing revealed his aristocratic family background. Some six feet two inches tall with a mop of well-cared-for black hair and a back as straight as a ram-rod despite his seventy-nine years, he oozed authority and confidence as he went about his daily routine in Crickledale. He drove a rather battered old grey Volvo which carried his two labradors, and wore tweed jackets, cavalry twill trousers, brogue shoes and sometimes a green trilby hat with a jay's feather in the band.

Sir Eustace could often be seen on the grouse moors or following the fox-hunt but more frequently, he could be observed striding around Crickledale before ringing the council every few days about litter in the streets, blocked drains, holes in the road, overflowing waste bins or any other nuisance which caught his attention. He did a lot for Crickledale, did Sir Eustace. In spite of living in this small market town, he was considered a genuine countryman, a true country gentleman in fact, one of a dying breed but a man of comfortable means who supported charities, sat on committees and chaired a bewildering range of small-town meetings.

When the renowned Detective Inpector Pluke, the officer in charge of Crickledale Sub-Divisional Criminal Investigation Department, telephoned to ask for an appointment, therefore, Sir Eustace reckoned it must be in connection with something pretty damned vital to the well-being of Crickledale and so he agreed.

'Five thirty, Pluke, at my house. We can enjoy a malt or

two before I have to break off for dinner. Five thirty then. On the dot.'

And so it was that Montague found himself outside Kowscott-Hawke House. He was pleased to note a horse-shoe hanging on the wall to the left of the door – and it was the correct way up, i.e. its points were pointing upwards. Clearly, the occupants were anxious to attract good fortune. To the right of the doorway was a massive brass bell with a rope and clapper hanging beneath it; Pluke pulled on the rope, the bell sounded like something from an ocean liner and the solid dark green door with its highly polished brass fittings was eventually opened by a middle-aged maid wearing a white apron over her black dress. She also sported a rather fetching little white cap.

'I have an appointment with Sir Eustace,' Pluke announced.

'Yes, Mr Pluke, he is expecting you.' Clearly she recognized him. 'Follow me, please.'

Pluke, entering the superb house with his right foot first, removed his panama but the maid did not relieve him of it and so he carried it in his left hand, leaving his right hand free for shaking. He was led into a spacious lounge with a log fire blazing in the grate; the place seemed cluttered with old and very comfortable armchairs, ancient carpets and rugs bearing signs of wear especially in front of the fire, and small side tables bearing a selection of glasses. A trolley laden with a variety of malt whiskies and sherries stood in one corner, and after bidding him to take a seat, the maid said, 'I will inform Sir Eustace immediately, Mr Pluke.'

Pluke did not take a seat but took the opportunity to move around the room to examine the wonderful old paintings and etchings which adorned the walls; there was a pen-and-ink drawing of the family's former home which was now the museum in Pebblewick, some faded Victorian images of family members and, he noted, some fine original oil portraits of important-looking people from past generations.

'Ah, Pluke old chap,' said a voice behind him and he turned to find the impressive figure of Sir Eustace bearing down. 'Examining our rogues' gallery, eh?' and he came forward with his hand extended. Pluke shook it.

'I am always interested in matters of history, Sir Eustace, and I am eternally gratified that the Victorians, and indeed those before them, took such pains to record their families and homes in such a range of fascinating ways.'

'Couldn't agree more, old chap. Now, a malt? I have a very good selection.'

Pluke was not a person for drinking spirits, and was extremely wary of being bribed to the extent he would be unable to execute his duties, but, he quickly reasoned, he was not here on police business because he was still officially on holiday. Furthermore, he was a guest in the home of this most eminent of local personages and felt it would be bad manners to decline. And so he accepted the offer and chose an Isle of Jura single malt.

'A very agreeable choice, old chap,' said Sir Eustace. 'Now, sit yourself down over there, next to that side table, while I get the drinks and then we can talk.'

Pluke found himself sinking into an old green leather chair to the left of the fireplace with its massive blaze while Sir Eustace was clearly going to occupy the one opposite. Pluke, remembering his manners, placed his hat on the floor but no one had offered to take his coat; he kept it on and saw that as a message that he was not expected to overstay his welcome.

'I am here to discuss the snuff boxes which were stolen from the museum at Pebblewick, Sir Eustace,' he began when Sir Eustace was settled and the drinks were in place.

'Ah, well, there's not a lot I can say about that, Mr Pluke, ancient family history, you understand. My grandfather wanted them to go to the museum, a sort of memento of our family home. Having sold the house for conversion into a museum dedicated to local artefacts, he thought it would be a nice gesture to give them a gift. The snuff box collection was ideal for that purpose.'

'Most considerate, Sir Eustace,' and Pluke took a small sip from his glass. 'A very nice gesture.'

'It was, but all that happened when I was a very young man, Mr Pluke. More than fifty years ago. Neither I nor my father had any part in that, it was all the work of my grandfather. It means, of course, that I have no real knowledge of those boxes or of the circumstances under which they were donated; I did receive a recent call, last Wednesday in fact, to say the whole caboodle had been stolen, but really, it has nothing to do with me or my family. The call from the museum was more of a courtesy call, Mr Pluke, my family placed no conditions upon the presentation. It was a total gift from my grandfather, no strings attached; he was pleased to get rid of them, if we are being honest with one another.'

'Pleased to get rid of them? But why?' puzzled Pluke.

'Search me, old chap, probably they needed a lot of dusting!'

'Well, your grandfather must have had his reasons but I should point out, Sir Eustace, that I am not here as part of the ongoing investigation into their disappearance. I am officially on leave, you see, and the enquiry is being undertaken by other officers until I return. I must be careful not to appear to be undermining their efforts.'

'Really, then why are you here?' and Sir Eustace took an enormous swig from his malt.

'It is in connection with one particular snuff box, Sir Eustace. The Siena box. I am personally interested in that one, you see, due to its links with the Palio in Siena, and its horse trough associations.'

'Ah, yes, I keep forgetting you are the famous horse trough Pluke, are you not? I have heard your name spoken in awe, Mr Pluke, among horsey people. So tell me, what's so fascinating about that snuff box?'

Pluke, still sipping somewhat nervously at the strong whisky, provided a detailed account of the Palio, the vanished Golden Horse Trough of Siena, the artistry of the craftspeople of Siena and the plastic reproductions being sold to tourists, and then explained his growing belief that the original trough had not entirely disappeared as most people seemed to think. He proclaimed his theory that it had been removed from the piazza and probably retained elsewhere; anywhere in the world in fact.

'So you see, Sir Eustace, the Siena snuff box is, in my opinion, proof that the trough was still in existence long after it had supposedly disappeared from the Piazzo del Campo. It must have been available for that copy to have been made in the late eighteenth century.'

'You are suggesting that somebody might have had it, or might even still have it, and not know what it is, eh?'

'Possibly, Sir Eustace. I truly believe the ornamentation on that snuff box was copied from the actual Golden Horse Trough of Siena. It even carries an inscription, a feature of many troughs. It could be the only surviving link with the trough.'

'That is assuming the design is an accurate reproduction of the actual trough, eh, what?'

'I am sure it is, Sir Eustace, I cannot think how else that design, which has so many links with Siena, could appear on a snuff box. Thanks to the museum files, I have a photograph of it, and I found a plastic reproduction on sale to tourists in Siena. Most curiously, that tourist souvenir is a copy of the Siena snuff box, Sir Eustace, although lacking the frieze which surrounds the design. I'm convinced that both these reproductions owe their designs to the original trough.'

'But the plastic replica is surely a copy of a copy, is it not? Are you saying it was also copied from the original?'

'No, I believe the Siena snuff box was copied from the

original Golden Horse Trough, and that the plastic replica was later inspired by that same snuff box, Sir Eustace,' and he explained how that had occurred.

'Well, I'm dashed glad to learn the snuff box could be so important. So what is your purpose in coming to see me, Mr Pluke?' Sir Eustace was taking very large sips from his glass; in fact, he drained it and refilled it, noting Pluke had scarcely made any impact on his own supply.

'I would like to hear your personal knowledge of that snuff box, Sir Eustace, your family memories, it might help me trace the original golden trough.'

'Well, old chap, as I said, my knowledge is almost nil. The boxes were handed over to the museum when I was a very young man and my only recollection is that the family were glad to get rid of them.'

'I find that very curious, Sir Eustace.'

'Grandfather must have had his reasons. I know they took up precious space in the house and after all, they were nothing but trinkets collected by one of my ancestors on his travels overseas.'

'If they were regarded as mere trinkets at the time your grandfather disposed of them, Sir Eustace, with him having no wish to keep them, they have become extremely valuable with the passage of time. Most certainly they are not trinkets now. But their monetary value is of no concern to me. I am trying to discover whether you or any member of the family knows the history of the Siena box.'

'I very much doubt it. So far as I am aware, all the information our family possessed was handed over to the museum. I have to say, Pluke, that when my ancestor, whoever it was, first gained possession of that snuff box, he would have bought or received it as a trinket. He would have regarded it as nothing more than that, a mere souvenir of his journey, rather like those plastic things one gets nowadays. I very much doubt whether he would have concerned himself with its history, or any of its local folk associations, and it's hardly likely he would have recorded anything about it on paper. People don't do that with cheap souvenirs, do they?'

'That's just as one might expect, Sir Eustace. However, my desire is to trace the history of the Siena box as far as possible in the hope it will lead to the whereabouts of the Golden Horse Trough of Siena. That is my mission.'

'Well, old chap, I wish you the very best of British luck.'

'As a specialist in horse troughs, Sir Eustace, it would be my great desire to find it and restore it to its proper site in the Piazza del Campo.'

'A very worthy and noble thought, Mr Pluke, very worthy indeed. So what you really need is some knowledge of the Siena box *before* it came into my family? You are trying to convince yourself and everyone else that it must have been inspired by the original trough, and that the original was still extant at the time the Siena box was made?'

'Exactly, but I need to know all about it before it *left* your family too, Sir Eustace. I am hoping I can discover which of your family acquired it and how he came by it. Where did it come from? Who made it? Is it in fact a genuine copy of the golden trough? What is its provenance? I must know everything about it.'

'Then I am going to disappoint you, Mr Pluke. I know nothing about the Siena box as you call it. Nothing at all. I can't ask my father or my grandfather, they're both dead and gone, and I am sure my younger brother will know even less than me. I would guess he's never even heard of the snuff boxes. And none of my cousins will know about it, they live overseas, Australia in fact. Been there for umpteen generations. Sorry not to be more helpful, old chap.'

'Would you object if I contacted your brother, just in case?'

'Not at all, Pluke, old chap, not at all. I'll give you Seymour's telephone number and address, he lives in the

Lake District, not far from Keswick,' and Sir Eustace wrote the relevant information on a piece of paper he took from his pocket, and handed it to Pluke.

'Give him my regards if you call him, and tell him it's time he came to see his elder brother. He never comes to see me, you know, I think he hates driving on roads full of slow-moving tourists.'

'Yes, of course.' Pluke could sense the meeting was drawing to a close and so he drained his glass even if it made his throat burn and his eyes water, and then stood up. 'Well, Sir Eustace, I must thank you for your co-operation. I will continue my enquiries in the hope I can find an answer to this problem.'

'Let me know if you do turn up any surprises, old chap,' beamed Sir Eustace. 'Sorry not to have been of more help but I will ask around members of my family just in case some snippets of gossip have filtered down the generations and if I do come across anything, then of course I shall contact you.'

And so Montague Pluke left the cosiness of Sir Eustace's home with no further advancement to his quest. It was time to go home. Millicent would have his evening meal ready. The world seemed to be spinning rather faster than normal, or was it something to do with that malt whisky?

On his way home, he reckoned he had a few minutes to spare so he decided to pop into Crickledale Police Station on the off-chance that Detective Sergeant Wayne Wain was there, or perhaps Sergeant Cockfield pronounced Cofield. The latter was in charge of the Control Room at the police station. As it transpired, Wayne Wain was in the CID office and so, with fumble-footed hesitancy, Pluke made his way up the stairs to speak to him.

'Hello, sir,' welcomed Wayne Wain. 'Can't you keep away? I thought you were on holiday until Monday.'

'I am indeed, Wayne,' smiled Pluke, feeling instantly at home in these familiar surroundings. 'But I have a good reason for calling in.'

'I never doubted that for a moment, sir,' said Wayne, a very tall and very handsome man with black hair, dark eyes, a huge white smile and a magnetic personality which drew women to him like bees to a honey-pot. Everyone liked Wayne Wain; he was the only officer whom Pluke saw fit to address by his Christian name and that was only because his surname and forename sounded alike. 'And what, might I ask, is that reason?'

Wayne was sure he could smell whisky on Pluke's breath. If so, that was something quite remarkable, but after all, the fellow was still on holiday. Wayne decided not to mention the matter.

'It is about the snuff box theft, Wayne.'

'So you've heard about it? Well, sir, there's no need for you to worry yourself about that, everything's been taken care of. Full circulation of the stolen goods, Crimestoppers notified, links with Cumbria established due to a similar break-in in their area, relevant websites supplied with information, all other forces notified with specific requests that their Antique Squads be alerted, Interpol informed . . . whatever has to be done, has been done, sir. Scenes of Crime has examined the scene and photographed it . . . it's just a case of waiting for one of those snuff boxes to surface in an antique shop or car boot sale and bingo, we'll catch the villains responsible.'

'Did the perpetrators leave any evidence behind? Have we any intelligence on the motive behind the crime? Is there a mad collector of snuff boxes at large, collecting them for his personal and secret hoard?'

'Nothing, sir. It was a very clean and well-executed raid, no useful evidence left behind at all. Just like the Cumbria job in fact, although in their case miniature paintings were stolen.'

'Small collectables in both cases, Wayne, easily transported and easily disposed of. When did it happen, precisely?'

'Our crime was last Wednesday, sir, committed in the early hours of the morning, so we believe. The museum closed at 5.30 p.m. on Tuesday and the raid was discovered next morning by the curator when he opened up. They got in through the roof, a clever job, sir, very professional. Cumbria's was the Wednesday before – we're hoping there won't be another one this coming Wednesday.'

'Thank you. Now, I should explain that I have a particular interest in this crime because there is one snuff box, among those stolen, which is linked to my recent research in Siena. Hence my visit to the museum this morning.'

'Ah!' said Wayne Wain, now realizing this was more than a courtesy visit.

'It is the one known as the Siena box, Wayne.'

'I remember seeing its picture, sir, yes. With the Virgin Mary on the front surrounded by racehorses. Most unusual. I fail to see why such a picture should adorn a snuff box, sir.'

'It wasn't a picture, Wayne, it was an embossed image, a bas-relief sculpture with something akin to a frieze around it. Probably an inscription of some kind. The snuff box is a miniature replica of a famous horse trough. Lots of troughs did have inscriptions, Wayne, in honour of those who donated them. I had better explain my interest, then you will understand my deep concern about that snuff box.'

A strong whiff of whisky fumes filled the office as Pluke opened his mouth and then, with just the slightest slurring of his words, he proceeded to tell Wayne all about the Palio and the Golden Horse Trough of Siena. Wayne Wain, being polite, listened with as much interest as he could muster and it did not take him long to appreciate that the stolen miniature image of *l'abbeveratoio del cavallo dorato* had now assumed massive importance. For Pluke to find the snuff box – and even the famous golden trough – was akin to solving a murder on his own doorstep.

'You must understand, Wayne, that I am not suggesting it has been stolen due to its prominence in the horse trough world, but you will appreciate that I have sound reasons for making the greatest possible endeavours to recover it.'

'Of course, sir, you know us, you know the skills and dedication of your officers, they have never let you down yet, sir, and never will. If it is possible to find that snuff box – and even *l'abbeveratoio del cavallo dorato* – then we shall do it. You may rest assured about that.'

'But you were not given any special information about that particular snuff box, were you?'

'No, sir, nothing extra, just the information we received from the museum. I must admit I had no idea of the importance of that particular box.'

'Well, that defect has now been rectified, Wayne and you will have a better understanding of the significance of this crime. But I shall trouble you no further. You will have a lot to do. I shall now go home and will see you on Monday.'

'Have a nice weekend, sir,' Wayne wished him as he departed, and smiled as Pluke almost misjudged the size and position of the doorway.

On his way home, Pluke halted at Crickledale's impressive Coachman's Trough with its triple capacity, cobbled standing area, brass inlet valves and stone carving of a lion's head; this dated to the mid-seventeenth century, he knew, and had been a gift to the town by the then mayor. But the age of the Crickledale trough was nought when compared with *l'abbeveratoio del cavallo dorato*; if the legend was correct it was about four hundred years older than the Crickledale gem. Four hundred years! Nearly half a millennium.

But this trough was still in prime condition, still producing an endless supply of pure fresh water, still a feature of the town and still a focal point for horses being ridden in the town. He felt sure that if *l'abbeveratoio del cavallo dorato* had survived vandalism, then it too would be functional even after the passage of so many centuries, just like this Crickledale trough. So where was it now? Had it been spirited out of Siena rather as the Elgin Marbles had been spirited out of Greece? Was it now reclining in some museum somewhere in the world without anyone realizing what it really was?

Pluke turned for home and decided to ring Sir Eustace's brother. He would do so immediately, this evening in fact. Strike while the iron is hot, he told himself. If Sir Eustace had no interest in the former family heirloom, then his brother might show more concern for the fate of those snuff boxes. He hiccuped and turned for home, placing his hand in his pocket – the rabbit's foot was still there, he was pleased to note. Good luck would surely be his.

Chapter Six

At home, and while Millicent was sipping her small sherry before dinner, Montague rang the Keswick number given to him by Sir Eustace. A crisp and rather high-pitched male voice answered. 'De Kowscott-Hawke, who is that?'

'Detective Inspector Pluke from Crickledale Sub-Divisional Criminal Investigation Department.' Pluke, generally loath to use his position as a senior police officer for the furtherance of his own private ends, felt that on this occasion he could justifiably combine the business of investigating the snuff box theft with his vital research into the Golden Horse Trough. 'To whom am I speaking, please?' He felt the announcement of his high-profile public role in Crickledale society would persuade this de Kowscott-Hawke to listen. It did.

'Ah, the police. What can I do for you, Constable Pluke?'

'Detective Inspector Pluke,' Montague corrected him with as much polite firmness as he could muster. 'And who are you, sir?'

'Me? I'm de Kowscott-Hawke. That's who you are ringing, isn't it, man?' The voice sounded short and anxious not to be bothered by this humble policeman.

'Seymour de Kowscott-Hawke?' Pluke persisted.

'Yes, man, that is me. For heaven's sake, what are you ringing about?'

'I have just been speaking to your brother in Crickledale, Sir Eustace . . .'

'Good old Eustace. Tell him it's time he came to visit me, he never comes here, you know, I think it's because he doesn't like fighting his way along roads full of slow-moving gawping tourists. So what can I do for you, Sergeant?'

'Detective Inspector, I am a detective inspector.'

'So you said, now get on with it, man. Why are you ringing me?'

'It is about your family legacy to Pebblewick Folk Museum, Mr de Kowscott-Hawke, the snuff boxes.'

'Trinkets, Superintendent, mere trinkets.'

'Detective Inspector actually, sir.'

'So what has happened to them that requires you to ring me, Sergeant? It's more than half a century since my family donated those useless bits and pieces to the museum, glad to get rid of them if you ask me. Worth nothing, not antiques worthy of credence, always a nuisance, a load of bother, all that dusting and cleaning . . . I would not want them around this house, Chief Superintendent. And if you are asking if I know anything about them, then I don't. I can't even remember seeing them let alone claim any detailed knowledge about the damned things.'

'They have been stolen, Mr de Kowscott-Hawke. The museum was broken into during last week, a very skilful operation which avoided the alarm system, and all the snuff boxes were stolen.'

'Well, I hope you're not suggesting I am the culprit, Detective Constable Pluke. So far as I recall, from family gossip when I was a mere stripling, my grandfather was glad to get rid of those things. Not a scrap of use to anyone, so I must say I am not too worried about this turn of events, not too worried at all. And if you think I took the damned things, think again, I wouldn't have them in the house, Detective Sergeant Pluke.'

'I am interested in one particular snuff box.' Pluke decided it was a waste of time trying to educate this man about the hierarchy of ranks within the police service. 'It is known as the Siena snuff box.'

'All the same to me, old chap. One snuff box is just like another to me, never touch the stuff anyway, it seems a crazy idea, shoving powder up your nose to make you sneeze, but what's so special about that box?'

'I believe it depicts a scene based on the Golden Horse Trough of Siena,' Pluke said with as much conviction as he could muster. 'In historic terms, it could prove to be a most valuable item, and I am ringing you to ask if you had heard any reference to that snuff box during your time at the house in Pebblewick.'

'Siena? Did you say Siena, Detective Sergeant? But that's in Italy.'

'Yes, it is. I believe the snuff box design was taken from the original Golden Horse Trough which was given to the people of Siena around 1347, to be used by the horse which won the Palio . . .'

'Ah, the Palio, yes. Wonderful stuff, what a race. But sorry, Mr Pook, I know nothing about your horse trough or your snuff box. As I said, the family got rid of the things years ago. My grandfather said he didn't want them in the house, so I was told, and when the family home was sold, he let the snuff boxes go with it. Very generous, everyone said, but he wasn't a generous man, Mr Cook, if he got rid of them he would do so with some very good reason. Sorry I can't help any more, Commissioner. And do tell that brother of mine to get himself over the Pennines to see me one of these days, tourists or no tourists.'

And the phone went dead even before Pluke could thank him. He stared at the handset for a second or two and then Millicent called to say she was ready to serve dinner. As they ate, she pressed him for an update on the day's events since they had last spoken, and he told her about all his adventures, including the telephone conversation just completed. She listened in good-mannered silence as he recounted his experiences in considerable detail, and then stated, in the form of a question, 'There must be some reason for thieves stealing those boxes, Montague?'

'It's their monetary value, my dear, they are worth a lot of money. They are collectors' items, worth a huge amount as a collection but also worth a lot as individual items. If any of those found their way on to the legitimate market, they could command huge sums. Just like those Cumbrian miniatures.'

'Then why did the family want rid of them, Montague? You have just told me that Mr Seymour and Sir Eustace both said their grandfather wanted rid of them. If they were so valuable why would their grandfather want to dispose of them?'

'It seems to me, my dear, that grandfather de Kowscott-Hawke had no idea of their worth or their historic importance. By all accounts, he thought they were trinkets, not worthy of space in his house. I can't see that the dusting and care of them would present a problem to a household with maids, but when he sold the premises, he gave them to the new owner – which happened to be a museum.'

'But it does seem to me, Montague, that his apparent benevolence was not entirely due to his generosity.'

'What are you trying to tell me, Millicent?'

'I wonder if he could have wanted rid of that collection for some other reason. Maybe he did so in a manner which made him appear generous. That shows double standards, Montague, a certain deviousness that is not becoming in a true gentleman but I believe such behaviour was commonplace among the Victorians and those who wished to present an acceptable face to their public. It seems to me that he wanted rid of them and this was one way of doing so in a manner befitting his station in life.'

'Offload them on to some unsuspecting person? But we don't know that with any certainty, do we? All we know for certain is that he gave the entire collection to the museum. We are not aware of an ulterior motive for doing so.'

'I think, Montague, that if you are so keen to find out more about your Siena box, you should endeavour to discover why de Kowscott-Hawke would want rid of those snuff boxes, all of them that is, including the one from Siena.'

'Are you trying to suggest there is something unsavoury about those boxes?' he puzzled, wondering if they had been stolen by someone else at some stage in their distant past.

'We know nothing of their previous history, Montague, nothing at all. I am aware, though, that it has been known for curses to be associated with certain ancient or historic objects, and you above all people should know that. I mean, what about the Curse of Tutankhamun? People said there was no such thing but the Earl of Carnarvon died during the excavations into Tutankhamun's tomb at the very time there was a power failure in Cairo, and his dog died at the same time!'

'Coincidence, Millicent, nothing more than coincidence, I am sure.'

'All the same, it is very odd. And don't forget there's the Curse of Cain and the Curse of Scotland, and isn't there some kind of curse which affects anyone plundering the pyramids?'

'Maybe, but I have never heard any reference to the Curse of the Snuff Boxes, even if there is a fungus called the Devil's Snuff Box,' said Pluke.

'I was thinking more of a curse involving the Golden Horse Trough,' persisted Millicent in her quiet way. 'And even things associated with it. Or possibly a curse affecting the people who possess images of it.'

'Good heavens, whatever gave you that idea? The Curse of the Golden Horse Trough? I know there are some fascinating examples of superstition around the world, but I doubt if the Golden Horse Trough of Siena was tainted in that manner. After all, it was a gift to the people, a thing of merit.'

'Nonetheless, it does seem to me that someone wanted rid of the Golden Horse Trough all those centuries ago for reasons we do not know. And they succeeded. Whoever it was, or whichever authority it was, they succeeded in getting *l'abbeveratoio del cavallo dorato* removed and written out of history to such an extent that even today no one will talk about it in Siena. It's no longer part of their culture or their history; you could ask any resident of Siena today, and they would know nothing about it. You've tried, remember. And now, here in England all those years later, someone wanted rid of a snuff box which carries the very same image as that trough – that's if your theories about the origins of that image are to be believed.'

'From what the records tell us, Millicent, de Kowscott-Hawke gave it to the museum out of the kindness of his heart, despite what Seymour suggests. I have not come across references to curses or evil of any kind associated with the trough. But if we are talking of curses being associated with images, or linked to people who possess such images, don't forget we bought a plastic trough bearing that same image. I doubt whether plastic souvenirs can carry curses! But even if there is a curse on us because we possess that same image, then I believe my own rituals to ensure good luck will counteract any evil forces. A rabbit's foot is a very good safeguard, Millicent, so I have no fears, not to mention that horseshoe near the front door of Sir Eustace's house. I have great faith in horseshoes and rabbits' feet.'

'I am pleased to learn of your confidence, Montague,' she smiled. 'I respect you for that.'

'The threat of ancient curses does not worry me, Millicent. However, there is one small aspect to all this which might have been overlooked,' and he looked steadily into her eyes. 'If there is a curse on those who possess the trough, or even an image of it, why did it not affect the museum?'

'But it did, it got broken into.'

81

'But the image arrived on the premises more than fifty years ago, and nothing appears to have happened since then – until the break-in.'

'But have you asked about that? Did you ask Mr Porter about any troubles the museum might have suffered since inheriting the snuff box?'

'Well, no, I must admit I did not, the thought never occurred to me. But if there is a curse on that image, Millicent, the person or persons who have stolen it will now suffer, will they not?'

'Quite likely, Montague, quite likely. If such things really happen.'

'Then I think I must ask the curator if he is aware of any odd incidents since the arrival of the snuff boxes at the museum, and then perhaps another word with Sir Eustace is in order, to ask about any of his family tragedies or unhappy events. Thank you, Millicent, you have raised an entirely new prospect about the Golden Trough of Siena. It might even enable me to trace its source.'

'That's if it actually existed!' she smiled cheekily. 'It might be nothing more than a wonderful legend, Montague, you must not overlook that possibility.'

'I am increasingly sure it did exist, my dear, and I believe that snuff box is proof of that. If there is a curse, then it must have been on the original trough. I wonder if it is anything to do with that supposed inscription? Is that the wording of the curse? I doubt if a copy of it, like something on a snuff box, could carry a curse. And, of course, our plastic replica does not carry that inscription or frieze or whatever it is. In spite of any likely curse, though, I still wish to find both.'

And so they settled down to complete their meal, each nursing their own private thoughts. Next morning, Montague rang the museum to check Sunday opening times and to ascertain whether Neil Porter would be in attendance. He was, and so Pluke arranged a second meeting; it was timed for 10 a.m. He would contact Sir Eustace later to fix an appointment with him.

Millicent decided not to accompany Montague even though Sunday was still part of their holiday – she had all their dirty washing and the aftermath of their trip to deal with. And so it was that Montague Pluke, still in holiday mode, caught a bus because his car driving was appalling and arrived for the second time at Pebblewick Folk Museum. As before, he ran the gauntlet of the old men sitting beneath the lych-gate as the man with the black and white cur laughed. 'Here again, eh, Mr Pluke? You've not caught him then?'

'All in good time!' waved Pluke in response. Once again, the meeting was in Mr Porter's office with Pluke sitting before the curator's desk as coffee was offered. Pluke accepted because he was still on holiday and attending in a non-police role.

'Well, Mr Pluke, this is another pleasant surprise. Have you brought some good news for us?' said Porter as he organized the coffee from an office percolator.

'I'm afraid not, Mr Porter. I am still on holiday although I did visit my office last night to check on progress but there is nothing to report. Everything that can be done to trace and recover your items is being done, I can assure you.'

'Thank you, so what can I do for you?' Porter carried two cups of coffee to his desk and placed one before Pluke, along with milk and sugar. Then he settled down.

'I am still pursuing my special interest in the Siena box, Mr Porter, but it means I shall be paying very close attention to your break-in when I return to duty and ensuring it receives the very best of investigations. It goes without saying that it is my wish to recover all your snuff boxes, but especially to find the Siena box and hopefully establish whether it has genuine links with the Golden Horse Trough.'

'My knowledge of the Golden Horse Trough is nil, Mr

Pluke, it is well beyond my professional brief. We do not concern ourselves with folk artefacts from foreign countries unless there is some special or strong link with our locality.'

'I realize that, but there is one aspect which intrigues me, Mr Porter. Now, can you tell me this. Have there been any untoward incidents in the museum or associated with the museum since it received the snuff boxes?'

'Untoward incidents, Mr Pluke? I'm not sure I understand.'

'Well, the break-in would, in itself, be considered an unfortunate event, but I am wondering whether there have been any other unwelcome occurrences since the boxes were given to you.'

'Well, it's an odd sort of question, Mr Pluke, and I am not sure how to answer it. I have not been curator for very long, there have been five or six curators since we received those snuff boxes, but I do know the museum has had its fair share of unwelcome events. Every establishment like this has its ups and downs, periods of prosperity followed by what the business world calls downturns. We're in the middle of one right now, I don't mind admitting. We're struggling to pay for the most recently installed of our thatched buildings just at a time when attendance figures are down. Well, they were down, there is a slight upturn just now. All one has to do is read the annual reports, they provide a very accurate account of our progress with all our problems and successes.'

'And the reports will be available should I wish to study them?'

'Yes, of course, we keep a modest library of our own achievements, Mr Pluke, and if it will help the investigation you are welcome to peruse them. But might I ask you about the kind of unfortunate incident to which you are referring? I might be able to help without you having to plough through all those reports.'

'Well,' said Pluke, racking his brains to provide an

example, 'there might have been gale damage to the buildings, floods from the moors, a chimney stack falling through the roof, theft of irreplacable objects, unexplained upsets . . .'

'Good heavens, Mr Pluke, you're not suggesting the snuff boxes are jinxed, are you? That they brought a curse to the place?'

'It was just a thought . . .'

'I know of your specialized knowledge of our folklore and superstitions, Mr Pluke, but to be frank I have never believed that an artefact of any kind, even if it did come from the pyramids or somewhere in ancient Greece, Rome or India, could exert any kind of malevolent influence, especially in modern times. Inanimate objects are not filled with evil spirits, Mr Pluke, I am quite sure of that. I can state that fact unequivocally, bearing in mind that among our exhibits are witch posts and objects used by witches such as witch bottles and broomsticks.'

'I am not suggesting such things exert evil influences today, but all I am curious to know is whether any unexplained incidents have occurred on these premises since you inherited the snuff boxes.'

'Might I ask why you have raised this matter, Mr Pluke? It hardly seems the sort of thing that would form part of a police investigation.'

'It is not part of the police investigation, it is part of my private enquiries into the background of the snuff boxes, the Siena box in particular. You see, there is just a hint – and it is nothing more than a hint at this stage – that the de Kowscott-Hawke family wanted rid of those boxes.'

'Wanted rid of them? You mean you *do* think there is a curse on them?'

'Well, I wouldn't put it quite like that, Mr Porter, I cannot say I believe in curses although it is one area of folklore I have not studied in depth; might I say I have an open mind on the matter? But nonetheless I am interested in any

85

untoward incidents which might have occurred since you inherited those snuff boxes.'

'Well, yes, now you have explained it like that. There was one year when all our staff caught influenza at the same time and we had to close for a fortnight. A very costly exercise, Mr Pluke, it cost us a lot of money in lost income. 1967 it was. And three years ago, a cleaner fell down those stairs just outside the room where the snuff boxes are . . . er, were . . . kept. She had been cleaning the boxes, and for some reason stumbled and fell down the stairs and broke an arm. And in 1963 one of the moorland streams got blocked and its waters, swollen by heavy rains, overflowed and flooded our ground floor, and then in 1972 lightning struck the gable end, and in 1980 the drains were blocked and we had a terrible smelly overflow into the museum, and in 1986 the roof of the thatched cottage in the grounds caught fire. There is our current financial struggle of course, not to mention the effect of the foot-and-mouth disease outbreak . . . so yes, Mr Pluke, we have suffered several unwelcome incidents since we received the snuff boxes, but surely no one can blame the boxes for any of them? There was nothing abnormal about any of those unfortunate occurrences, I can assure you, they could have happened to anyone. I see them as nothing more than a normal sequence of events, some good, some bad. That kind of thing happens all the time.'

'So it is a fact that there have been several unfortunate incidents, Mr Porter?'

'Well, yes, but there is no way I would associate any of those with the presence of the snuff boxes. That is being silly, Mr Pluke. They were the sort of misfortunes that could have happened to any similar organization.'

'Quite. Now, might I examine those annual reports? Just to read up the accounts for myself?'

'By all means. I could have got my secretary to make photocopies of the relevant reports and send them along to you, Mr Pluke, but it is Sunday and she is not working today. She can do it tomorrow, if you wish . . .'

'I would prefer to examine the reports now, Mr Porter, if that is possible. I must return to duty on Monday when my leisure time will be severely limited. Are your reports indexed? If so, it will not take me long to find the relevant entries and jot down a few details.'

'As you wish, Mr Pluke. I can take you into our rather modest library immediately, there is a table and chair in there and everything you need for research purposes. Ballpoints and even paper for you if you need it. Just help yourself. There might be other publications of interest to you too. And yes, our annual reports are indexed. It shouldn't take long to examine every one and find what you seek.'

'I am interested only in those published since the arrival of the snuff boxes, in fact, since the date the museum moved into these premises.'

'Good, then follow me.'

And so it was that Montague Pluke found himself sitting at a bare table in the small but efficient library of the folk museum. Mr Porter showed him the shelf containing the annual reports and left Pluke to his studies. He began immediately with the 1952 Annual Report and it didn't take many moments to locate the item which recorded the presentation of the snuff boxes. There was a black and white photograph of Sir Joshua de Kowscott-Hawke standing beside a table which bore the display case containing snuff boxes. The glass case had been propped up in a sloping position so that its contents were visible to the camera, and standing beside Sir Joshua was a rather plump moustachioed gentleman with a bald head who wore a smart, dark suit. According to the caption he was the then curator, a Mr Clarence Gardner, and the caption added that the presentation had occurred on Wednesday, 30th April 1952, the day the museum had officially opened in new and enlarged premises. Hitherto, the museum had occupied a small cottage in the same village.

On the day of that presentation, which coincided with the formal opening by Sir Joshua, there had been a party for the villagers and staff. Clearly, it had been a day of celebration, a happy occasion for everyone to remember. In this way, therefore, Pluke now had a precise date for the arrival of the snuff boxes at the museum and he made a note on the paper supplied by Porter.

He realized, of course, that the boxes might have been on the premises a few days before the official opening, but equally, Sir Joshua could have brought them with him for the formal handover. In the circumstances, he had to accept 30th April as the day of their arrival; there was nothing to indicate otherwise. In studying the reports in chronological order, Pluke soon realized that news of untoward incidents was always recorded in the Curator's Foreword; the rest of the report was split into various sections dealing with aspects of the displays, both indoors and outside, recording donations of new artefacts and the appointment of staff or the recruitment of specialist advisers. And so he read each foreword. In 1956, he discovered the then curator, still Mr Gardner, had suffered a broken leg in a road traffic accident and so he made a note of that, including the date; in 1963 there were the floods mentioned in passing by Neil Porter; in 1967 the outbreak of influenza closed the museum for a couple of weeks; and then in 1969 there had been a fall of soot from one of the chimneys of the former house. That had smothered many exhibits with a thick coating of black which had required costly and expert cleaning. In 1972 there was the lightning strike which damaged a gable end of the building with more expense. In 1976 all the goldfish in the pond died mysteriously, and in 1980 the village drains had become blocked, resulting in gallons of appalling effluent flooding into the museum. A messy time. Then in 1986 the thatched roof of one of the external cottages had caught fire; it was the one used to house period furniture as well as a real live lady who worked on a spinning wheel. And then in 2000 a cleaner fell downstairs and broke an arm after cleaning the snuff boxes.

Porter had recalled most of these, Pluke remembered; probably he hadn't thought it necessary to include the broken leg of a previous curator or the fall of soot. And the foot-and-mouth outbreak. Wasn't there an outbreak on the moors nearby at the end of April 2001? But, in Pluke's mind, all these events were worthy of record for one astonishing reason – they had all occurred on the same date. 30th April, the anniversary of the arrival of the snuff boxes.

Rather oddly, there was no comment on that curious fact. Not one report drew attention to that peculiar set of coincidences. Pluke flipped through the indices to see whether he had overlooked any aspect of his search, and also searched the other documents, all indexed, to see whether any contained a detailed history of the Siena box. None did. Then he let himself out of the tiny room and made his way back to Mr Porter's office. The door was open and Porter, at his desk, noticed Pluke's arrival.

'Come in, Mr Pluke, sit down. A successful search, was it?'

Pluke said it had been very successful and completed far more speedily than he would have expected; he explained the additional incidents he had uncovered – the soot and the curator's broken leg – and then produced his *coup de grâce*.

'Mr Porter, a remarkable thing has emerged. The formal presentation of the snuff boxes occurred on Wednesday, 30th April 1952, the day the museum officially opened the doors of its new premises – this former house. The date may not be significant to you but all the other incidents, without exception, occurred on 30th April. Every single one of them. Even the epidemic of influenza began on that date and the outbreak of foot-and-mouth, not recorded in your report of that year, had an outbreak at the end of April, if my memory serves me correctly.'

'Oh my God . . . I had no idea . . .'

'I would have thought someone would have commented on that, Mr Porter, someone must have noticed the somewhat remarkable coincidence.'

'Well, if they have, they have never mentioned it to me, and I must admit I did not absorb the fact of the dates. My studies of our past have not embraced such details, many of our tragedies occurred before my arrival anyway and no one has pointed out that oddity.'

'Perhaps no one thought it was of any significance?'

'Certainly some of these country people can be tight-lipped, Mr Pluke, they're not ones for reading unrealistic things into ordinary events. And, of course, we do have a fairly rapid turnover of staff, long-term gossip is not very prevalent here. This kind of thing appears not to have been passed down by word of mouth. But good heavens, what a weird coincidence . . .'

'Perhaps it is no more than a coincidence, remarkable though it is, Mr Porter,' smiled Pluke. 'However, thanks for allowing me access to those reports. Now I must speak again to the de Kowscott-Hawke family to see whether they have experienced similar unsettling events.'

'Mr Pluke, as an expert on folklore and superstitions, what do you make of that series of coincidences?'

'At this early stage, that is how I see it – a series of remarkable coincidences. Perhaps I will have further views after speaking again to Sir Eustace.'

And he left the puzzled curator as he went to catch a bus back to Crickledale for another chat with Sir Eustace de Kowscott-Hawke.

Chapter Seven

Even before going home, Pluke went straight around to Sir Eustace's house, rang the bell and was admitted by the maid who had previously attended him. She assured him that Sir Eustace would be pleased to see him, that the time was convenient and settled him in the chair he'd used earlier.

'Ah, Pluke, old chap.' Sir Eustace's impressive form soon loomed in the doorway. 'Got some news for me, have you? About those missing snuff boxes?'

'No, Sir Eustace, not news exactly, but a theory about them, or about one of them, for which I need your help.'

'Well, you know me, Pluke old chap, always willing to help the constabulary, but before we settle down for our chat, how about a nice malt? I've got a rather good Royal Lochnagar all the way from that distillery near Balmoral, Victoria used to enjoy a tipple of it, you know, but she mixed it with her claret . . . damned silly thing to do if you ask me, spoiling two rather splendid drinks, not that one could or would say that sort of thing to the old Queen. Now, let's share one. Neat.'

'Well, I er . . . it's a bit early for me . . .'

'Nonsense, man, it's never too early, it's lunch-time anyway, well, near enough, Sunday lunch should always be a celebration, Pluke,' and with that Sir Eustace went across to his malt-bearing trolley, poured two generous glasses and passed one to Pluke, saying, 'Cheers, old chap. Glad you could call. So it's help you want, is it?'

'Yes, it's a very delicate question, Sir Eustace, bordering on the personal, I may say, but it has arisen due to my preliminary researches into the stolen snuff boxes.'

'Well, don't be timid, Pluke, out with it! I won't bite your head off, personal or not. And if it's too personal for comfort, I won't answer, it's as simple as that, so fire away.'

Pluke took a sip at the aromatic whisky and said, 'I have just come from the museum, Sir Eustace, your former home where this matter arose. Tell me, did your family – and I am speaking of your grandfather's era – experience a lot of bad luck?'

'Bad luck, Pluke?' boomed the other. 'Of course his generation experienced bad luck, it was like poverty, always with them. That's why my grandfather sold the house at Pebblewick. He said the place was accursed, he wanted to move out and so he sold it. And, so I am told, things improved from that point onwards.'

'What kind of things happened to make him want to leave?'

'Well, I wasn't there for most of the time, you understand, and I was just a youngster enjoying occasional family visits while he lived at the Pebblewick house but he did have a series of misfortunes. I heard my family discuss them from time to time, not that most of them meant anything to me. I was more concerned about playing in the woods or exploring the rooms, and there were lots of them. But problems, yes, I remember one occasion when one of my grandfather's horses put a foot down a rabbit hole and broke a leg, it had to be put down. He was devastated, I'd never seen my grandfather show such emotion. Then there was a fire in the east wing but luckily it was noticed before it did too much damage – but the thing which made him sell the Pebblewick house was financial.'

'Money problems?'

'Yes, we, the family that is, don't object to talking about it. It was no fault of grandfather's, he was a good manager of his finances but for reasons beyond his control he lost everything. There were those who said it was due to ill-considered investments, and some said he squandered all his cash or drank the proceeds, but that was not true. In the end, when things settled down and a cool assessment was made, we could see it was due to the bad luck which had dogged him all his life, Mr Pluke. Sheer bad luck.'

'He could have taken steps to ward off the bad luck, Sir Eustace.'

'The odd thing was that he did not consider himself superstitious, and wouldn't be bothered with things like horseshoes on the wall or elder trees growing around the house or any other good luck charms. In spite of that, he always said the Pebblewick house was cursed. Not haunted, nothing like that, just cursed to the extent that he was constantly faced with unsettling problems. He called it his accursed house. For all his common sense and down-to-earth attitude, he did feel the house was somehow working against him and his family. That's why he sold it along with other properties in the village such as the pub and gardener's cottage – and the odd thing was, so family history tells me, things did change for the better once he was in his new home. He had a very happy and contented few years before his death. My father did not live at Pebblewick, of course, except as a child. He left to marry and buy his own house and he didn't seem to have grand-father Joshua's run of bad luck.'

'That makes it even more curious that the museum has also had a series of misfortunes,' said Pluke. 'They have all occurred since it transferred into your former home, it does look as though that house is somehow jinxed.' Pluke pulled his museum notes from his pocket and listed the incidents as Sir Eustace sipped his malt.

'Well, blow me!' Sir Eustace said. 'It seems my grandfather was right after all, there was something uncanny about that house. And still is, so it seems.'

'Or its contents,' said Pluke.

'Contents?' puzzled Sir Eustace.

'The snuff boxes,' said Pluke. 'When I spoke to your brother yesterday evening, I got the impression he believed the family was pleased to get rid of them. I wondered if your grandfather blamed them for his misfortune, rather than the house.'

'I remember he was most insistent they were to remain with the house but I never heard him suggest they were somehow associated with his problems,' admitted Sir Eustace.

'It would not have been a nice thing to do, would it?' Pluke smiled.

'I don't follow.' Sir Eustace was clearly enjoying his malt and his chat.

'If your grandfather was a true gentleman, he would not wish his bad fortune to befall anyone else. It would seem to me that if he thought the snuff boxes were somehow responsible for his bad fortune, he would have thrown them away, disposed of them or destroyed them, not deliberately imposed their bad luck upon someone else.'

'Well, yes, he was a kindly old cove by all accounts, I can't see him wishing bad luck on anyone, certainly not a museum who had just bought his former home.'

'I am pleased to hear you say that.'

'I agree with you on that, Pluke old chap, so you don't think the snuff boxes were the root of his troubles? They were not cursed, if that's the right term. I know you are an expert on these matters . . .'

'I can't rule it out,' Pluke admitted. 'I would like to know the source of each of those snuff boxes, the Siena one in particular. There may be some legend or reputation associated with one or all of them. But there may be another reason for wanting to dispose of the boxes in that manner.'

94

'Another reason? What other reason?'

'That is what I must ascertain. It does seem odd that several mishaps have occurred to the museum since it moved into your family's home.'

'Pure coincidence, old chap. That's what any logical person would say. You can't go around believing in curses or the forces of evil. Anyway, it should stop now, shouldn't it? Now someone's taken the snuff boxes away!'

'It will be interesting to see if anything further happens, but there is one further thought-provoking aspect to all this which you should know about,' Pluke added quietly.

'I'm all ears, Pluke old chap, all ears.'

'Every one of the museum's mishaps occurred on the same date. Different years spanning several decades, Sir Eustace, but on the same date each time.'

'And if you're going to tell me it was 30th April, then I know there is something mighty peculiar about all this. The family always said it was their unlucky day – we avoided taking risks then, even as children. Nonetheless, lots of things happened, small annoyances, not the sort of thing to be recorded or remembered.'

'That date is exactly what I was going to tell you, Sir Eustace, but it is even more spine-tingling when I hear you speak of it like that. Yes, all the museum's mishaps have occurred on 30th April, your family's unlucky day. Or the house's unlucky day. . . . Oddly, due to changes of staff and curators, and with long gaps between each incident, the significance of the dates had not been noticed. I spotted it only this morning.'

As if digesting this news, the two men lapsed into a long silence, each with his own thoughts, with Pluke taking tiny sips from the mighty potion in his glass, and Sir Eustace absorbing rather larger quantities. In fact, before responding to Pluke, he went across to his sideboard and refilled his own glass, offering a refill to Pluke who signalled 'no' with wave of his hand.

'Pluke old chap,' said Sir Eustace eventually. 'This sort of thing is beyond me, I am not superstitious, I don't believe in things like ghosts or the paranormal or jinxes or gypsy curses or the Curse of Tutankhamun or anything like that, and if you ask why I have a horseshoe on the wall near the front door, then my answer would be that it was here when we bought the house and I saw no reason to remove it. I might add I have not suffered any of the problems you have mentioned – but I might have done, had I inherited that house.'

'You can understand why I am so interested in the history of those snuff boxes, Sir Eustace.'

'Indeed I can, old chap, indeed I can.'

'Now, of course, I am equally interested in trying to understand why anyone would steal them – I know they are valuable, but they are only valuable if they are sold and these are so identifiable that it would a huge risk, putting them on sale.'

'You think they might not have been stolen for purely financial reasons?'

'It is one possibility I have to bear in mind, Sir Eustace. Any attempt to sell them would surely alert the buyer, assuming they are not sold through car boots or junk shops. Any reputable dealer would recognize the boxes as valuable commodities, and our circulations have surely alerted everyone within the antiques trade. I doubt if they were stolen with a view to an eventual sale.'

'But why else would anyone steal those boxes, Pluke old chap?'

'That is what I must try to determine, Sir Eustace. I am due to return to my police duties tomorrow morning and will give this crime my undivided attention. It seems to me, though, that I need to know more about the origins of all those boxes, and for that I need to know where your grandfather, or one of his ancestors, obtained them.'

'Oh, grandfather didn't acquire them, Pluke, it was one of his relations way back in the mists of our family history, long before his time. He inherited them from his father.

They were handed down through the family but I must admit I did not want them, old chap, not in view of their reputation.'

'You knew of their reputation?'

'Well, yes, we all did, even if it was regarded as a family joke.'

'A joke?'

'You know the sort of thing, Pluke old chap, the sort of stuff you trot out at dinner parties and family gatherings, always done in a jocular way, you understand. If things went wrong, especially on 30th April as they often did, we blamed the snuff boxes. I never thought it was anything to be taken seriously . . . mind you, I was glad grandfather got rid of them.'

'So you *did* believe in the possibility they bore a curse of some kind?'

'I'm not saying that, Pluke old chap, I was just being careful, not taking chances. And I was just a youngster, remember, when grandad disposed of them, it was more than fifty years ago. If he believed they were cursed in some way, then so did I at the time, as a youngster, but I grew out of that kind of thing as I matured.'

'So can I return to my basic question, Sir Eustace? How did those snuff boxes come to belong to your family?'

'My ancestors – great grandfather and his father and grandfather before him, and several great uncles and great great uncles – were all great travellers, Pluke. I've heard tales from India, Europe, most parts of Asia, Australia, even the South Pole and South America. And they returned with souvenirs: the snuff boxes are just a few of those souvenirs.'

'And where did they live?'

'My cousins lived at Tillabeck Hall, that's now an hotel not far away from here, but generations of my direct ancestors lived in the Pebblewick house. I believe the first de Kowscott-Hawke settled there in the fourteenth century. Of course the house has been altered, extended and modernized down the years. The museum has altered it too, so it bears no resemblance to the original.'

'With regard to that snuff box, we're talking of the eighteenth century and later, are we not?' Pluke put to Sir Eustace.

'Are we? My knowledge of the history of snuff boxes isn't as good as yours.'

'Well, tobacco came to Europe in the sixteenth century when it is widely accepted that the Irish were first to manufacture snuff in the 1560s. It is generally accepted that snuff, the powdered form of tobacco, became highly fashionable, among both sexes, in the eighteenth century, around 1750. That's when specially constructed and very ornate snuff boxes – which became exceedingly valuable – were part of a person's attire.'

'I can't say I've ever been tempted to stuff my nose full of that brown powder!'

'The habit was highly fashionable, Sir Eustace, and the boxes were made to conform to that high fashion. Some were made of gold or silver, others of wood or ivory, and all with ornate decorations or painting – they were even made to match a gentleman's clothing. And the very smart ladies would often carry a matching spoon, sometimes made of gold, with which to extract their snuff – it meant their fingers did not get discoloured. Did you know that Count Von Bruhl, the prime minister of Saxony and director of the Meissen factory, had three hundred suits, each with a matching cane and snuff box? And Lord Patersham had one different snuff box for every day of the year. So, Sir Eustace, we are talking of the period from, say, 1730 until around 1830 or 1840. That was the heyday of snuff boxes and if your ancestors were travelling Europe, it is quite feasible they would collect fine examples and bring them home, either as part of a collection or for their personal use.'

'So they are not purely an English fashion accessory?'

'By no means,' said Pluke, airing the knowledge he had

checked as recently as yesterday evening from his own library of books. 'The French were fanatics, as were most Europeans including the Poles and Prussians. So if your ancestors travelled in Europe during the heyday of snuff taking, then they were highly likely to have brought examples home with them. And they would bring them to the Pebblewick house, I suspect.'

'Well, yes, that was our family seat, unless some went to Tillabeck too.'

'Perhaps your grandfather wanted those snuff boxes to remain with the Pebblewick house for some reason we do not know? It might not have anything to do with curses or bad luck. Something in keeping with his generous nature?'

'Yes, it would, Pluke, but even so I seem to remember family members believing the boxes were a nuisance . . . maybe it was my childish interpretation of adult talk.'

'Whatever the reason for them staying with the house, Sir Eustace, I would like to track down any or all of those boxes – to date them, in other words, and to trace their sources.'

'That's a tall order, Pluke old chap, because I don't have any family records from that period – the fire, you know, at the Pebblewick house. It destroyed a lot of family records.'

'Another accursed tragedy?' said Pluke.

'Yes, and it happened on 30th April. I'm coming to believe that house really was accursed, it would explain a lot.'

'There is such a thing as bad luck, Sir Eustace. And good luck.'

'Well, I've always believed that the harder you work, the luckier you get. But if you hang on here a few seconds, I have a family tree somewhere, one that survived the fire. I might have a name for you and some useful dates. Help yourself to some more of that Lochnagar while I'm gone – and have a look at our family portraits on those walls . . .'

Old Whatsit, whom I hope I shall soon name, might be among them.'

Old Whatsit, as Sir Eustace had called him, turned out to be the Earl of Tillabeck, Halbert de Kowscott-Hawke, who was a distant uncle. He had been born in Northamptonshire on 14th May 1721, at the family seat of Nenneford Hall on the banks of the River Nene, but he died in Yorkshire in 1788. A run of bad fortune meant he had to sell his estate in Northamptonshire, which he had inherited from his father, and he had moved to Yorkshire in 1751, having also inherited, from another distant cousin, that estate and title of Tillabeck. Sale of the Northampton pile had enabled him to secure the future of Tillabeck while also permitting him to travel widely on the Continent where he lived for a time in Italy.

'This is our family Bible.' Sir Eustace held up a huge volume with a black leather cover and gold-faced leaves. 'One of my forebears gathered as much of our family history as he could, and I've done my best to maintain it. Those notes about Halbert are in here.'

'It's a good starting point for further research,' agreed Pluke. 'For example, I had no idea you were related to the Earls of Tillabeck. The title is extinct now, of course.'

'Died out in the nineteenth century. Tillabeck Hall is now an hotel, as I am sure you know. It's never easy having to admit defeat when one owns a big country house and estate but there are times when one must be realistic and not romantic. But I hope you can do something with those few snippets, Pluke old chap, they're not my work, I have to admit, but that's all there is about him. To be truthful, it's far from complete.'

'A hero of the family perhaps? Great great uncle Halbert or whatever degree of uncle he is,' suggested Pluke.

'Oh yes, by all means. He is still held in high esteem, we often talk about him and his exploits at family gatherings. Mostly hearsay, I might add, and a good deal of embroidering of the facts. I believe his forebears were also great travellers, spending time in, and exploring, places like Rome, Athens and other classical sites. He is known to be the family's great traveller and there is no doubt he brought home lots of souvenirs. Now, whether he brought home any of those snuff boxes, Pluke old chap, is something that is not stated here. I rather suspect he did, and they came down to us in due course. Have a look,' and he handed the weighty tome to Pluke. Pluke scanned the entry but found nothing more than Sir Eustace had told him.

'Did the Earl of Tillabeck ever live in your house at Pebblewick?' asked Pluke.

'The answer is no. When the Earl came north, he and his descendants always lived in Tillabeck Hall on the southern edge of the North York Moors. That was their home, although, as you know, he travelled widely. I think he rented homes overseas if he intended to stay in any particular area for any length of time. When that branch of the family died out we inherited Tillabeck and its contents, so we suddenly found ourselves full of surplus furniture and artefacts. We kept some and sold the rest; we sold Tillabeck Hall as well. But as for my branch of the family, a generation of the de Kowscott-Hawkes has always lived in the Pebblewick house. When we sold Tillabeck, it helped the family finances immensely.'

'A stroke of good fortune?' smiled Pluke.

'I know what you are thinking, Pluke, and yes, it was a stroke of good fortune. I am pretty damned sure that some of the snuff boxes were part of our inheritance from the Earl's estate or house, collected from all over the place; it was all a long time before I came into the world but that slice of good luck enabled my direct ancestors to modernize the house and accommodate all our belongings, extend the house and grounds and so on . . . and we were there until we sold it to the museum in 1952. You know what, Pluke old chap, you've certainly caused my old brain cells to revive themselves, I thought I'd forgotten most of this.

Amazing what one can dredge up from the sump of one's memory, eh?'

'There must be something about those events in local history books?' Pluke suggested.

'I would expect so, important families like mine was in days of yore would always attract the attention of historians. I have no objection to you conducting your own research into my family, Pluke. And, by Jove, I will set about doing some more research of my own, this is most interesting, you know. I ought to find out just what did happen on 30th April, and make a full list. Just for the hell of it.'

'I am very pleased to hear you say that, Sir Eustace.'

'It will give me something to occupy me. I will try to find out some more by chatting to my brother and our cousins in Australia, one never knows what will turn up. And I will contact you. If I hear anything about snuff boxes, I will make sure you are informed.'

'Thank you, Sir Eustace. And I would also like to know of any family links with Siena, or the Golden Horse Trough of Siena, *l'abbeveratoio del cavallo dorato di Siena* as it is called. That has disappeared although some maintain it never existed. There is a strong belief in Siena that it is nothing but a legend, but whatever the story, I am sure the Siena snuff box bears an image from the trough . . . Now, in your ancestor's travels he might have come across the legend, or even the trough itself. That would indeed be staggering news. And if I could prove one of your ancestors had found the actual trough . . .'

'By Jove, Pluke, you are a fountain of knowledge. Yes, you have given me reason for doing some detective work on my ancestors. I must thank you for that. Now, I think you had better have another malt by way of celebration.'

'I'm afraid I don't have the time.' Pluke had glanced at his watch and realized Millicent would have his Sunday lunch ready for serving. 'My wife will have prepared lunch, I daren't keep her waiting.'

'Well, cheerio, old chap, and what a fascinating insight you have given me, truly inspiring. Keep in touch, promise me you will keep in touch.'

'I will indeed, Sir Eustace, and thank you for all your help.'

And so Montague Pluke left his host and hurried home for Sunday lunch; he was late and so he broke into a trot, a strange sight. A gentleman in a long flowing coat of black and yellow pattern, with a panama hat clamped on to his head with his left hand, black and yellow trousers, white spats, pink socks and brogue shoes. A man on a mission. An inspired man in search of a fabled horse trough last thought to have existed in a foreign country.

But his quest might be delayed for some time because tomorrow he had to return to police duty.

Chapter Eight

When Montague Pluke arrived at the police station that Monday morning, he made sure he entered its mighty period portals with his right foot first and, in keeping with his workaday routine, went directly to the Control Room.

'Good morning, sir,' greeted Sergeant Cockfield pronounced Cofield, the officer in charge of that modest but highly efficient nerve centre of Crickledale Sub-Divisional Police Station. 'Welcome back. I trust you had a nice holiday?'

'Good morning, Sergeant,' returned Pluke. 'Yes indeed, Mrs Pluke and I had a most interesting time in Tuscany. Very brief but rather stimulating and definitely thought-provoking. But now it is time to resume work. Have we had any reports of any overnight suspicious deaths, serious crimes, fraudulent behaviour, rapes, racist demonstrations, unexplained incidents, train crashes or major catastrophes?'

'No, sir, it has been a very quiet night indeed, with the exception of old Mrs Carruthers at No. 7, Market Terrace. She has reported her tabby cat missing. It is five years old and answers to Puss.'

'That is not a very nice name for a cat, Sergeant, it suggests a rather messy kind of fluid of the kind associated with abscesses.'

'I am sure she had no such thoughts when she named

the cat, sir, but it is a very common name for a cat. A very popular name, if I might say so.'

'I can never understand why but I am sure Mrs Carruthers had a very good reason for naming her cat in such an odd way. Now that it has absconded without her consent, I am sure our uniform patrols will be keeping an eye open for it.'

'Details have been circulated around the town, sir.'

'Well done. If that is our only prevailing problem, I shall head for my office where I can be contacted if necessary.'

'Very good, sir.'

And so Montague Pluke made his way upstairs and stepped over his threshold with his right foot first, hung his panama on the hat-stand and his voluminous coat on a hook and then approached his desk. He spent the first few moments rearranging things because the office cleaner always managed to move his essentials to undesirable places. On one occasion, he left a note asking her to be more careful with his tidy desk arrangements, but she had ignored it. He inched his blotter slightly to the right along with its pile of correspondence awaiting his attention, moved his pen-rack to balance it symmetrically with the blotter, made sure the edges of his in- and out-trays were equidistant from the edge of the desk and then resited the coaster which bore his official coffee mug. Finally, he centralized the plastic horse trough containing his paper clips; he had left the model of the Golden Horse Trough at home because it was far too important and significant to lodge in his office even if that man Green had said it was a paper-clip holder. The pile of correspondence on his blotter, this morning's post by the look of it, was the next to demand his attention. It was weighted down with a witch stone, sometimes called a hag stone. This is a round stone with a hole in the centre and these treasures can often be found in open places on the North York Moors. Hag stones make very good paperweights and they deter troublesome witches; this one prevented them interfering with his correspondence.

Not that Mrs Plumpton was a witch, for indeed it was she who had placed the hag stone there – it was, of course, Pluke's very personal hag stone and she had found this additional and very practical use for it. Mrs Plumpton was Pluke's secretary, a rounded lady of ample proportions who seemed to float everywhere in a cloud of rising, falling and wafting purple fabric which somehow managed to contain most of her unseen moveable parts. Some of those parts, however, did become eminently visible whenever she bent forward but being a true gentleman, Pluke always endeavoured to glance in another direction. There were times he never quite succeeded, she was often far too quick for him. Sometimes he thought she did it on purpose, a sort of teasing ritual to make his sap rise, especially if he had been away for a while.

He did wonder today, though, what she would have been like in the heat of that piazza in Siena. Perhaps she would have worn far less and exposed far more? That would have caused him to perspire even more profusely than he had so it was perhaps a good thing she had not accompanied him. Not that Millicent would have allowed him to take another woman on holiday, no matter how pure his intentions . . .

'Good morning, Mr Pluke.' Mrs Plumpton, in a ravishingly lightweight enclosure of low-necked deep purple frothy fabric, sailed into his office. 'How nice to see you back and how nice to see you with a tan. Even in such a brief time, that Italian sunshine has clearly done you a lot of good.' And she bent down to place two more letters before him; at least, he thought it was two but couldn't be sure. His attention was momentarily elsewhere and the sight made him perspire just a little, and then she righted herself with a large smile and everything sank home.

There were times, he admitted to himself, that he did wonder what really occurred beneath all those layers of fabric but he told himself not to be misled by erotic thoughts. He was a senior police officer with immense responsibilities and a faultless reputation to maintain; he had to remain aloof from every kind of temptation, especially temptations of the flesh. It was quite a struggle, therefore, to remain calm as he responded:

'Thank you, Mrs Plumpton. It was a very nice break, if rather too short, and I am sure Mrs Pluke enjoyed it. But it is all over now, and I must not be distracted from my duties. So have we anything important in this morning's mail?'

'No, Mr Pluke, it's all routine correspondence. Weekly crime circulars, a new Home Office directive about accommodating stray donkeys, a note from the supermarket with a special offer on perfumes and ladies' lingerie, and a letter from a fan who wants you to autograph your book about civic horse troughs. Oh, and there is a circular letter from the Prime Minister about road accidents involving nuclear materials and the theft of articles that might be used in chemical warfare or for making weapons of mass destruction of the human race.'

'All very quiet then, but I cannot autograph that book in duty time, Mrs Plumpton, I shall take it home and deal with it in my private house. It is wrong that readers continue to confuse my private life with my police duties.'

'As you say, Mr Pluke. So is there anything I can get you now?'

'I think a nice hot coffee would be a very good idea. It will not be easy, getting back into my stride after a holiday. A coffee will help.'

'The kettle is already on, Mr Pluke.'

'Good. Now, has Detective Sergeant Wain arrived?'

'Yes, he is in his office, shall I call him?'

'Yes, we must talk about those major crimes which occurred during my absence. I need to be fully briefed. So perhaps coffee for us both? Here in my office. I am told

107

there was a sickening raid on the Pebblewick Folk Museum last week and I feel we must exercise our minds on detecting that atrocity.'

'Yes, it was dreadful and I know Sergeant Wain has been paying very close attention to it. I will call him, Mr Pluke, and then, when you have read your mail, I will see you again in case there is any dictation or other instructions you need to issue,' and she turned away with a twirl of her skirts and more than a flash of an ample thigh.

He settled down to read some of the correspondence and then, following a tap on the door, Wayne Wain arrived bearing a file and settled on a chair.

'Good morning, sir, nice to see you back.' They had already discussed Pluke's holiday during his unscheduled visit to the station. 'Nothing much has happened in your absence, except the museum raid, of course. There were one or two minor thefts in town – a set of garden gnomes taken from a council house garden, some underwear from a clothes line on that new housing estate, a carved wooden figure of Mickey Mouse from a garden shed behind the High Street and two bottles of home-made wine from a chap's greenhouse. We have issued a warning about the wine, it seems it's liable to explode if the bottles are shaken.'

'Are you sure it was wine, Wayne?'

'The loser claimed it was wine, sir.'

'He wasn't a terrorist, was he? Making bombs? The loser, I mean.'

'No, sir, it was old Henry Pilchard, he's eighty-five years old, he made the stuff when he was only twenty-five, gallons of it. It's very mature and pretty potent, rather like Henry himself, so he tells me. It was his last two bottles, he's very upset about it. He reckons it's kept him alive all these years and says it keeps his arteries free from blockages. He said it was good for cleaning brass too.'

'Well, I am sure you have dealt very efficiently with

those matters. So, the museum, Wayne. That is our major unsolved crime, is it not?'

Wayne drew his chair closer to Pluke's desk and opened his file, then Mrs Plumpton arrived with two mugs of steaming coffee. With the open neck of her dress seeming ever lower, she bent down in front of Wayne to present one to him, and repeated the performance in front of Pluke as she stood his mug on the awaiting coaster. The two men went very quiet during her masterly performance.

'Thank you, Mrs Plumpton,' said Pluke when she had finished, his mind still puzzling about what lurked beneath those acres of purple gossamer.

When she had left and closed the door behind her, and when Wayne had restored his attention to Pluke instead of the retreating rotund figure of Mrs Plumpton, Pluke asked, 'Well, Wayne, now that our morning entertainment is over, shall we begin?'

'Sorry, sir, yes. It's very difficult not to look at her . . .'

'Don't I know it!' and Pluke laughed, his first overt sign of happiness today. 'But I am too old to be distracted by such massive displays of feminine charms.'

'One is never too old, sir!'

'One is, Wayne, believe me. But of course, I do have Mrs Pluke, such a treasure . . .'

'Yes, sir, you are very fortunate.'

'Well, that is our distraction dealt with. Now, Wayne, the museum. What developments have there been since we last spoke?'

'Nothing positive, sir. We have conducted house-to-house enquiries around the village in the hope of finding someone who heard or saw something suspicious but we've drawn a blank. We've also visited that plastics factory in Rosklethorpe, sir, apparently a lot of their shift workers travel through Pebblewick in the early hours of the morning on their way to and from work, but again we've drawn a blank. I've also asked the Road Traffic Division to inspect their records of vehicles which were checked or stopped during the material time, but I've not yet had a response from them.'

'So it's not looking very promising, is it? What about scientific evidence? Did the scene yield any useful material?'

'I'm expecting the formal SOCO report very soon. I've had no authorized advance information about their findings, but, as I said, their report is due soon, today in fact. They sent some items to the forensic lab and I asked them to seek DNA as well as any other evidence; those findings will take a little longer.'

'Examination of the scene is vital, Wayne, as you well know. Every criminal leaves some evidence behind when he or she commits a crime, and it is our job to find it and make full use of it. Now, what about the staff? There is a small complement at the museum from the curator down to the caretaker by way of several attendants, the secretary, a gardener and receptionist. And there will be members who have left too, don't forget, including some who have left unwillingly. Those who have been dismissed, in other words. Could one have returned with a vengeance to steal something valuable and easily disposable? Or do any of the current staff bear a grudge, something strong enough to make them steal that collection of snuff boxes?'

'Well, sir, I interviewed them all, including some who had departed involuntarily. All have alibis, sir, and I've checked them. I've not found a prime suspect, sir. Furthermore, no one noticed anything untoward, but you will appreciate they all go home at five thirty and not all of them live in the village. They are not likely to be aware of anything happening at the museum in the late evening or early hours of the morning. I have given this case some very close attention during your absence, sir, and I doubt if any of the staff can be suspected of committing the crime. It bears all the hallmarks of being done by a very professional thief or thieves.'

110

'I believe you have reached that conclusion due to the lack of evidence at the scene?'

'Yes, that has a strong bearing on my conclusion, sir. It was a very skilfully executed crime because it left no obvious clues, the scene appeared to be very clean, as SOCO told me at the time, that was their provisional assessment.'

'I trust they did their usual thorough job?'

'So far as I am aware, yes, sir. Once they have analysed their findings we might have additional clues. Their formal report is due later today, as I said. It will take account of the results of our liaison with Cumbria Police about their raid.'

'Good, then I shall await it with interest. Now, the widest possible circulation of details of the stolen snuff boxes? That has been done, I presume?'

'It has, sir. The Antiques Squad from Force Headquarters has been provided with details, and they are liaising with all their specialist contacts, both within the police service and in the antiques world. Magazines and newspapers have been informed, antique dealers given details, second-hand shops notified . . . you name it, sir, and we've done it.'

'And can our case be linked to the Cumbrian raid?'

'The MO was similar, sir, but not identical. Both entries were through the roof by the removal of tiles; both the attacked premises were museums; in both cases small and valuable collectables were stolen; and in both cases no useful evidence was left. The lack of evidence at the scene makes it impossible to state categorically that the same person is responsible. It remains a possibility, however.'

'So in spite of all that, and in spite of some good publicity, we have no leads? No positive suspects? Is that the correct assumption?' Pluke demanded.

'Well, put like that, sir, yes. We've got no leads or suspects in view, it's just a case of slogging along with the laborious process of routine enquiries and the elimination of suspects.'

'Which brings me back to the staff, Wayne. You have interviewed the staff as witnesses?'

'Yes, as I said just now, sir. They've all been interviewed.'

'And have they been eliminated from the enquiry? Surely they are all suspects, Wayne, until formally eliminated. We need to look at each one of them very carefully. I am still of the opinion that this could be an inside job, as the saying goes.'

'Oh, I doubt it, sir, this was a professional crime. A very professional crime, achieved without leaving a clue, without any witnesses and with enough skill to avoid the alarm system.'

'Exactly. And could one of those members of staff be a professional criminal, Wayne, working in the museum, say as an attendant, with the sole purpose of acquiring sufficient knowledge to steal some valuable artefacts? Or be a friend of such a criminal? Providing the criminal, or even a rogue family member, with the necessary background information? I think we need to check the background of the staff's families and friends, including the curator, and any criminal records they might have. We need to interview each one again, in depth, with a view to establishing whether he or she has an alibi, or knowledge of the museum's routine, or links with a criminal capable of this crime, or has even committed the crime. I am determined to leave no stone unturned, Wayne, in the pursuit of the offender or offenders.'

'I do realize you have a special interest in this case, sir, but everything we have done so far is standard procedure.'

'I want more than standard procedure, Wayne. I want imagination and determination to solve this dreadful assault on our local museum. And yes, I admit I have a special interest in the whereabouts of the Siena snuff box

112

but I trust that will not influence my overall commitment.'

'Understood, sir.'

'So, Wayne, while you await the results of the Scenes of Crime Officers' report, I shall revisit the museum.'

'I thought you had already been to see the curator, sir?'

'Yes, but that was on a private matter. This time it will be upon official police business. In particular, I want to examine the route by which the criminals got on to the roof and I want to see how they managed to remove the tiles to break in at exactly the right place.'

'I do have photographs, sir, in my file. Taken by SOCO.'

'Then let me see them, Wayne.'

From his file, he produced a set of half-plate size coloured photographs bound in stiff board covers. The front of the booklet bore a title saying these were taken at the scene of a burglary at Pebblewick Folk Museum, and this was followed by the date of the break-in and the relevant crime reference number. Pluke knew the pictures would have been taken prior to any disturbance of the scene and so they portrayed things exactly as they had been left by the villains. That was vital. Wayne led him through the set of pictures.

The first four or five comprised a selection of exterior views of the building and its grounds, but these offered no obvious clues. Then they came to a shot of the roof depicting the point of entry; it showed the blue slate tiles with a gaping hole, large enough to admit a full-grown man. A ruler had been positioned alongside to act as an accurate guide. The point of entry was on a sloping section near the north-west corner of the building; it was sufficiently high from the ground below – four storeys – to shield the point from the view of anyone directly below, while a wide chimney stack, with eight pots, offered further secrecy from anyone walking or working in the grounds. Some four feet below the hole in the roof was a walkway, one of several which were linked by a network of paths upon the roof. These allowed workmen to carry out the necessary maintenance, such as replacing tiles, clearing gutters and spouts, removing old birds' nests or painting any wooden sections. There was little doubt the thief had stood on that walkway, removed the tiles with comparative ease and then placed them neatly on the walkway.

'I had a look up there, Wayne, a thief could work unseen from below, he could remove the tiles without anyone seeing him.'

'Some of those roofs are like public parks in themselves!' Wayne explained. 'Lots of footpaths leading to interesting places, you can spend ages up there, ideal for sun-bathing too, sir, I'm sure the gentry often went up on to their roofs to take advantage of the privacy in the height of summer. They are very sturdily built.'

'I know, Wayne, there were times it was the only peaceful place they could find. You are aware that there is access to the roof from within the museum?'

'Yes, sir, a wooden staircase provides access. It allows maintenance staff into the loft which contains the water tanks, and then it leads outside on to the roof.'

'And you know my next question, Wayne?'

'I do, sir, and yes. That door was locked at the time of the raid, it is kept locked until it is needed for work on the roof. The only access to that loft and the roof door is through the house itself, through the museum as it is now. At the time of the raid, the museum was locked with the alarm set. There was no way any intruder could reach the outside of the roof via the inside of the museum without setting off the alarm. It did not go off, and there was no sign of a break-in, except for the roof tiles.'

'I have noted that, Wayne.'

'I thought I should stress that I am confident the thieves climbed on to the roof from the outside, sir, under cover of darkness. It's a considerable feat but there is no other way they could have got on to the roof.'

'Right, then continue, Wayne.'

The next shot showed the pile of removed slates; they had been carefully stacked on a flat area just to one side of the point of entry.

'A neat job, Wayne. Why did he not just throw the tiles down to the ground?'

'They would have attracted attention, sir, the noise they would make. It would sound very loud at night, the crashing of the tiles as they broke into small pieces. This was done carefully, the hallmark of a skilled burglar, sir, like those who remove entire windows to gain access. They remove the windows in one piece, in silence.'

'An identifiable MO?' smiled Pluke.

'We've checked with CRO, sir, both locally and nationally. This MO has not been widely used, but it was used for the Cumbria crime. The last occasion before that was about five years ago, a liquor warehouse in Liverpool. Tiles off and down into the storage area without setting off the alarm. In addition, there have been lots of instances where raiders have removed glass panes or even complete doors, and in complete silence.'

'And fingerprints, Wayne?'

'None, sir. The face of the tiles is in itself smooth enough to carry prints, fingerprints and palmprints, but there were none. Either the tiles were levered off with tools which left no marks, or the raider wore rubber or plastic gloves, or else the tiles were handled only at their edges, not on the flat surfaces.'

'Either a very clever villain, or a lucky one, Wayne.'

'The reason for the lack of prints is pure speculation, sir. The short answer is that no prints were found. That is a simple fact.'

'And after being examined, the same tiles were replaced?'

'Yes, sir, that was necessary, due to the vulnerability of

the premises, if only from the weather and wildlife. The hole could not be seen from the ground, by the way.'

'And how far below is the ground, Wayne?'

'In the region of forty-five feet, sir, equivalent to four storeys and a bit extra for the upper lofts, with the water tanks in them . . . what's that in metres? Thirteen and a bit.'

'Then it was a remarkable feat of climbing, Wayne, from the outside, even with the best of extension ladders,' said Pluke pointedly. 'And, of course, the ladders would have to be transported to the scene . . .'

'I know what you are thinking, sir, you think it was an inside job, that someone avoided the alarm, crept up through the lofts and out on to the roof, did the job and escaped the same way.'

'One has to consider every possibility, Wayne.'

'But the alarm was set, sir, all the museum doors were locked, there was no break-in at any door or window, we've checked the whereabouts of all the keys at the material time . . . Security is adequate, sir, so I must disgree about it being an inside job.'

'That is a healthy attitude, Wayne, you must not be pressured into accepting everything I say. So you may conduct your enquiries along your favoured route and I will do likewise with mine. Maybe we have been visited by burglars who are agile climbers, cat burglars as they used to be called and probably still are. It cannot be ruled out. So, when you examined the ground below the house, did you find any evidence of a ladder being positioned there?'

'No, sir, I have to say not. But the immediate surrounds of the building form a wide footpath made from York stone. It is some seven yards – well over six metres – wide, a ladder would not leave an impression there, sir, not even one extending to such a great height or of such a great weight. Had it been standing on the lawns or gardens, then we might have found evidence of that. We didn't, sir. Cat

116

burglars use ropes, too, remember, and make use of window ledges, balconies, iron grilles, ivy.'

'Point taken, Wayne. So let us continue. That pile of removed tiles was reused to repair the breach, you said?'

'Yes, sir, by the groundsman when SOCO had finished with them. The groundsman does repairs to the exterior and acts as caretaker for the internal jobs. One man, two jobs, indoors and outside. The tiles are big ones, sir, bigger than those on a normal private house. When they were removed, the hole would accommodate a large person.'

'Good. Pray continue.'

Wayne showed Pluke photographs depicting the cutting away of the roof felt immediately below the tiles, and then several slender wooden laths had been cut out to leave a gaping hole.

'The roof felt has not been found, sir, it was cut away with a very sharp instrument, like a Stanley knife perhaps, and removed from the scene. The lengths of lath fell inside, sir, after being sawn off. They, and samples of plaster, have been preserved in case we need to re-examine them. Other than revealing they had been cut with a small saw, the laths offered no other clues. We do not think they had been handled, sir, there were no prints on them. They were just cut away to drop into the room below.'

'Accompanied by a shower or two of sawdust, Wayne?'

'Yes, plenty of sawdust, sir.'

'And plaster?'

'And plaster, sir, old and very dusty.'

'As one would expect. Now, Wayne, for a thief to descend through that hole would not be the easiest of tasks. Lowering oneself down, bearing in mind the fragile state of its edges, those raw, thin slate tiles, would be hazardous, and then – most important, Wayne – there is the problem of getting back out again. How do you think he, she or they did that?'

117

'With ropes, sir, or portable collapsible ladders, or an assistant or two. These perpetrators are skilled climbers, remember, sir, they scaled the outer walls somehow . . . they knew exactly which room to enter, they knew precisely which tiles to remove. They came fully prepared, sir, clearly they did lots of advance planning.'

'Or they entered that room from the inside of the museum, Wayne, and removed the tiles to make it look like an outside entry. There is indeed food for thought here. All right, proceed.'

Most of the remaining photographs depicted the interior of the snuff box room, showing the smashed display cabinet, the barred window, the carpet which contained a good deal of debris from visitors but which might also reveal something of the villains, and the door with its sturdy locks. There were also photographs of the security alarm system showing it when primed and when in 'off' mode. It was operated by a coded number which was known to some staff members and the control box was on the wall to the left of the main door.

In the booklet, there was also an enlarged photograph of each of the stolen snuff boxes; each showed some point of identification for that box and a written description was also included, as provided by the museum's literature.

The enlargement of the picture of the Siena trough showed the frieze which ran around three sides of the scene in the Piazza del Campo. In its enlarged form, there was no doubt it looked like lettering, albeit with the figures worn by the passage of time until they were almost illegible. Pluke pulled open a drawer of his desk, ferreted about inside, pulled out a Sherlock Holmes type of magnifying glass and stared at the photograph.

'Look at this, Wayne,' he said peering through the thick lens. 'This is an inscription and I know what it says! It is in Latin, an inscription which appears on many horse troughs . . . very common nowadays, I know it well . . . it says, "*De torrenti in via bibet propterea exaltabit caput.*" Now,

118

Wayne, this is very exciting indeed, have you any idea what it means?'

'No, sir, not a clue.'

'Those words form the world's best-known horse trough inscription. It is said to be a Latin translation of Verse 7 of Psalm 110. The English version is "He shall drink of the spring in the way; therefore shall he lift up the head."'

'Really, sir, fancy that.'

'There have long been arguments, within the upper echelons of horse trough society, about the precise translation of that phrase, some believing the word "spring" should be "trough" or "well", and some thinking there is no reference to precisely what the horse is drinking from – that he is just drinking along the wayside. But this is tremendously exciting, Wayne, tremendously important.'

'Indeed, sir? Can I ask why?'

'As I said, Wayne, this inscription is to be found on ancient horse troughs throughout the world. Indeed, there is one in the Yorkshire Dales which bears it, on the road between Appletreewick and Burnsall.'

'Really, sir?'

'But you are a detective, Wayne, don't you see the importance of this? It means that this snuff box is genuinely modelled upon a horse trough. I believe this is further evidence that this snuff box is actually designed from the facia of the Golden Horse Trough of Siena. That in turn means that the Golden Horse Trough must have borne this legend all those years ago which logically means the Siena trough *must* have existed. It means the trough is not mere fantasy or legend as many would lead us to believe – and I believe that that famous golden trough set the pattern for others which followed. Ever since that time, horse troughs of prime importance have carried those very same words.'

'Well, fancy that, sir.'

'Fancy that indeed, Wayne. This makes it even more vital that I recover it.'

119

And then Mrs Plumpton tapped on the door and entered the room. 'Mr Pluke,' she said, 'I thought I should interrupt your meeting. The report from the Scenes of Crime has just arrived. I thought you might like to see it.'

'Yes, please show me what you've got,' beamed Pluke and she bent forward to oblige.

Chapter Nine

The formal report from the Scenes of Crime Department concentrated upon two main areas. One was the exterior of the museum, in particular the grounds which were to the rear. Although the grounds were open to the public during the day, both as gardens and as the setting for extra-mural parts of the museum, they were secured by the grounds-man each evening. Unauthorized access was not impossible but it would not be easy – a ten foot high wall surrounded the grounds and the solid wooden double gates were the same height. The gates, securely locked at night, opened on to the main street at the side of the museum in full view of neighbouring parts of the village while private houses surrounded three sides of the grounds, the museum's main building occupying the fourth side. For thieves to gain admission without anyone knowing or without seeing them would be unlikely. A thorough search had been conducted with especial emphasis upon evidence of the raiders' presence either in the grounds or upon the surrounding walls or gate. Nothing had been found; there was no evidence of anyone climbing over to gain access. Furthermore, there were no impressions from the feet of any ladder standing on the grass or earth, and none of the museum's walls, ledges, roof extremities or ivy bore any recent signs of having an extension ladder resting against it. A search of the grounds had produced a surprising amount of rubbish – papers which had wrapped everything from toffees to sandwiches; apple cores, orange and banana skins and plum stones; coins; several combs; some cheap ear-rings; a pair of dark blue woollen socks and a baby's rattle.

There were several plastic shopping bags too, all of which had been examined in case they had been used to carry the loot down from the loft or placed on the tops of walls to ease over the passage of the ladder or climbers. But nothing useful had been found. The conclusion was that either the raiders had been extremely careful and knowledgeable about the need not to leave behind any kind of evidence, or they had not gained access to the roof via the grounds. It was pointed out, however, that access to the roof could have been achieved from the front of the building, but had that been done then it would probably have been witnessed either by villagers or passers-by: as with access from the rear, very lengthy ladders would have been required. No evidence of access via that route was found; any ladders used there were unlikely to leave indentations on the solid frontage of the museum. The report did point out, however, that access to the roof through the main building could not be ruled out, however unlikely that appeared to be due to the in-house security measures.

The second point of reference was the snuff box room. The report highlighted its position in the top storey of the museum and made due reference to the security methods deployed. Pluke already knew what they were and nodded his agreement with the content of the report. The display cabinet, which had been made from toughened glass, had been smashed with a very heavy instrument, probably a hammer; the locks had not been smashed, however. That had not been necessary. The mere smashing of the glass had made it quite simple for the thief or thieves to remove all the snuff boxes.

Particles of broken glass had been found inside the cabinet and on the floor, but none had borne any useful fingerprints. Further fingerprints had been found on several larger pieces of glass and on the unbroken sections of the cabinet itself, and these were currently being checked; it was thought, however, that some were from members of the staff or attendants and cleaners, but most would have been left by visitors when resting their hands on the top of the cabinet as they viewed the contents. The carpet inside the room had been treated to the services of a powerful vacuum cleaner and lots of small items of debris had been recovered. Most of the bits and pieces had come from the feet of visitors – particles of grit from outside the building, human hairs of various colours, black and white dog hairs, black, white and ginger cat hairs, dandruff, fibres of various colours and types such as wool or cotton, dust from clothing, lots of unidentified pieces of dirt, pieces of squashed flies and beetles, remnants of stinging nettle flowers, old seeds from dandelions, a couple of pine needles, several tiny chunks of chewing gum and other minuscule particles of dust and debris which could not, in this short time, be identified. Efforts would be made to do so in due course. In all relevant cases, the particles would be tested by the Forensic Service for DNA, especially the human hairs, but that would take some further time. There was also a lot of sawdust which had been recovered from among the fibres of the carpet. This had been compared with that from the sawn-off laths in the roof and it matched; it also corresponded to the more considerable heaps of sawdust on the floor below the attacked roof space. Likewise the plaster dust matched that from the roof's interior.

The tiles had been neatly positioned outside on a flat area of the roof space, although the felt had been removed entirely from the roof and taken from the scene. Also recovered were the cut-away pieces of lath, narrow strips of very old wood, two inches wide and half an inch thick, which had lined the roof for generations to support the tiles . . . but one comment caught Pluke's eyes.

It confirmed what he believed – it said, 'The pieces of

lath recovered from the snuff box room floor were checked against the cuts made in those remaining, and in all cases they matched. The sections of lath which had been cut away were of uniform length (2' 6" long or 75 cm approx) and, in their original positions, would have filled the hole made by the intruders. The laths had, however, been cut from below; this was proved by direction of cutting as evidenced in the marks made by the saw.'

'See this, Wayne?' Pluke pointed to the relevant paragraph and read it out aloud, just to be sure Wayne was aware of its contents. 'Those laths were cut from below, from inside the room in fact.'

'All of them?' he asked.

'All of them,' said Pluke.

'Oh,' said Wayne. 'So whoever cut them could not have descended into the room before doing so?'

'No, he could not, Wayne. Those laths would have prevented him.'

'So it is an inside job, sir?'

'I would stake my reputation on it, Wayne,' said Pluke in a rare show of emotion. 'And that puts a lot of people under suspicion. But before we try to produce a short list of suspects, I suggest we establish a motive.'

'I thought we'd already done that, sir. Money. The high value of the stolen goods?'

'That is feasible if it was an outsider, but if the crime was committed by someone working within the museum, there might be another motive. We've already considered revenge but might there be something else?'

'Revenge is one of the most frequent of motives in this kind of establishment, sir, where people seek to get their own back for some bad previous treatment they believe they've suffered. The high resale value of stolen goods is always another likely motive, I agree with that. What else have you in mind?'

'I'm aware that the museum is going through a tough time financially, Wayne. That could have some bearing on

124

the case. The stolen goods were very valuable, a most useful asset.'

'You're thinking of an insurance claim, are you?'

'Among other things. There might be other reasons, very personal to some member of the staff, something strong enough to compel a person to steal the snuff boxes. And remember, the thief is cunning enough and skilled enough to make the crime look like the work of an outside raider. What we need to do now, Wayne, is to find out all we can about every member of staff and we must, at the same time, consider a variety of motives.'

'You're thinking the curator might have upset someone who has hit back in this way?'

'Who knows the mind of a criminal, Wayne, or a person under intolerable personal pressure? Or even professional pressure.'

'You're not thinking the curator himself did this, are you?' frowned Wayne Wain.

'Everyone is a suspect until eliminated from our enquiries, Wayne.'

'So what are you proposing?'

'That we reinterview every member of staff, past and present, with a view to establishing a possible motive and whether they might be guilty. It will not be easy, Wayne, I hate to place such dedicated members of staff under suspicion, not only from us but also from one another. The actions of just one person have that dreadful effect, everyone is suspected. So I think we must proceed with extreme caution, we must not let any one of them believe we think one of them is guilty. We need to let them think we are trying to prove their innocence . . . to eliminate them from the enquiries. So, that is our task for the immediate future, Wayne. Now let me consider further aspects of this report.'

He turned to the paragraphs about the pile of slates left neatly on the roof; each had been examined for fingerprints or other evidence but nothing had been found. The puzzling point was that the underlying piece of felt had been cut away and removed from the scene; it had not been traced.

'Why would anyone take away that felt and yet leave the tiles and pieces of lath behind, sir?' puzzled Wayne.

'It would be done for a purpose, Wayne, it is important not to forget that. So why did the thief remove it from the scene? That is the question you must ask yourself. That kind of waterproof roofing material is hardly the sort of material that would be used to wrap the stolen goods but, if it was removed from that roof, then it must be somewhere else.'

'Unless it has been destroyed, sir, or thrown away.'

'If it has been destroyed, Wayne, fire is perhaps the only means by which that could be effectively and safely done so do we need to look at people's garden bonfires or domestic fireside ranges? Parts of the felt might remain among the ashes.'

'If we visit the staff's private houses to interview them, sir, we might come across it.'

'I doubt it. If it was removed because the thief thought it might provide evidence, then it will have been destroyed although, of course, remnants might remain. Let us be vigilant, Wayne. If it was thrown away, it has surely gone with the dustbins in which case it will be in some landfill site beyond our abilities to find it.'

'If it's there, it can be found, sir.'

'Would you fancy searching among thousands of tons of domestic waste, Wayne?'

'No, sir, most definitely not.'

'Me neither, and I don't want to burden the Task Force with such a ghastly job if it can be avoided.'

'You're very considerate, sir.'

'One tries, Wayne, one tries, so let us hope our enquiries do not depend upon finding that piece of felt. Having said that, however, we must not let it out of our minds. We must believe it was removed for a sound criminal reason, such as the removal of incriminating evidence.'

'Right, sir. So any suggestions?'

'I rather suspect it became contaminated with some kind of evidence which could lead us to the culprit.'

'Fair enough, sir, I'll bear it in mind during my enquiries.'

Apart from the tiles, no evidence was found on the roof. There was nothing to indicate that the raiders had climbed on to the roof from below, no scrub marks, no footmarks, no disturbed pieces of guttering or roofing, no trampled mossy growths or damaged ivy. The single door which led on to the roof from inside the museum had also been examined, but had revealed no clues. It was a stout wooden door reinforced with metal bands across its width inside and fitted with twin bolts plus a stout mortice lock. No attempt had been made to force it, although the key was kept in reception. The sturdiness of the door meant it was highly unlikely anyone could smash it down from the outside or force it open from the inside. If the door had been used to allow the thief to make his exit from the museum on to the roof, then he or she must have had the key.

In turn, this suggested the thief or thieves had been concealed in the building while it was being secured that Tuesday night or else they had found a means of entry which had not activated the alarm system. Or else they were members of staff, or just a solitary member, with a knowledge of the security procedures. The possibilities of identifying the villain were narrowing.

The Scenes of Crime Officers had examined the routes from the museum into the water tank loft, the loft itself and the wooden staircase leading up to that rooftop door, but no material evidence had been found. It was accepted, however, that the route was used from time to time by the caretaker as he went about his maintenance tasks but Wayne said he had denied using it on that day.

The report concluded with notes to confirm that SOCO had examined the entire surrounds of the museum and had found no signs of any attempted forcible entry, no discarded snuff boxes and no further evidence. There was a brief résumé of the Cumbrian break-in but no scientific evidence to link it with this one. It was a competent report signed by Detective Sergeant Tabler, the officer in charge of the Scenes of Crime Department.

'Well,' said Pluke when they had finished examining it. 'What do you make of that, Wayne?'

'It tells us what we know already, sir,' smiled Wayne. 'Except that it supports your suspicion that it looks like an inside job.'

'Yes, it does, but that report contains items which are of interest to me. I shall not burden you with this now but it is something I shall bear in mind.'

'You could always tell me, sir, if it's important . . .'

'I need to make a few more enquiries, Wayne, and to interview all members of the staff and all the volunteers, then I shall be in a position to assess the import of the information provided by the report. I think that is my next task – another visit to the museum. Are you free to drive me there?'

'Yes, sir, I was going to Pebblewick anyway today, to wind up a few outstanding enquiries.'

'It will be useful to have you with me. Having interviewed them already, you will know whether any of them change their stories when I speak to them.'

'I understand, sir.'

'Good. Then let us go.'

Making sure his rabbit's foot was in his pocket, that he left his office with the right foot first and that he touched the wood of the door upon leaving, Pluke felt good fortune would accompany him during today's enquiries. This happy situation was reinforced during their journey because a black cat scampered across the road as Wayne was driving into the village, and he did not run it over. That was lucky for the cat. Running the gauntlet of the old men sitting beneath the lych-gate, they arrived at the museum where the lady at the ticket desk, Mrs Collins, recognized them immediately. She said Mr Porter would be pleased to see them. She offered coffee and biscuits but Pluke, now in formal police mode, declined without giving a reason, and so they were eventually ushered into the curator's office.

'Good morning, Mr Pluke, Detective Sergeant Wain. This is an official visit now, Mr Pluke, eh?' smiled the ever-cheerful Neil Porter as he invited them to be seated.

'It is indeed, Mr Porter,' said Pluke. 'I am now back at the helm with the intention of pursuing your raider with every ounce of vigour at my disposal. And so is Detective Sergeant Wain. Having completed the preliminary investigations, it is now time for us to concentrate on the details and for that, I must eliminate every member of your staff from the ongoing enquiry.'

'I thought that had already been done, Mr Pluke, when Detective Sergeant Wain carried out his investigation during your absence?'

'Detective Sergeant Wain was undertaking the essential task of trying to find reliable witnesses. When a crime is committed, it is essential that any possible witnesses are traced with the utmost speed so that the investigation can be carried out right from the start with the greatest efficiency. Sadly, we did not find any.'

'Because the criminal or criminals were experts, you said?' Porter looked at Wayne. 'Your view was that they were so skilled at their task that they left no clues behind and attracted no witnesses.'

'Yes indeed, Mr Porter,' Pluke interjected swiftly. 'That is the most logical conclusion but, due to that very fact, we must now adopt a slightly different approach, in other words, a studied process of elimination.'

129

'Like a murder investigation?' Porter smiled thinly.

'Very similar, yes. We need to eliminate from suspicion each and every member of your staff and all your volunteers, past and present. This is perfectly normal, I assure you, in any major crime investigation.'

'But I do hope you are not suggesting that any member of my staff, full-time or otherwise, could be responsible for this outrage, Mr Pluke!'

'Good heavens no, that is far from the case. To eliminate someone from the enquiry is the very opposite of pointing the finger of guilt, surely? The finger of suspicion does, at this moment, point at everyone who has worked on these premises, and their friends and relations. That will be the situation until we can prove them all innocent beyond all doubt. That, I assure you, is our purpose.'

'Well, clearly I will co-operate as much as I can, I am as anxious as you to get this matter cleared up. So what do you want of me?'

'I need a complete list of your current staff, Mr Porter, names, addresses and dates of appointment. Part-time staff too, volunteers, everyone associated with the museum, even in the tiniest way. And it might be an idea to include details of anyone who has recently left your employ, someone who might bear a grudge.'

'We do have details on file, Mr Pluke, I will ask Miss Chapman to run off a list immediately. It will be on our computer and she will let us have it very soon. But I thought Sergeant Wain had dealt with all that kind of thing?'

'Consider it a double-check, Mr Porter, an essential matter in any elimination process.'

'Sorry, I do not mean to be critical of your methods, Mr Pluke.'

'I am sure you don't and this is not mere duplication of the previous interviews. Now, we shall need to interrogate you too, Mr Porter, in depth, and also Mrs Collins on the

130

ticket desk, and your secretary. Miss Chapman, you said?'

'Yes, Dorothy. Of course, we have nothing to hide, Mr Pluke. Our sole desire is to work for the good of this museum. So, let me ask Dorothy to prepare that list, it will be a copy of the one we gave to your sergeant.' He pressed the intercom and asked her to arrange it as soon as possible and to bring it to his office. 'There we are, the list is on its way. Not everyone will be on the premises just now, of course, we have part-timers who work either mornings or afternoons, they're the attendants, but we do have some full-time staff. Mrs Collins, Miss Chapman, myself of course, the caretaker-cum-groundsman and the gardener.'

'Where possible, I would like to conduct the interviews in their homes, Mr Porter, although I appreciate that is not always feasible. Sometimes, it is much better to do that than to carry out very personal interviews at one's place of work; besides, there is your own essential work to be done here and I am sure the public would not take kindly to a key member of staff being removed for an hour or more by the police. I do respect the work they do here, you see.'

'I am more than happy to allow you the time to interview my staff at work and a spare room for your interviews, Mr Pluke, if you think it will help your enquiries.'

'Thank you. May we begin here, Mr Porter, to prepare the way, as it were?'

'Certainly, let me set an example to the others. You can make your main points while we await my personnel list.'

And so Pluke began his interview, with Wayne Wain at his side taking copious notes. The preliminaries were straightforward. Pluke asked for Neil Porter's date and place of birth, his home address, his home telephone number, personal email address and then the museum's email and website addresses. His marital status was determined too – he was forty-five years old and had a wife, Gillian, and two children, a boy and a girl, Simon and Emma, both of whom were away at university. He lived in a converted farmhouse on the outskirts of Pebblewick, and kept a few hens and ducks, along with a black and white dog called Sally and two tabby cats, Mouser and Buster. He had been curator for the past five years and provided details of his previous posts since leaving York University. All perfectly normal background material but it did enable Pluke's staff, if necessary, to delve into his background to determine whether or not there were any shady areas. Sometimes, when an employee of a large organization behaved dishonestly or caused trouble, they were moved to other departments or 'advised' to resign or even retire without any police involvement. On occasions, this kind of quiet and unpublicized treatment was not a genuine solution – serious criminal behaviour could often remain undetected and unrecorded or never be made known to the police. Pluke, therefore, made sure Wayne made careful records of all the salient details.

Then he said, 'Now, Mr Porter, we come to last Tuesday evening. The eve of the crime. I know you have told us what happened but we'd like to hear it again.'

'There's not a lot I can say, Mr Pluke, and certainly nothing to add to what I've said already.'

'But I have not heard it in my official capacity as the officer in charge of the Criminal Investigation Department of Crickledale,' said Pluke. 'I have talked to Detective Sergeant Wain about it and I have read the official crime reports, but this is my first official interview and by this means I hope you will be eliminated from our enquiries. So, if you please, go ahead. What happened last Tuesday?'

There was a hardness in Pluke's voice; it did not go undetected by Wayne Wain and it seemed to have the desired effect upon the curator. He told his story all over again. He said how it had been quite a busy day with a commendable number of visitors, none of whom had

132

caused any problems. In keeping with the practice of the museum, he had locked the doors at 5.30 p.m. but only after carrying out his usual search in case anyone had got left behind, locked in the toilets, lost in the grounds or corridors of the big house or, of course, was lurking in some secret place for ulterior motives.

'Where do you search when you lock up?' asked Pluke.

'Everywhere, Mr Pluke. The whole premises, inside and out. Display rooms, stock rooms, rooms marked private, offices, toilets, buildings in the grounds, even behind bushes and flower borders, the lot.'

'It must take up a considerable amount of your time?'

'It does, but it has to be done. Sometimes, if the staff are available, I will ask one of them to help me, but usually I do it alone. As I did on Tuesday.'

'So take me through that routine, Mr Porter, if you please.'

'Well, the last admission is at 4.45 p.m., we close the entrance at that time. This allows anyone admitted then to take a leisurely tour in time to leave at 5.30 p.m. Three-quarters of an hour. Five minutes after the final person has entered, I begin my tour, telling the attendants they can leave and checking each room along the route.'

'So you follow the route taken by the visitors?'

'Yes, it's the best way, well tried and tested, the result of several years' experience. And there are other rooms along the way, stock rooms, storage spaces, our little shop, the toilets, the boiler room and so forth, so I am not treading on the heels of the final visitors. This is what I did on Tuesday. Even though we'd had a busy day, I found no one lurking anywhere or dawdling. I checked everywhere along the route, including the grounds even though our groundsman, Bob MacArthur, had already checked the outside buildings and gardens.'

'And am I right in thinking that after every room has

133

been checked, the door is closed? I noticed locks on the doors of most of the exhibit rooms.'

'Yes, as I check each one, I close the door. The locks are automatic, they lock without keys,' and all the time, the curator was smiling.

'So a mischievous child could slam a door on a school-mate, and he or she could be locked in?'

'If that happened, the attendant is always nearby, he or she would see that and deal with it. I've never known that sort of thing happen. In any case, the attendants carry keys to open the doors; they leave them at reception when they go home.'

'So a locked and closed door means the room has been thoroughly checked and secured for the night?'

'Yes, Mr Pluke. On Tuesday I did exactly that. I completed part of the internal route, went outside into the grounds, checked the gardens and grounds and returned to the house to complete the tour. I locked the rear doors, they are very secure and protected by our alarm system. I check all windows too, by the way, even if they are barred. Then, as always, I went upstairs along the visitors' route, and finally downstairs which brings me back to the reception area and ticket desk. As I am doing that, the staff are moving out and by the time I finish my rounds, the staff have all left except for Mrs Collins. She collects the cash takings from the shop and the entrance fees and drops them into a night safe on her way home. When she is ready, we set the alarm and exit by the front door. We do that every working day, Mr Pluke, and during the evenings if we have a special event, and we've never had any cause for concern. Until now.'

'And what about the loft, Mr Porter? The place which contains the water tanks? Do you check that?'

The expression on Porter's face told Pluke that that part of the house was not checked.

'Er, no, Mr Pluke. It's well signed with notices saying it

134

is a private area with no members of the public admitted. Only someone very familiar with the house would find their way via that route to the loft. Besides, even if someone did hide in there, there's nowhere they else can go and they can't get out on to the roof . . .'

'Unless they have a key for that roof door,' said Pluke. 'So you are telling me that space, quite a large space, was not checked?'

'No, I have to admit it wasn't, Mr Pluke. I think it must be included in the future . . .'

'I am not here to issue recriminations, Mr Porter, I just want to establish the facts. You see, if that place was not checked, then someone could have hidden there and remained there until all of you had left the premises.'

'A member of the public, you mean? A criminal?'

'Anyone, Mr Porter,' said Pluke, pointedly.

'But why hide there, and go out on to the roof to remove the tiles when all they had to do was walk along the internal corridors . . . there's the question of keys, of course, and the alarm system . . .' Porter was struggling to find answers.

Pluke helped him. 'Think of a man hiding there, Mr Porter, with an accomplice outside in the grounds. How would the accomplice know which room contained the valuables? Easy, Mr Porter. The man left inside the museum goes into the room in question having found the key in reception and he is able to make contact with his pal outside who, one must assume, managed to ascend to the roof, probably after being shown the room in question. Mobile phone perhaps? Just loud voices? Lights from inside even. A torch shining through that window in the snuff box room would easily tell an accomplice on the ground outside that this was the room to break into. He could then make his way up his extension ladder or rope or whatever, get in through the roof, empty the display case and depart the same way, this time with his com-

135

panion. His companion could not exit by ground-floor doors because that would trigger the alarm system. But they could move around inside the building without triggering the alarm, I believe?'

'Yes, that's true. All the external doors and windows are alarmed, and display rooms containing valuables have locks on their doors. It is possible to move around inside the building without triggering the alarm – but if anyone breaks in through a door or window, then the alarm will sound. So, yes, someone could have hidden there and moved around inside the museum. . . . I suppose, you know, the keys are accessible too . . . if you are already inside, they're kept in reception.'

'Yes, Mr Porter, a rather unsatisfactory system, might I suggest.'

'In the light of this crime, Mr Pluke, we are already reconsidering the replacement of our alarm system and have adopted new internal security procedures. I know it sounds like locking the stable door after the horse has bolted but it is better late then never. I must admit we've never regarded ourselves as holding objects of high monetary value. Things like Stone Age tools, witch bottles, medieval farming implements, wartime hairdressing aids or 1950s kitchen utensils are not considered particularly valuable, certainly not in purely cash terms.'

'Perhaps when your insurers originally decided to accept your security measures, they had no idea you were sitting on a hoard of valuable snuff boxes?' said Wayne Wain.

'I think that is highly likely,' agreed Porter. 'We've had the same insurers for decades and valuation of the snuff boxes was not undertaken until fairly recently.'

'I am assuming you have reported the theft to your insurers?' said Pluke.

'I have, yes. They have already said they will want to commission an independent assessor to evaluate the snuff boxes, but they've made no mention of upgrading our security measures. We shall do that before they demand it from us, Mr Pluke.'

'Good. Now, let me put this to you. Would a pay-out by your insurers solve your immediate financial worries?' Pluke did not flinch from that question. 'And safeguard a few jobs?'

'That is one way of looking at things, Mr Pluke, but I do hope you are not suggesting we staged our own robbery to raise money!'

'I am not suggesting anything, Mr Porter. I am just considering the facts. Now, having accepted that someone could have concealed themselves in the museum that Tuesday night, might I now ask you to detail your own movements that same night? For elimination purposes, of course.'

'I'm not sure I like the tone of this interview, Mr Pluke. I get a distinct feeling that I am under suspicion . . .'

'You must not think like that, Mr Porter. Please, your movements for last Tuesday.'

He told them he had gone straight home from work, walking the half-mile or so to get a little exercise, and he and his wife had gone into their own garden to enjoy the evening sunshine with a glass of wine. They had talked over their respective day's events, and had enjoyed their evening meal in their garden.

After clearing up and washing up, they had gone for a walk through the village, popped into the Marble Trough Inn for a quick half-pint of beer for him and a glass of wine for her, and had then returned home in time to watch the news at ten o'clock. Their stroll had taken them past the museum but they had seen nothing untoward. They had gone to bed around 11 p.m. and he had remained there until leaving home for work next morning, and he then discovered the break-in shortly after 8.30 a.m. A typically mundane evening but far from a typical morning.

'So, Mr Porter,' said Pluke, 'let me put you on the spot now. It does appear that the museum could benefit considerably from this crime, financially I mean, so if you did not commit the crime, who did? Who do you think broke into your museum and stole those snuff boxes?'

Chapter Ten

'If you expect me to suggest it was one of my staff, Mr Pluke, you are going to be disappointed. Their loyalty is total, both to me and to the museum, but no matter how fiercely they will protect their place of work and all that it stands for, they would never stoop to crime as a means of solving our cash-flow problems. They are worried about the future, as indeed I am; they have noticed the reduction in visitor numbers and the fact were are not replacing staff who leave, but the solution is not to commit a crime in the hope it will rectify matters. The solution is simple – we need to attract more paying customers and find more ways of increasing our income. So, Mr Pluke, even if someone did secrete themselves in the loft overnight, it would not be one of my staff. I suggest you look elsewhere.'

'Well spoken, Mr Porter, it's reassuring to find a senior official who is not afraid to support his work force at times of great uncertainty. Nonetheless, we must interview them all, we should be failing in our duty if we did not. You have spoken of financial concerns. I must ask just how serious is your cash-flow problem?'

'I cannot see it has anything to do with the fact we were raided, Mr Pluke, the raider would not be aware of our dilemma. It has not been made public.'

'Mr Porter, I am investigating a serious crime, I must examine every avenue and I expect your co-operation, even in this most delicate of matters.'

'Our revenue, Mr Pluke, comes mainly from admission

charges and in addition there are sales of memorabilia from our shop, plus the renting of space to groups for special meetings.'

'Like the old manor house in the grounds? I have attended events there.'

'Yes, several local societies like to use our external facilities in the evenings but even with this bit of extra income, it is not sufficient, at the moment, to cover our running costs.'

'There is a reason for this downturn?'

'It stems from the time of the foot-and-mouth disease outbreak. People went elsewhere when the movement restrictions were in force around us, to the seaside mainly or to theme parks and city attractions. Having changed their leisure practices, they haven't reverted to their former habits, they have not returned to the countryside in their former numbers. That is the chief reason for the downturn. Our purpose is to woo them back; we have to sell ourselves all over again.'

'But apart from that, you have also incurred some high expenditure?' Pluke said. 'You told me you had spent a lot of money on a building?'

'We did. We learned of a thatched cottage, the former home of a peat cutter which was high on the moors in a near derelict state. The owners, a local estate, were going to demolish it chiefly for safety reasons because ramblers had discovered it and were using it to sleep in, light fires for cooking, shelter in bad weather and so forth. The walls were unsafe and most of the roof was rotten, it could have fallen in and injured a rambler. The estate didn't want to get sued and decided to demolish it. We heard about it and decided it would be an asset to the museum – the estate said we could have the entire building free of charge provided we removed it, stone by stone, at our expense. As the place was historic from a moorland folk lifestyle point of view, we decided we should do that – and re-erect it in our grounds. Our income at the time, four years ago, was sufficient to justify half the cost and would cover the repayments if we borrowed the rest. We secured a donation from the Heritage Lottery Fund and also a grant from the Yorkshire and Humberside Museums Council, but we still had to borrow substantially from the bank.'

Pluke began to think that horse troughs appeared much less expensive to maintain, and his mind wandered for the briefest of seconds, pondering the possibility of a grant from the Heritage Lottery Fund for the conservation of horse troughs. He would consider that . . . but Mr Porter was continuing,

'Even though much of the demolition, labelling of stones for their rebuilding, transportation and the rebuilding itself was done by volunteers and supporters, it did cost us a lot of money.'

'How much?' asked Pluke.

'In round figures, £300,000. It became more expensive than we had bargained for. We had to borrow half that amount, £150,000 in fact. We negotiated a ten-year term for the loan, which means our repayments of capital and interest charges come to around £1800 per calendar month. With some prudent housekeeping, we could initially just meet that out of admission charges – now we can't. It's as simple as that. The bank has allowed us a breathing space, though, and we are paying what we can. We are able to find £1000 a month or thereabouts but it means there is still a considerable shortfall and, of course, we are not making much headway in reducing the debt. Much of our repayment money is merely keeping pace with the interest charges. But we are working hard to raise our profile and this summer has seen a modest increase in the number of visitors and, of course, we are always looking out for more grants for which we might apply.'

'And have you any assets, apart from the exhibits? The building and its grounds must be a considerable asset?'

'It is, yes, and we do have other assets. There are the buildings in the grounds, of course, but they are part of the museum and we could never realize their capital, but we do have a cottage in the village. The gardener rents it from us, but we have no intention of mortgaging that for what is really a short-term problem. It came with the house when we bought the estate from the de Kowscott-Hawkes.'

'I see, so you have substantial assets in Pebblewick? But, like other organizations, you also have your running costs?'

'Yes, wages, National Insurance, routine maintenance, heating and lighting, various insurances such as public liability, buildings and contents, the purchase of exhibits although many are donated to us, council tax, income tax, administrative costs – there are lots of outgoings, Mr Pluke, but we can cope with those if we are careful. Volunteers are so important to us, most of our attendants are volunteers who demand no wages for their work. We couldn't function without them.'

'So a sudden influx of insurance money to compensate for the loss of a handful of snuff boxes would be a great salvation?'

'I can see how your mind is working, Mr Pluke, I can see how the suspicious police mind views our loss as a means of solving another pressing problem, but what can I say? I did not steal the snuff boxes and do not believe any of my staff did either.'

'Who knows about your financial dilemma, Mr Porter?'

'Very few people, it is not the sort of thing I discuss with the staff and certainly, it has not reached the public domain. I know, my secretary knows and our board of trustees also know. And the bank of course. No one else. I do feel, however, that the more alert of local people have recognized our reduction in visitor numbers and our failure to replace outgoing staff. It is a message which is not easy to conceal, Mr Pluke; it may have started rumours.'

Pluke, recalling he had been told about the museum's troubles by Mr Green in Siena, thought the rumour was

142

more widespread than Porter realized. So who had informed Green? He was now wondering if he should question members of the board of trustees just in case one had seen an opportunity to solve the problem, then there was a knock on the door. It opened to admit the caller; it was Dorothy Chapman, Porter's secretary. She was a heavily built middle-aged woman with a shock of auburn hair, and was dressed in a sober grey skirt and jacket, a white blouse and black shoes.

'The list of staff and volunteers you asked for, Mr Porter,' and she passed the file to him. 'It is up to date and includes those who have left in the past eighteen months.'

'Thank you, Dorothy. This is Detective Inspector Pluke and Detective Sergeant Wain, by the way, they are here about the break-in. This is Dorothy Chapman, gentlemen, our museum secretary. I think it is fair to say we could not function efficiently without her! There's nothing she doesn't know about the running of this place, there are times I think she could run it on her own!'

'I just do my job to the best of my ability, Mr Porter,' and there was a faint flush of pride on her face. 'And I enjoy what I do, that's so important.'

'We shall need to talk to you at some stage, Miss Chapman,' said Pluke. 'We are interviewing every member of staff as a matter of routine.'

'Yes, of course, I shall be pleased to help in any way I can, although Detective Sergeant Wain has spoken to me already. Last week, just after the break-in, when he talked to us all.'

'Quite, and now we are working on what we call the elimination process, we need to record your innocence in our files, Miss Chapman. So when would be convenient? It would take about half an hour, give or take a few minutes.'

'I am here all day, Mr Pluke.'

'I realize that, but whenever possible I prefer to speak to

witnesses in their own homes, Miss Chapman, I do not like to interrupt their work, and I am sure you are very busy.'

'Well, I go home for my lunch hour, Mr Pluke, I live in the village, just across the green in fact, almost opposite here. Howe Cottage.'

'That would suit us, would it not, Wayne?'

'Fine, sir,' agreed Wayne Wain, wondering if Pluke would venture into the local pub for lunch.

'Then, if it does not interfere with your lunch break . . .'

'No, I usually have a sandwich and a cup of tea, I have my main meal in the evening but I go home each lunch time at twelve thirty to let my dog have a run in the garden.'

'All right,' said Pluke, glancing at his watch. 'I see it is approaching twelve o'clock now and we have almost finished our chat with Mr Porter, so shall we say one fifteen at your house?'

'If it takes a while, Dorothy, don't rush to get back to work,' smiled Neil Porter. 'I know Mr Pluke will want you to concentrate on this enquiry, and of course it is important to us all. Take an extended lunch hour if necessary. I know Mr Pluke will not detain you without good reason.'

'Oh, thank you, Mr Porter but there is not a lot I can say about the break-in. I'm sure I won't be late back. Now, Mr Pluke, you'll have no trouble finding my cottage, it has a green gate and there is a lilac tree in the front garden. I look forward to seeing you at quarter past one,' and she left the room.

Pluke quickly scanned the list and saw that Dorothy had done a good job: full names, dates of birth, special skills or knowledge, home addresses, dates of appointment or dates of departure where necessary were all included.

'I think we have concluded our chat with you, Mr Porter,' said Pluke, putting a tick next to his name on the list. 'Thank you for your time and for allowing us to talk during your working day.'

'I hope my contribution was useful.'

'It was of immense help, but we have others to see. It is our lunch-time now, then we shall talk to Miss Chapman and maybe other members of staff later in the day. If we need to speak to you again, might we visit you at home?'

'Yes, of course. It's wise to ring beforehand, I go out a good deal, to give talks to all sorts of organizations and groups, that sort of thing. It's an important way of generating interest in our work, but I've no commitments this evening.'

And so they left, having given Neil Porter something to ponder. Until now, he had never considered he could be employing or using a person with criminal tendencies. He had been remiss in not checking the loft but he'd never done so since his appointment. It was hardly likely a staff member would have hidden there – they'd have been missed by the others and in any case it was such an out-of-way place for a casual visitor to find. It seemed the raider knew his way around the museum's inner parts including the alternative route to the loft. So was it someone who had worked here, even as a builder or electrician? Or as an occasional helper? A villager related to a staff member? Family members helped out on occasions, especially at evening events. The range of probabilities raised by Pluke would exercise his mind in the following hours and days. Or had he, for example, inadvertently spoken to someone about the financial crisis?

He was always extremely careful about speaking of confidential professional matters outside the premises, but had one of the staff overheard him talking on the phone or speaking to Miss Chapman? Could this crime really result from a warped sense of responsibility towards the museum? Were the signs of the cash-flow problem so very evident to everyone? The villagers especially? The worried families of staff members? All kinds of questions with unpleasant answers were now forming in his mind and so Neil Porter would do some detective work of his own.

Outside the museum and clutching Miss Chapman's list, Pluke took a deep breath and said, 'My word, Wayne, this moorland air is invigorating. A walk across the heather would be most enjoyable, a very nice change from the mental stress of conducting demanding criminal enquiries. And did you know that a sprig of white heather is the key to good fortune and that it protects one against danger? Not that much white heather grows wild on these moors, you can walk miles without ever seeing a single sprig. It is certainly well worth the effort seeking it, though. There is much merit in finding a sprig of white heather.'

'Well, sir, for all that, I think a walk to the pub would be most enjoyable. I missed my breakfast and I'm starving. I could do justice to a steak pie, chips and peas, and a nice pint of bitter. For that, I'll willingly forgo the chance of finding a piece of lucky white heather.'

Pluke, recalling the happiness of his holiday in Siena and the joy of sitting in the sunshine with a tasty Italian meal, felt a twinge of desire for a repeat of those moments because he saw several tables outside the inn. They were in a small garden surrounded by a fence, and not one of them was occupied. They promised peace and tranquility.

'You know, Wayne,' he said, 'that might be a very nice idea. Yes, lunch in the open air on this warm June day. A time to relax and consider what we have learned. I wonder if they do Italian meals here?'

'I doubt it, sir, but I am sure they have something very similar on the menu,' and so they walked over to the pub. 'See that, sir, the name?'

'The Marble Trough? Yes, Wayne, I researched the name and inn sign some years ago and it seems there used to be a trough on the roadside near the inn, probably until just after the First World War. By all accounts, it was a very handsome edifice, so I was told years ago when I made enquiries, but there is no picture of it and no record of it in local history books. Horse troughs weren't considered to be worth recording or preserving in those days. The inn sign bears an image but that, it seems, is purely from the imagination of the artist. He'd heard the name and assumed the trough must be a white one if it was made from marble. No one knows whether it depicts the actual trough which stood here, or whether the artist used some other trough as his model. I never saw the trough which once stood near this inn, it vanished many years ago, long before I developed my interest in troughs. I managed to glean my rather scant information from people with long memories, now sadly passed on.'

'What happened to it? Have you any idea?'

'Who knows, Wayne? With the decrease in horse traffic and the increase in motor vehicles, it would have been removed so the road could be widened. That was the fate of many troughs, removed and destroyed, or merely thrown away and forgotten. It is a pity this one was not donated to the museum.'

'It's the sort of thing they would welcome, sir, I'm sure.'

'Absolutely. A few horse troughs were given to museums, you know, but most of those which survived finished their working lives as gigantic plant pots in suburban gardens, or cemented into stone walls.'

By now they had reached the tables outside the Marble Trough; each bore a menu and Wayne said, 'I'll go inside and order, sir. What are you going to have?'

Pluke considered the menu, bearing in mind he and Millicent would be eating at home this evening, and said, 'I see there is a salad, with tomato, cheese, spring onions and beetroot . . . not unlike some of those in Italy. So, yes, I shall have that, Wayne, and a glass of red wine.'

'A glass of wine, sir?' Wayne was astonished. Pluke rarely drank alcohol of any kind, let alone red wine. And certainly not on duty. His holiday had clearly transformed

Pluke, although it could be argued he was off duty temporarily, having his official refreshment break.

'Cheese salads go down very well indeed with a nice red wine, Wayne, Italian preferably.'

'Fine, sir, I'm sure they have an Italian red in stock,' and off went Wayne to order the meal. Pluke settled down at one of the tables and took deep breaths of the pure moorland air. He found it invigorating as he sat there taking in deep breaths so that every part of his inner self was fortified with the benefits thus offered. There were times it was so beneficial, being a detective in the open air of North Yorkshire.

'Hello,' said a beery male voice very close to his right ear. 'It's that detective chap again. I knew you were in the village again, you never came to see me.'

He turned to find a stocky man at his side with his face very close to Pluke's ear and a half-consumed pint of beer in his right hand. It was one of the men who had accosted him earlier from the seat under the lych-gate. Pluke's gift for observation now leapt into action – there was a piece of sticking plaster on the index finger of his left hand, his ancient grey jacket was torn at both sleeves and ragged at the collar, he wore no tie over a collarless shirt, his trousers were filthy and the fellow needed a shave. He wore a flat cap too, and a black and white collie dog, known as a cur, was at his side. His beery breath was strong enough to knock over anyone weaker than the powerful Pluke. In his mid-seventies, estimated Pluke, and probably from a moorland farming background, the fellow had managed to approach Pluke without him realizing, so wrapped up had he been with his thoughts. It's a good job the fellow meant him no harm. Pluke decided that one should never drop one's guard, not even out here in a remote and peaceful moorland village.

'Detective Inspector Pluke,' responded Montague, rising to his feet to speak to his visitor.

'I know who you are, we've met. Just now I saw you

148

from t'bar, that mate o' yours is in there getting t'drinks,' said the man without volunteering his name. 'You never came back to me last time, but I just wanted to say it's time you lot caught that chap what broke into t'museum.'

'We are working very hard on that enquiry,' countered Pluke.

'Not from where I'm standing you're not,' said the fellow. 'From where I'm standing I'd say you were eating and drinking and having a good time instead of getting him caught. And at t'ratepayers' expense.'

'And from where I'm standing,' said Pluke, 'I think I'm talking to a very unobservant and rather stupid old man. We have been engaged on the enquiry since the moment the raid was discovered, and this morning my colleague and I have been conducting extremely delicate enquiries in the museum while you and your friends have done no more than sit around doing very little. And we must eat or we die.'

'By gum, Mr Pluke, that's what I like to hear, a chap what speaks 'is mind,' and he promptly sat down at Pluke's table. 'You and me'll get on, Mr Pluke, you can't beat calling a spade a spade, can you? Or a bloody shovel or summat worse. No good pussy-footing about. So what are you going to ask me about it?' and he took a long drink from his pint pot as the dog came closer and sniffed at Pluke's trouser leg.

'Ask you?'

'Aye, ask me summat. Go on. Ask me summat about t'break-in at our museum, owt you like.'

'Well,' said Pluke, 'I would like to know who broke in.'

'Now I can't rightly help you wi' that, Mr Pluke, 'cos I've no idea. But it's a good start. Well, I must be off now that I've been quizzed by the police. Can't stop the constabulary from making their enquiries, can we? Come on, Jess.'

And off they went, man and dog.

'What did he want?' Wayne was now approaching the

149

table with a pint of beer in one hand and Pluke's red wine in the other. 'Isn't he one of those old chaps who sit under the lych-gate? He was in the bar when I went in.'

'I think he wanted to be part of the ongoing police investigation, so I asked him a very difficult question, he did his best to answer it, then left.'

'Apparently, he's in there every day, for most of the day when he's not sitting outside the museum,' said Wayne. 'The barmaid says he's single with nothing to do now he's retired but when the detectives came around asking questions last week, he'd just popped down to get his pension from the post office so they missed him. Anyway, now he's been questioned, he'll be happy. He wouldn't want you to ignore him, he likes to know what goes on.'

'He liked me being rude to him,' and Pluke actually chuckled.

'He's a Yorkshireman, sir, he respects blunt talk. I suspect you knew that. So what was the difficult question you asked him?'

'I asked if he knew who had broken into the museum, and he didn't.'

'Ah, well, that includes us. Now, the meals will be here in a few minutes.'

'We need individual receipts, Wayne, so we can make our subsistence claims as per Police Regulations. Now, as we are not likely to be overheard here now that our friend has returned to his bar, what did you make of Mr Porter?'

'He struck me as being a very honest and decent man, sir. I think the raid has shaken him, and I think he was even more shaken when you suggested it might have been done to pay off the museum's debts. I doubt if that occurred to him until that moment.'

'The raider, if he is from outside the museum, did it a favour but at the price of casting suspicion on every member of staff. Now, Wayne, I might be wrong in thinking this but when I asked if he knew who the culprit was, he did

150

not try to blame any of his colleagues. That makes our Mr Porter a very honest man; so many guilty people, when they think they are about to be caught or exposed, try to shift the blame. He did not. Furthermore, he was quite open about not checking that loft. He could have lied about that, but he didn't. If he claimed he had checked it, to cover his own tracks, it would have spoilt my theory about it being an inside job. The fact he told us the truth means that the villain could have hidden there, Wayne, and it could also be someone who is working there. Or has previously worked there.'

'I go along with that reasoning, sir.'

'Good, I'm pleased we agree. For those reasons, I think Neil Porter was not involved in the raid – and I'm sure he has no idea who did it.'

At this point, a waitress emerged from the inn carrying a tray with their meals on board. They halted their conversation and discussed the name of the pub as she approached; she laid out their cutlery, presented each with their meal and left. And as she returned to her chores inside, the flat-capped man reappeared, this time clutching an almost-full pint pot as he approached them again with his dog at his heels.

'Aren't you blokes going to ask me owt else about them missing snuff boxes?' he demanded as he stood above them.

'What do you know about them?' asked Wayne, hoping to humour the fellow into leaving them in peace while they ate.

'Why don't you ask me?' smiled the man, taking a massive drink which left a moustache of white foam on the whiskers of his upper lip. Framing the right question was therefore something of a challenge as the fellow stood before them in defiant pose, but Pluke, having a knowledge of the way some of these moorland characters thought, rose to the occasion.

'What do you know about the missing snuff boxes?' he asked.

'Well, it's good riddance, I say. They brought nowt but bad luck so I say good riddance.'

'Bad luck? How can snuff boxes bring bad luck?' Pluke smiled at the fellow, hoping to coax him into saying something useful.

'Have you asked my brother about that?' was the response. 'I'll bet you haven't asked our Fred about that. He knows, you know.'

'Your Fred? Who's your Fred?'

'Our Fred? Everybody knows our Fred! I thought you blokes had been here asking questions, so how come you don't know our Fred?'

'What's he got to do with this enquiry?' asked Pluke.

'What's he got to do with this enquiry? Only that he works for the museum and has done all his life, well, he worked for the de Kowscott-Hawkes before that but he's been there ever since . . . should have retired years ago, our Fred, but he keeps going, it's all he has, you know, working there for the museum . . . if he stops working there, he'll drop dead . . .'

'Ah,' said Wayne producing the list of names from his inside pocket and scanning it quickly. 'Frederick Cullingworth, the gardener. Is that him?'

'Well, who else would it be? I've only one brother, you know. I'm Ted and he's Fred, older by five years. Grand chap, is our Fred, salt of the earth.'

'So what does your Fred know about the snuff boxes?' pressed Pluke.

'Know? He knows everything about them.'

'He must be a very clever man,' smiled Wayne.

'He is, he hasn't got where he has without being clever, he was the brains in our family, I was the dumb cluck.'

'I have spoken to him,' said Wayne. 'Last week, when I made my initial enquiries. I asked if he'd seen any disturbances in his garden or grounds, signs of people

152

climbing over the walls to get in, or using ladders to get up to the roof.'

'And he said no?' grinned the old man.

'Right,' said Wayne. Clearly these two characters had been talking about the raid. 'So what's he know about the snuff boxes that's going to help us find the thief?'

'Like I said, he knows everything, Mister Detective. That's why you should ask him about them.'

'Ask you, you mean? So what do you know about them?'

'Not as much as our Fred, not by a long way.'

'So what does your Fred know?'

'He knows they bring bad luck, like I said, so that's why he said good riddance when they'd gone.'

'All right,' said Pluke. 'We'll talk to Fred again, he's on our list of experts who have to be seen again.'

'Aye, well, I'm pleased about that. You get nowhere if you don't ask, do you?' and he trotted back to the bar, delighted that his brother was regarded as an expert. Pluke knew how to talk to such characters.

'So has someone really got rid of them because they bring bad luck?' asked Wayne, thinking this was hardly the reason for such a sophisticated raid.

'A person from outside would not steal them for that reason,' Pluke reminded him. 'He'd steal them because they have a high resale value.'

'Right,' said Wayne. 'But a member of staff might want to get rid of them, eh? If it was widely thought those snuff boxes were responsible for their run of bad luck, with jobs at risk? I can imagine someone thinking it was best to get rid of them, then things would be all right. That kind of simple logic is not uncommon, sir.'

'We need to talk to Fred, Wayne, but first let us enjoy our meal while Ted is otherwise engaged, and then we have to visit Miss Chapman. I do like visiting suspects in their homes, you know.'

'So she's a suspect, sir?'

153

'A witness then, that is perhaps the right word, although they are all suspects, Wayne, until we eliminate them.'

'Fair enough, so why do you like visiting them in their homes?'

'A person's home is so revealing, it tells a lot about the person who lives there. Much better than their office or place of work. I can tell what a person likes or dislikes, their interests, the way they care for their home and personal belongings . . . I am looking forward to seeing what Miss Chapman's cottage is like.'

And so they tucked into their meal; it was splendid and as they ate other people came to the surrounding tables and they ceased their discussions about the case. Pluke made no comment about Wayne drinking a pint of beer when he had to drive the police car. But, of course, their enquiry was likely to continue throughout the day, by the end of which Wayne's modest alcoholic intake would have been dissipated.

Prompt at one fifteen, therefore, Pluke and Wayne presented themselves at Miss Chapman's cottage door with its horseshoe-shaped knocker.

Chapter Eleven

There was no response and so Pluke knocked again, and waited.

'Do you think she's all right, sir?' Wayne Wain asked with concern in his voice. 'I mean, you don't think some harm has come to her?'

'This is not a piece of crime fiction where the bodies turn up all over the place as vital witnesses get murdered for the silliest of reasons, Wayne. I am sure Miss Chapman is all right, she asked us to call at one fifteen, and one fifteen it is.'

'I just wondered if we should check round the back . . .' and he walked a few yards along the footpath to peer over the garden fence, but a laurel bush obstructed his view into the rear of the premises. Then their patience was rewarded.

Miss Chapman opened her door, smiled a welcome and said, 'Do come in, gentlemen. Sorry if I kept you waiting, I was in the garden with Sally, my young spaniel, I've left her there, she gets so excited when I have visitors.'

She led the way into her neat little cottage; it was decorated rather in the style of the 1970s but was clean and tidy. She led them into the lounge and bade them be seated in the easy chairs, one at each side of the fireplace, then asked, 'The kettle has boiled, would you like a cup of tea?'

'No, thank you.' Pluke was quick to decline her offer

with a smile. 'We've just had a nice lunch at the Marble Trough.'

'It would be no trouble, Mr Pluke, no trouble at all.'

'Thank you, but we couldn't,' and so she settled down on the settee which faced the fireplace.

It was a cosy room, modest in size and furnished only with necessities. There were no antiques, Pluke noticed, and no sign of expensive tastes but a small TV set occupied one corner to the right of the fireplace, a full bookshelf lined the wall to the left and the small size of the room forced the settee to dominate the rear wall. One or two pictures hung on the neutral-coloured emulsioned walls – watercolours of the moors by a local artist – and there were family photographs on the mantelpiece. They looked like her parents and a man about her own age. A brother perhaps? On the wall above the centre of the fireplace hung a mirror and he noticed a sprig of white heather attached to its chain. There was a vase of roses on the mantelpiece too and several potted plants on the window ledge. The general atmosphere was of sparseness, but it seemed very functional. A modest house, the home of a careful spinster.

The fire had not been lit – after all, it was June and she was out at work during the day – although there was a floral screen before the grate, and the hearth was decorated with pine cones and assorted greenery. A nice touch, homely and rustic.

'I will come straight to the point,' said Pluke. 'I know your time is precious, Miss Chapman, and you know why we are here – it is in connection with the theft of the snuff boxes. My prime purpose is to eliminate all the museum staff from our enquiries but let me begin by making reference to the financial state of the museum. I regard that as very important.'

Pluke repeated the background supplied by Neil Porter and observed her face as he revealed the extent of his knowledge. Then he delivered the body punch.

156

'There is no doubt, Miss Chapman, that the insurance money will solve the museum's immediate financial problems. Assuming, of course, that the claim is paid in full.'

'I must admit that had never occurred to me, Mr Pluke.'

'Few people are aware of the financial situation, Miss Chapman. You are one of those who is. Mr Porter has provided me with the details.'

She studied him without replying, tightly clutching her knees with her hands as she sat forward on the settee with a deep frown on her face, and then she said, 'I do hope you are not suggesting I committed the crime, Mr Pluke, to solve our financial crisis. I did not, I can assure you, and I had no part in it.'

'It is just one of the motives I must examine, Miss Chapman. It cannot be ignored, and I am sure you can understand how important it is for me to eliminate you from our enquiries. I am aware that thieves could have broken in to steal the valuables out of sheer greed, but the issue of the museum's finances does add another dimension to our enquiries.'

'But Mr Pluke, surely you don't think I climbed on to that roof, took off those slates and carried out the most daring of raids? It would have been suicidal. I have no head for heights and I very much doubt if I could have carried heavy ladders all that way . . . it's absurd, Mr Pluke, to even suggest I could have done it. Or been party to such a crime.'

'I am not suggesting you did, Miss Chapman, or that you were involved. I am trying to eliminate you from suspicion. Now, suppose I told you that it was possible – just possible, but possible nonetheless – that access to the roof was gained by someone hiding in the museum at locking-up time, and going out on to the roof via the water tanks' loft doorway.'

'I'd say that was ridiculous, Mr Pluke. No one could hide like that, Mr Porter checks the whole place before he locks up, and all of us, the entire staff, keep an eye open for people going astray or wandering into the private areas, especially near closing time. No, I don't think that would be possible. Besides, you need keys to open the door on to the roof, it's always kept locked. We pay very close attention to our security.'

'Mr Porter did not check the roof loft on Tuesday night, Miss Chapman, he is quite honest about that. He has never checked it, he tells me, it was one area which has never featured in his daily checking routine. In view of that, I am sure you understand that someone could have hidden there that evening, waited until the museum was deserted, obtained the necessary keys from the reception area, dealt with the alarm system and committed the crime.'

'But they came in through the roof, surely? They took the tiles off, that's what we were told.'

'It is possible they did not enter by that route, it is possible the tiles were removed as a decoy tactic, to make us believe there had been a break-in.'

'Oh my goodness . . . this is dreadful, Mr Pluke. Do you mean it could be one of our own people?'

'Or a clever thief who was able to conceal himself inside the museum and then perhaps to make use of an accomplice outside. We are looking at every possibility, Miss Chapman, we have to explore every likely means by which the crime was committed.'

'Oh dear, this is dreadful, it really is. I just thought we had been the victims of clever criminals, like that other museum, but to think someone I know, someone I work with even, might have done this, well, it's dreadful, really too dreadful to contemplate.'

'You can see now why I wish to eliminate you from our enquiries, Miss Chapman; through no fault of their own, suspicion has fallen upon everyone employed there or even associated with the museum, so I must ensure that all the innocent parties are eliminated from my enquiries. I think perhaps you understand that now.'

158

'Yes, I do, of course I do. I fully understand. I'll help in any way I can.'

'So, Miss Chapman, as one of the few people with knowledge of the museum's finances, did you know the value of those snuff boxes?'

'Yes, I did. We'd had them valued for insurance purposes. As secretary I attended the meetings and dealt with the correspondence but it would never occur to me to use them to solve our problems, not in such a criminal way.'

'I suppose, if the museum was really desperately in need of money, the snuff boxes could have been sold on the open market?' smiled Pluke. 'Had that option ever been considered?'

'Oh, no, Mr Pluke, we never dispose of any of our exhibits. We might loan some of our surplus items to other museums on a temporary basis or even on a long-term agreement, but we never sell anything. I can't imagine our trustees would ever consent to such an idea. It would be like selling the family silver or valuable paintings to pay income tax or inheritance tax; those snuff boxes were one of our finest exhibits, certainly the most valuable – except for the buildings in the grounds. They have always attracted a lot of interest, people come a long way to see them, so it would have been folly to sell them to ease what is really a short-term financial problem.'

'Were they regarded as your most valuable asset?' Pluke asked.

'Yes, undoubtedly, they were the most valuable of our portable assets. None of our other exhibits is worth so much, not in financial terms. Some are irreplaceable from an historic viewpoint and we can't put a financial value on those. And, of course, Mr Pluke, we were given those boxes, they were a gift, we did not have to buy them. We regarded them as very special and very precious, all of us. All the staff and volunteers, that is.'

'And so their high value could provide a solution to

your museum's financial plight?' Pluke was not smiling now. 'It would be a neat solution.'

'Mr Pluke –' she stiffened visibly – 'we are a dedicated staff. None of our attendants, volunteers or full-time staff would ever countenance such a dreadful plan.'

'I am pleased to hear you echoing Mr Porter's support for them,' Pluke said. 'So, Miss Chapman, I need to know your whereabouts on the night of the crime. Can you detail your movements after leaving work?'

'Oh dear, this sounds like establishing an alibi. Tuesday? Well, I spent the night in. Came home from work, got Sally something to eat, let her out for a run in the garden, got my own supper, watched the early television news, read a book because there was nothing else worth watching, took Sally for a late walk about nine thirty and went to bed about eleven. Not a very exciting evening, Mr Pluke.'

'Can anyone verify that? Did anyone call? Ring you? Did you ring anyone?'

'No, Mr Pluke. I had no phone calls, no callers, no contact with anyone except Sally. And she can't talk.'

'Did anyone see you taking Sally for her walk?'

'I'm sure someone must have done, not much happens in this village without someone noticing, but if so I was unaware of it. I took her round the green, it wasn't quite dark. These June evenings are light until very late, aren't they? There were people about, there always are. Visitors mainly, just wandering about or perhaps going to the pub, or leaving for their drive home. I can't say I recognized any of them. I spoke to no one, Mr Pluke.'

'Did you pass the museum? I am wondering if you noticed anyone lurking nearby, vehicles perhaps, unusual lights, people hanging about.'

'I was asked that question by Sergeant Wain last week, and have to say I saw nothing suspicious, nothing that would have worried me.'

'That's right, sir,' chipped in Wayne. 'I did ask Miss

Chapman about that and she told me she'd been walking her dog that evening but had seen nothing untoward.'

'And later?' Pluke continued. 'Did anything wake you? Noises outside your house in the early hours? Vehicles moving? Voices? People clanking ladders?'

'Not a thing, Mr Pluke. I slept very well indeed, and if there had been unusual noises, I think Sally would have barked. We're just opposite the museum, and unusual sounds do carry in the night air. But she never barked, and I never heard anything. Sorry I can't be more help.'

'Negative information is often as valuable as positive information,' Pluke smiled. 'Now, as a local person living in the community, and working for the museum, have you encountered any gossip or theories which might help us trace the culprits?'

'Well, clearly it is the talk of the village, Mr Pluke, and further afield, but everyone says how shocking it was and everyone's convinced it was clever criminals who'd toured the museum in the guise of ordinary visitors before planning to break in. Everyone thinks they got in through the roof, by climbing up from the grounds out of sight of the village, just like the Lake District raid. They think it's one of a new series of such attacks and it looks like that to me. I've never heard anyone's name mentioned as a suspect, and certainly no one in this village, or working for the museum, would have done this. No one. I think the general view is that experts were responsible, with a ready market overseas and the snuff boxes being out of the country first thing the following morning, to be lost for ever.'

'That is distinctly possible,' agreed Pluke. 'Well, Miss Chapman, I think we need not trouble you any further. If we have any more questions, we will contact you at work if we may, or of course, here at your house, depending on the time of day.'

'Any time will be suitable, Mr Pluke, any time at all.'

And so they left. As they were walking back to the car

161

well out of range of the cottage, Pluke asked, 'Well, Wayne, what did you make of Miss Chapman?'

'Very straight and honest, sir,' he said. 'Her story tallied with what she'd told me just after the crime was discovered. She made no attempt to create an alibi, her account of that evening has a ring of truth about it. I saw no reason to disbelieve her, or to think she is in any way implicated.'

'She is dedicated to her work, to the museum, you think?'

'I'm sure she is, sir. She would never wish any kind of harm to befall it.'

'Good. Well, now I think we must find another person to interview. How about the gardener?'

'Frederick Cullingworth himself,' smiled Wayne. 'He's not very like his brother in my opinion.'

'He's on our list so I'll soon find out. Let's go back to the museum. I think I can interview him in his garden without unduly interrupting his work, and I doubt if he has much contact with visitors. We won't be getting in their way.'

The old men had not yet returned to their seats beneath the lych-gate. No doubt they were still in the pub and so Pluke's passage up to the museum was not subjected to their ribald comments. Once inside, they explained their mission to Mrs Collins and she allowed them through the barriers without charge, pointing the direct way into the spacious grounds.

'He'll probably be in his shed,' she smiled. 'He spends a lot of time in there. It's at the far end of the grounds, in an area marked "Private" behind some small fir trees.'

'We'll find him. You have a groundsman as well, I believe,' Pluke said. 'Two men to look after this area full time?'

'Mr Cullingworth is very old, Mr Pluke, he came with the museum, in a manner of speaking. He's well past retirement age but we keep him on, almost an act of charity, I suppose. He often says he's one of the exhibits!'

He doesn't do a great deal to be honest, looks after the Wild Garden, the borders and a small greenhouse near his shed but the rest of it, lawn cutting, hedge trimming, the heavier work, maintenance of all our outside attractions, care of the footpaths, all that's done by Bob MacArthur.'

'Thanks for telling me,' and so they left the museum and entered its magnificent grounds. Their width was greater than the length of the museum and they extended up a gently sloping rise for about a hundred and fifty yards. Much of the area comprised well-kept lawns and small patches of garden, a relic of its days as the showpiece of a country house, but now there were interlinking footpaths between the museum's added attractions.

Those consisted of some former outbuildings which were now converted into period shops such as a cobbler, chemist, grocer, post office, sweet shop and rural garage complete with a 1936 Austin 10. In addition, there was the lovely old thatched cottage which had brought about the present financial crisis; it was now occupying a prime site and was popular with visitors who enjoyed its tiny rooms, inglenook, cramped bedspace, stone floors and genuine witch post. Another big building was the former medieval manor house, also removed stone by stone from its previous site; little more than a huge barn-like structure with a sleeping area upstairs at one end, it was popular as a meeting place for societies and social functions. It provided extra income for the museum. As Pluke and Wayne walked through this fascinating place, they were surrounded by visitors of all ages including a party of chattering schoolchildren. There was a witch complete with black pointed hat and broomstick sitting in a tiny heather-thatched hovel, always popular with children and adults alike; the nymph on her plinth in the middle of the fish pond was spouting water from an upraised finger; and a former glassworks had been recreated with startling accuracy. Museums like this, especially the one at Hutton-le-Hole at the other side of the moors, were popular with people of all ages. Some had lived and worked with objects like those on display and youngsters were now learning about a former lifestyle on the moors, one experienced by their grandparents or even parents.

'Up there on the left, sir, at the top of the grounds . . .' Wayne had spotted the wooden garden shed behind the line of conifers.

There was no sign of the gardener or groundsman as they made their way up the gentle slope, but near the top Pluke halted and turned around. He wanted to see how much of the roof of the house was visible from this elevated position.

'We get a good view of the house from here, Wayne,' he said after a few moments of studying the scene before him. 'A clear aspect of the museum and the rear section of the roof.'

'The right-hand corner, sir, as you are looking at it. That was the point of entry. It's been repaired now, a neat job, you can't see where the tiles were removed but they were just to the left of that chimney stack, seen from this angle. The chimney hides it from most aspects; it's possible the culprit could have removed those tiles quite unseen, even in daylight.'

'Quite so, Wayne. I went up there, you know, on my first visit. It's a considerable height from the ground,' said Pluke, having identified the place. 'A very long extension ladder would be required to reach that height, not to mention the angle it would have to create when positioned against the wall. Too narrow an angle, with the base too near the wall against which it was resting, would result in a risk of it toppling over backwards or even sliding sideways, especially with a man upon it, and climbing. I remember my old geometry master explaining such things – he always maintained there was a special and important technique which was necessary when siting ladders and then climbing them. From a safety aspect, I mean. A badly positioned ladder is a danger and remember, whoever had to climb it would also have to descend while carrying the stolen goods.'

'I appreciate that, so what's the point you are making, sir?'

'That it would take a very skilled ladderman to position and climb a ladder to such a great height. And in my opinion its feet would have to be on the lawn, not on the stone surrounds of the building. They are too narrow to accommodate a ladder when extended to such a great height, I believe.'

'But no prints of a ladder were found in the earth, sir, either the lawn or any of the borders.'

'Precisely, Wayne. It all supports my conclusion that the crime was committed from the inside, with no access from outside and without ladders even being used as decoys. Now, let us see what this gardener has to say.'

The gardener's shed was a sturdy structure of brick and creosoted wood complete with window and door. The bricks formed the lower walls while the wood formed the upper section and roof, the roof being covered with felt. Outside there was a kind of staging which was full of plant pots all containing plants of some kind, and above the doorway was a wooden roof supported by a couple of pillars: a sort of cabin-style portico to provide added protection against the weather. As they approached, they could see at the rear a further extension on posts, but without walls; this contained an assortment of tools, several wheelbarrows, a mechanized lawnmower, piles of clay plant pots, bits of fencing and much more besides. A gardener's domain.

Pluke made his way to the open door by crossing the staging, at which a voice growled, 'This is private property, young man.'

Pluke, rather delighted at being addressed as 'young man', was not surprised by this welcome and said, 'Police, Mr Cullingworth. I'm Detective Inspector Pluke and this is Detective Sergeant Wain, whom you have met before.'

165

'You'd better come in then, I'm just finishing my bait.' He used the old word for his lunch-time snack. 'I got delayed, some chap wanting to know what to do with clematis in winter. We get all sorts here, you know. So what do you chaps want now?'

'We'd like another word about the raid if you can spare the time.'

'Well, I'm a busy fellow, allus up to the neck with work and stuff, but I reckon I can spare a few minutes. You'd better sit down.' Cullingworth was sitting on a three-legged stool in front of a workbench which bore his flask of coffee and sandwich box. He snapped shut the lid as a sign that his meal time was over. The rest of the bench was littered with trowels, small forks, pruning shears, paint brushes, tins of weedkillers and pesticides, plastic plant pots, bits of wire and string, the head of a rake, several lengths of what looked like broom handles, mole traps, a few tools like screwdrivers and hammers along with countless other treasures of value to a gardener. They were things that might come in useful one day. But hanging from the roof was something that caught Pluke's eye – an ancient hot cross bun suspended in a piece of bird netting.

Fred Cullingworth indicated a couple of stools which were in fact old dining chairs with their backs missing. Covered in dust, they offered some kind of position from which Pluke could ask his questions and so, dusting off the seats, the two detectives sat down.

Although Cullingworth did not stand up to greet them, Pluke reckoned he was smaller than his brother. He was not quite so tall as Ted nor quite so broad; in fact, Pluke did not think they looked at all like brothers. Fred had a round head which was almost bald except for some wisps of long white hair around the ears and nape of the neck, but his eyes were large and very blue and he wasn't wearing spectacles. Those big eyes regarded Pluke from a round, tanned face which hadn't been shaved recently.

Fred was wearing a pair of dusty overalls and black leather boots, undoubtedly his working clothes, and his hands looked thick and strong, toughened by years of manual work.

'Well, Mr Cullingworth –' began Pluke.

'Fred, everybody calls me Fred, when folks ask for Mr Cullingworth I have to stop and wonder who they mean.'

'Fred,' said Pluke who was not normally accustomed to such familiarity. 'We're here about the break-in last week.'

'Well, I didn't think you'd come for some gardening advice, Mr Pluke.'

'You're the longest serving member of staff, I believe?' Pluke began, recalling the data provided on his list of employees.

'Been here ever since the museum started,' and Fred puffed out his chest. 'Came with the house, as they say, like a dog might do. Part of the scenery, I am, one of their best-known exhibits, I'd say.' And he chuckled at his own oft-repeated joke.

'Really? How is it you've been here all this time?' Pluke wanted to hear Fred's own account of his years of service.

'I worked for Mr de Kowscott-Hawke as under-gardener, that was until he sold the house. When he sold up, I didn't want to leave and besides, there was no work for me at his new place, so he came to some arrangement with the museum. They said they would keep me on as long as necessary. I was part of the deal, you see, like them snuff boxes that have gone missing.'

'How old would you have been then?' asked Wayne.

'In my thirties, Mr Wain. 1952 it was, when de Kowscott-Hawke sold up, I'm turned eighty now. I keep thinking I might retire, but what would I do with myself if I did? I've no wife, never have had, and no children or grand-children.'

167

'I'm sure that's a question many people have asked themselves, Fred.'

'I know I'm better off here keeping fit and doing summat, and they give me enough to live on. What more could a chap want?'

'What more indeed? And you live in the village? No long-distance travel to work?'

'Right, Ivy Cottage down by the beck. It belongs to the museum, you know. That was another of the things Mr de Kowscott-Hawke did for me. Sold Ivy Cottage to the museum along with the big house on condition I could spend my days there. Very good to me, Mr de Kowscott-Hawke was, he looked after me. And the museum has as well. So here I am, part of the scenery, Mr Pluke, and nearly a museum piece myself.'

'You pay rent for the house?' asked Pluke.

'A peppercorn rent, Mr Pluke, summat do with the law. It makes me a tenant and gives me security. A shilling a week as was, it's gone up to ten pence now. Ten pence a week, they knock it off my wages.'

Fred's cottage must be a valuable asset for the museum. Pluke had not seen it but whatever its size or condition, it must be worth many thousands of pounds, especially in such a desirable village. Even with such an asset, however, the museum would not be able to realize its value until Fred either died or voluntarily moved out. Would the trustees then sell it, or would it become another extension of this popular place?

'So, Fred,' Pluke's questions now began in earnest. 'Those snuff boxes.'

'What about 'em?'

'Who do you think stole them?'

'Me? How would I know that, Mr Pluke?'

'You live in the village, you work here, I thought you might have heard some gossip, had local people chatting to you about it, picked up some useful information perhaps?'

'Well, all that was said, Mr Pluke, was that somebody had spotted how valuable they were, cased the joint as they say, then broke in that night and ran off with 'em like a rat in the darkness.'

'Did any suggested names come to light? Motive, even?'

'Nothing, Mr Pluke, nothing at all. It's no good asking me, whoever did this came and went without a soul knowing a thing about it. But one thing I do know, I'd never climb up to that roof, ladder or no ladder. One slip when you're up there, and you're a gonner. Broken back as likely as not, a broken leg at the least. I never go up to the roof, that's Bob MacArthur's job. I leave all that to him.'

'You knew what the snuff boxes looked like?'

'Oh aye, Mr Pluke. I'd seen 'em many times, both in the museum – the bosses like us all to know what we've got in there so they tell us to look round from time to time – and also when Mr de Kowscott-Hawke lived here, they were in his house, brought home by some ancestor way back. I saw them then. He hated 'em, though, didn't really want owt to do with 'em, so I wasn't surprised when he left 'em behind when he sold up. If he wanted to give 'em to the museum, it was all right by me.'

'You weren't worried when he did that?'

'Worried, Mr Pluke? Why should a thing like that worry me? I thought it was quite a decent thing to do really, to leave summat behind from the old house.'

'A generous thing to do?'

'Aye, that's how I saw it. A generous thing to do.'

'You don't think there was some other reason for him leaving them behind?'

'Well, you never knew how his mind was working, Mr Pluke, he was a clever chap, fast-thinking, devious some folks thought, so he might have done it for some other reason. I know he sometimes said the boxes brought him bad luck, but I don't think he was serious about that. Joking, he was, whenever he said that. I told him to get

169

himself fettled up with a few horseshoes about the house and plant some elder trees around it, and mebbe a few rowans, that would bring him good luck, I said, but he just laughed at me.'

'I see you've got an old hot cross bun hanging up there,' and Pluke indicated the object.

'Aye, had it years, Mr Pluke. It's never gone mouldy and it stops my shed from catching fire. My mother always had an old hot cross bun hanging in the kitchen, to stop the place catching fire. And we never had one, you know, a fire, I mean.'

'I can well believe it. Now, Fred, the reason we are here is to eliminate all members of the staff from our enquiries. If none of them stole the snuff boxes, then we must look elsewhere.'

'Steal them? No one working here or even folks just helping out would do a thing like that, Mr Pluke, now you are talking daft.'

'I'm sure you are right but I have to make it all official, Fred, for our files. So where were you last Tuesday evening?'

'At home, where else? Well, nearly all evening, I went up to the Marble Trough with our Ted for a couple of pints, a regular trip for him and me.'

'And what time would that be?'

'Nine or thereabouts. We got home just before eleven.'

'And then?'

'Well, we went to bed.'

'We?'

'Me and our Ted, we live together. We've our own rooms and share the house, he's not bothered to get wed either. We couldn't see the point of it.'

'And did Fred work here then?'

'No, he was a builder's labourer until he retired and got his pension, and now he spends most of it on booze.'

'And the museum have no objection to you sharing the house with Ted?'

'No, why should they? It was for me, that house, well, for the family really, but it was when Mr de Kowscott-Hawke sold up he said I should have it for life, that's the deal he did with the museum. It was my house, in my name, so Ted pays me lodging money. Not much, just enough to cover council tax and so on, but it means I can chuck him out if he gets too much to cope with.'

Pluke did not seem to be getting very far with his in-depth investigation but realized that an old character like this, well into his eighties, was hardly likely to remove the tiles to conceal the true method of stealing the snuff boxes, and he was just as unlikely to conceal himself in the loft to commit such a crime.

He changed tactics. 'So what do you do here, Fred?'

'Potter about and keep things tidy, Mr Pluke. Bob does the heavy stuff, that lawnmower's getting too much for me to cope with, and he sees to the fish pond and fountain, keeps them clean. I can keep things neat and tidy like weeding the borders, planting out, pruning and so on. Me and Ted might help indoors if they're short-handed on an evening, keeping an eye on things. I enjoy all that, it's nowt strenuous.'

'Good, well, keep up the good work. Now, Wayne, is there anything you would like to ask Fred?'

'I don't think so, sir. We had a good chat the last time I was here and there's not much more that can be said. I asked you last time, Fred, whether you'd heard anything peculiar overnight near the museum but you said your house was too far away, you'd never hear anything any-way.'

'Right, Mr Wain, that's it. Neither me nor Ted heard a thing, we talked about it afterwards, but we've learned nothing, nothing at all. If we do hear owt, we'll tell you. It's shaken us up, has this break-in, I can tell you.'

'Thanks, we need all the help we can get. And remem-ber,' said Pluke, 'apart from finding the culprit, we want to recover those snuff boxes.'

'I had no idea they were worth so much, Mr Pluke, not until I read that bit in the paper about the break-in. Just like that carry-on in the Lake District, eh? We read about that an' all. There's some rum folks around, can't keep their hands off other folks' belongings. You're not safe in your beds these days.'

Pluke decided to ask this old character whether he knew anything about the Siena snuff box; if anyone was likely to have overheard talk about it during its time in the big house, it was Fred.

'Fred,' said Pluke. 'A change of direction now. I am personally interested in one of those snuff boxes. I came to have a look at it on Sunday, having just returned from Siena in Italy, but it had already been stolen.'

'I remember that 'un, Mr Pluke, a very nice-looking little box it was an' all.'

'I have been trying to trace its history. Do you know anything about it?'

'Not a lot, except it was brought back by some ancestor of Mr de Kowscott-Hawke's years and years ago. Hand-carved it was, mebbe in ivory or mebbe in wood, I can't be sure, it was a long time ago when Mr de Kowscott-Hawke was chatting to me about it, he was in one of his chatty moods. But yes, it came from Siena, so he said, he said it was unusual because it had the carving on the side and not on the lid like other snuff boxes. Like a horse trough, he said. Horse troughs sometimes have inscriptions or carvings on the front face.'

'A horse trough?' spluttered Pluke. 'What else did he say about that?'

'Well, it was a long time ago, Mr Pluke, I was only a lad. But I remember him holding that snuff box up and pointing to the image on the front, so I could have a good look at it, and he said it been copied from a horse trough years ago . . . that's why the picture wasn't on the lid, because the box, without its lid, was just like that miniature trough, same shape even with a horse's head for the water to come in, except there was no water with the snuff box.'

'Are you sure he said it was copied from a horse trough?' Pluke could hardly believe his ears. So the information in the museum's pamphlet seemed correct.

'Oh, aye, Mr Pluke, I remember that because it was different from the other snuff boxes, with the carving on the front, if you understand.'

'So which Mr de Kowscott-Hawke would that be? Not Sir Eustace?'

'No, it would be Eustace's grandfather, old Mr de Kowscott-Hawke as we called him. Grand old chap.'

'Did he say why his ancestor had brought that particular snuff box back to England?'

'Well, Mr Pluke, he had a passion for collecting trinkets, bringing things home from all over the world, but old Mr de Kowscott-Hawke said it caught his eye because it matched a trough owned by the family in England. He thought they would match.'

'Say that again!' demanded Pluke. 'Did I hear you correctly, Fred?'

'I just said the snuff box had caught the ancestor's eye in Siena because the family had a trough just like it, back here in England.'

'I don't believe this!' cried Pluke. 'You're saying it was a copy of a trough which was already here, in England?'

'That's what he said. I remember him saying that. And as you know, Mr Pluke, some English troughs were very ornate and very historic. But a lot have been lost, new road schemes have destroyed thousands, umpteen were thrown away when new roads were made or widened, like that one outside our pub, before I was born that was, and some people pilfered them for gardens . . . it was all very sad. I know you are a big trough man, but a lot have vanished, Mr Pluke, gone for ever.'

'So where was this trough in England?'

'It could have been that 'un on the roadside outside here,

just near the pub, but that vanished before I set eyes on it. Or it might have been in these grounds but there isn't one here now and there never has been in my time. Or it might have been at Tillabeck Hall, I couldn't swear to any of them places, to be honest.'

Pluke recalled that Tillabeck Hall had been in the family, albeit in the hands of distant relations.

'Was Killabeck a likely place, do you think?' he asked.

'I suppose it could have been, Mr Pluke, but I can't be sure. As I said, I never saw it and nobody has ever said which trough they copied from. Some do say the pub is named after it, but no one knows for sure. But why do you want to know about an old trough, Mr Pluke? It won't help you get our snuff boxes back, will it?'

'Every piece of information is of potential value, Fred,' said Pluke. 'But now, I think we should talk to your colleague, Mr MacArthur.'

'At this time of day, you'll just catch him in his shed, down near the back door.'

'Come along, Wayne,' said Pluke, clearly shaken and deeply excited by what he had just discovered. 'We have work to do.'

Chapter Twelve

As Fred Cullingworth had predicted, Bob MacArthur was in his shed. Compared with most sheds, however, it was more of an emporium because it had formerly been an outbuilding of the original house and was substantially built of stone. About twice the size of a double garage, complete with a radiator fed with hot water from the museum and with enough lights to equip an operating theatre, it was of the sturdy lean-to style with a sloping slate roof, windows along the length of its lower wall and a fine wooden door with a glass window.

Inside there were shelves along the two main walls, all neatly ordered with a mass of mysterious paraphernalia of the kind required by a groundsman and caretaker such as tins of paint, brushes galore, white spirit, jam jars containing umpteen varieties of screws, bits of electrical apparatus and wire, spare pieces of almost anything and a range of tools like screwdrivers, hammers, pliers, chisels and electric drills. Cans of oil, creosote, paraffin and other unnamed liquids stood on the floor, and there were bags of cement and sand near a wheelbarrow, not to mention an old electric oven, kettle, washbasin and selection of mugs whose cleanliness might not have impressed the most relaxed of food inspectors. There was enough space for some unwanted furniture too – spare chairs and a table occupied the far corner along with countless lengths of cut and dressed timber of varying designs and widths.

Some might say it was a glory-hole; but for Bob Mac-

Arthur it was a little corner of heaven, his own personal heaven in fact. In his shed, Bob was always content. In fact, he had one just like it at home. He knew precisely where anything and everything was, and had enough spare bits and pieces to cope with any emergency, whether it was something as simple as a blown fuse in the museum, an urgent repair to the fabric of the house or maintenance of the pathways around the grounds. Bob, in his dual role as both caretaker and groundsman, carried lots of responsibility but he reckoned there was nothing he could not cope with. Tall and thin, he was in his late forties with a mop of greying hair, wise grey eyes and a smoking pipe clenched between his teeth; summer and winter alike, he wore the same dark grey sports jacket over bib-style overalls and stout black leather boots.

'Mr MacArthur?' The door was open so Pluke tapped on the glass and called the fellow's name before entering.

'Aye, that's me.' MacArthur straightened up to see who had called; he had been working on something which was clamped in the vice on the workbench. It was something metallic which he was filing. 'Who wants to know?'

He laid the file on the bench and turned to Pluke, removing the pipe from his mouth and placing it in the breast pocket of his overalls. Pluke hoped he wouldn't set fire to himself, but there was a portable fire extinguisher on one wall, he noted.

'Detective Inspector Pluke and Detective Sergeant Wain,' he announced. 'We'd like to talk to you about the break-in.'

'Well, there's nowt much I can say about that, Mr Pluke, but you can ask. I can't tell you what I don't know but I want them rogues caught, whoever they are. Come in and sit down.'

He ambled across to the pile of old chairs, selected two and brought them closer to his bench, setting them down to face a chair which was already there. He occupied that one, stuck his pipe back in his mouth, made sure it was ignited and said, 'Well, Mr Pluke, what is it you want to ask?'

Wain sat with his notebook open, ready to act as the silent partner, while Pluke launched into his well-rehearsed preamble about wanting to eliminate all members of the museum staff. Bob nodded sagely amid clouds of smoke as Pluke emphasized various points. When he had finished, Bob said, 'Well, Mr Pluke, there's nowt much I can add to all that. It's not often I work in the museum unless it's to change a light bulb or deal with a dripping tap or get a radiator working in winter, so I was not too familiar with those snuff boxes. I have seen 'em, mind, when I fitted that display cabinet. It's all glass, to give a better view, the first one was mainly wood with a glass top. You couldn't see much then. I know the boxes were left with the house when it became the museum, but that was before my time. I've only been here about fifteen years.'

'Have you any idea who might have stolen them?' Pluke asked.

'Sorry, no idea, Mr Pluke. No idea at all. I wish I had. It wasn't me, though, if that's what you're thinking. I was at home that night, Tuesday wasn't it? I'm making a kitchen cupboard for my wife so I was in my shed at home, not this one, I've one at home, not as big as this by a long way, but a good shed, Mr Pluke. I do like good sheds.'

'So what time was that? When you were working in your home shed?'

'I went in just after tea, sixish I suppose, and stayed there till bed time. Elevenish. You can ask my wife, she was at home all evening and brought me a cup of tea, and told me not to stay out too late.'

'Thank you, I hope we won't need to interview her. Do you live close to the museum?'

'Not really, I live at the far end of the village, Ashtree it's called. Just Ashtree. It's about three-quarters of a mile from here.'

'I am interested in the time the museum was closed, Mr MacArthur. I am very anxious to learn of any unusual incidents in that time, during the hours of darkness especially, and of course I am keen to know of anyone showing undue interest in the grounds and house itself.'

'Well, I must say that has bothered me, Mr Pluke, ever since I learned about the break-in. I saw nothing and heard nothing that night, nor was I aware of anyone wandering around the grounds during the daytime, any daytime I mean, looking as if they were planning anything, like climbing on to the roof. I'm out and about in the grounds most of the day, and if somebody had been planning something like that, I should have seen them. If they did it without me noticing, then they must have been very professional, that's all I can say. You can always tell when folks are standing there considering doing summat out of the ordinary.'

'There is a possibility the thief or thieves could have hidden inside the museum, Mr MacArthur. Hidden there until everyone had gone home and then stolen the snuff boxes.'

'It's funny you should say that, Mr Pluke, that's what I've been thinking. When Mr Porter told us all what had happened, I went round the grounds looking for signs of them putting a ladder up against the wall but I found nothing, and neither did the police when they looked. If those raiders have put a ladder against any of those walls, it would have left marks in the ground, or even scratch marks on the stone surrounds, and there's no way you can get all the way up to that roof without a ladder, I don't care how good a climber you are. Even if they'd used mountaineering gear, like pitons, they'd have left marks on the walls. They didn't, Mr Pluke, they left no signs outside, nothing at all. That made me wonder if they'd got in from the inside. I told the police that when they came before, those chaps doing the scientific stuff.'

178

'And how could they have done that, Mr MacArthur? From the inside?'

'Well, they'd hidden somewhere inside. I know the curator does his rounds before locking up but I reckon anybody, once they knew their way around the place, could find somewhere to hide so as he wouldn't find them.'

'So how could such a person have carried out this raid?' Pluke wanted to test this man's knowledge of the museum and its procedures against his own theories. He wanted MacArthur to speak his mind and so he did. He said that in his opinion, a clever thief could have entered the museum as a paying visitor. With some pre-knowledge of the museum's layout, perhaps gained during earlier visits, he could easily find somewhere to hide; there were places which were out of bounds to the public and which were seldom, if ever, checked for people loitering without authority.

'There's the upper loft, Mr Pluke, where the water tanks are kept. You know that?'

'I do, I have been there. It has a door leading on to the roof.'

'You've done your homework.'

'But that roof door is kept locked, Mr MacArthur, and it is very secure. It wasn't attacked by the raiders.'

'The key is on a keyboard in the reception area, Mr Pluke, along with keys for the exhibition rooms, easy to find for anyone locked in. I think the raider opened that door with the key, got out on to the roof, removed some tiles and roofing felt to make it look as if they'd gone in that way. To throw you chaps off the scent. Then he came back into the house, locked the roof door and set about stealing the snuff boxes.'

'Leaving by which route, Mr MacArthur? Not via the roof. There was no ladder, you are convinced of that, so there was no way down from the roof and besides, he would be carrying those snuff boxes. He'd need something to contain them which makes it most unlikely he would try

179

to descend via a drainpipe or rope, and he wouldn't have dropped them to the ground. That would cause too much damage to the snuff boxes, I imagine some are very fragile. So he must have used a doorway to leave – and how could the thief get out of the museum if all the doors were locked and the alarm was set? And without being seen?'

'The alarm's no problem, Mr Pluke, not when you're already inside.'

'Go on, Mr MacArthur, I find this quite fascinating and most useful.'

'Well, it's quite an old system, Mr Pluke. We had it installed years ago because the insurers insisted on it. I helped the contractors, being a sort of labourer for them because they wanted me to have a good working knowledge of it in case summat simple went wrong. Then I could fix it instead of incurring unnecessary expense with a call-out if it was summat I could cope with.'

'That makes sense,' said Pluke. 'I am told it operates in conjunction with the windows and doors?'

'Right. Once it's set, if anyone tries to force an entry through any of the windows or any of the external doors, it becomes activated. It sounds a hooting sort of alarm noise at the museum as well as in the curator's house and in the local police station. Very effective really, especially when it was installed. I know modern alarms are more sophisticated and efficient but this one has always worked for us.'

'So am I right in thinking that even if it was set on the night of the raid, with a person hiding inside the building, they could move around without activating it?'

'Right, Mr Pluke. Unless they tried to open a window or one of the doors, either from the inside or the outside. You know that none of the displays are alarmed? Not even those snuff boxes?'

'Yes, I was told that. I must admit I was quite surprised.'

'It's all down to money and expense, Mr Pluke. No one

ever thought our displays were worth anything financially.'

'So the thieves have managed to steal the only really valuable objects?'

'Financially valuable, yes. We've other stuff that's important even if it's not worth a lot but it's hardly the kind of stuff a thief would want.'

'I understand. So in this case, the thief would not be able to leave the building without the alarm sounding? I mean by either a door or window?'

'Not unless he switched it off, Mr Pluke. I've been thinking a lot about this, it upset me that somebody would break into our museum and I've been wondering how it could be done. I reckon he hid inside until the place was deserted, more than likely in that top loft, then came down to reception and overrode the alarm system. Maybe he didn't know precisely how it worked and was taking precautions because he wanted to work as he wished, undisturbed for as long as he wanted. He wouldn't want to risk the thing going off while he was in there.'

'But when the curator came next morning to open the doors as usual, he noticed nothing wrong with the alarm system. If it had been disabled, he would have noticed.'

'He would, but it can be reset as you leave. The control box is near the door; you set the alarm the last thing before the door is locked. Just press a few buttons, it takes seconds if you know the code.'

'So how do you know all this, Mr MacArthur?'

'Like I said, Mr Pluke, I was there when it was installed and was shown how it worked, along with the routine sort of problems that might be expected.'

'Clearly, you were trusted?'

'The contractors had words with the curator, just to clear me for that sort of work. But as I worked here, and was caretaker, yes, I was trusted. This was before Mr Porter arrived, by the way. I must say, Mr Pluke, that it wasn't the most sophisticated of systems because we didn't have anything of great financial value on the premises, or we didn't think we had. It was later when the snuff boxes were found to be worth more than anyone thought, but even then the insurers were happy with our system.'

'And how many people know how to operate the alarm?' Pluke asked.

'Most of the staff,' admitted MacArthur. 'All the full-time staff and some of the volunteers. Sometimes the grounds are open in the evening, you see, when people use the old manor house for meetings or functions, and that means somebody has to work late to lock up. Volunteers and staff often get friends and families to help them, we've even used villagers if there's a really big crowd but it means we have to secure the museum afterwards. We let the people in that way, you see, through the main door and straight out into the grounds, then exit by the same route. Always supervised, I might add, we never let them look around the museum unless that's part of the deal for that occasion.'

'So are you saying this crime was committed by a member of staff?'

'It's a nasty thought, Mr Pluke, one I've been fighting ever since it happened, but it's either somebody who knows our system very well, or the friend of somebody who knows our system very well. Or even a family member who's mebbe helped us.'

'It is indeed a nasty thought, Mr MacArthur.'

'Very nasty indeed, Mr Pluke, it leaves a nasty taste in the mouth and puts us all under suspicion. Which is why you are here, eh?'

'I am here to eliminate the staff from such suspicion,' Pluke said. 'I must achieve that before I can begin to look elsewhere.'

'Well, knowing what I know about the system and how it works, I reckon it could be one of us. Now why would any one of us want to steal those snuff boxes? Think hard about that.'

'I will,' said Pluke. 'Now, I believe you repaired the hole in the roof. Can I ask for your reaction when you went to repair it?'

'I had to leave it until the police gave me the all-clear, from the evidence point of view. Luckily, we didn't have any rain or birds looking for somewhere to nest while it was open. Anyway, when I got up there, through the loft door we've been talking about, I found the pile of tiles, all neatly stacked up on one of the walkways, and a big hole where the felt and laths had been cut away.'

'And what were your immediate impressions?'

'Well, like the police I thought somebody had got on to the roof and cut their way in, they'd managed to pick exactly the right place an' all, right above the snuff box room. I doubt if even I could have done that, Mr Pluke, even if I do know the place like the back of my hand. I'm often up there, fixing tiles, clearing gutters and so on. It's one mighty big roof, with all its ups and downs and dips and hollows. It was only afterwards, when I got to thinking about it, that I realized they'd not gone in that way, it was done to trick us all.'

'To trick us?'

'Well, when I got to thinking about it, I thought the raider had come from inside, like I said, but he'd made it look like an outsider to throw you chaps off the scent. Clever stuff, Mr Pluke.'

'So what made you think the hole was not done by an outsider?'

'The tiles were placed neatly, Mr Pluke, just as if they would be needed again to reroof the hole. I doubt if a criminal would be so careful. I thought a thief would have chucked them off the roof; if he could work up there unseen and unheard, then a few tiles dropping on to the lawns below wouldn't make all that much noise. And that rear part isn't overlooked by anyone, not even the houses around have a view of that part of the roof. You know the felt was taken away?'

'We do, Mr MacArthur. Another peculiar thing.'

'Very, then the laths. Cut away to finish the hole. And dropped inside. They were cut from the inside, Mr Pluke. I can tell you that.'

'We know,' said Pluke. 'Our scientific experts have told us that.'

'It doesn't need clever scientists to tell you that, Mr Pluke. All you have to do is look at the angle of the saw cuts. They were done from below. So he couldn't have got in before he did that, and if he didn't cut them away, then he couldn't have got through the hole. It's an inside job, Mr Pluke, make no mistake about it.'

'So how did you repair it?'

'I had to put some temporary laths in, made from stuff I've got in my shed. It's a temporary job until the police say we can do it properly. I had to have some laths to support the tiles. I didn't put any felt in, I'll do that when I've got the go-ahead. Then I just replaced the tiles – although I had to remove some more from around the hole to get them all to sit properly. It's watertight and weather-proof for the time being, but I'll need to fix it properly before winter sets in. The weight of snow and all that. You need a proper job for that.'

'Thanks, Mr MacArthur. Now, one final question – why would anyone want to steal those snuff boxes? By that, I mean why would anyone working here want to steal those snuff boxes?'

'Now you've got me, Mr Pluke. I've racked my brains over that one. I've thought of revenge against somebody or the museum? Somebody stealing them to give to a friend who'll sell them? Somebody who is desperate for cash? Some fanatic of a collector who can't bear to see them in a museum? I even wondered about a member of the de Kowscott-Hawke family coming for them, thinking they had more right to them than the museum . . . but I've not come up with a real answer. If I did, it might help to trace them. All I hope is that we get them all back unharmed.'

Pluke was most impressed by this man's perception of events and decided that, with such a broad knowledge of the museum's inner systems, he might know more about the snuff boxes, the Siena box in particular.

'I would like to change the subject now, Mr MacArthur,' said Pluke.

'Aye, well, I'll help if I can.'

'The Siena snuff box. Do you know anything about that?'

'Sorry, Mr Pluke. I know nowt about them individually, except they were all given to the museum by the family who had the house. Oh, and some folks thought they brought bad luck, but I don't believe in that sort of thing.'

'And do you know anything about the family having an ornate old trough?'

He shook his head. 'Sorry, no. All I know is there used to be a trough outside the pub but it was moved when they widened the road. Years ago that was, before I was born. A right posh one, so my old dad said, but I've never seen it, not even as a lad, and I've no idea what happened to it. They say the pub's named after it.'

And so Pluke thought they had come to the end of their conversation with this highly perceptive man. He thanked him profusely for his help, most of his ideas being parallel to those of Pluke, and then Pluke asked Wayne:

'Detective Sergeant Wain, have you anything you want to contribute or ask?'

'Just one thing, sir,' said Wayne. 'Mr MacArthur, can I ask you this? Your theory about the crime being committed by an insider, have you mentioned this to anyone?'

'Not me, I thought better of it. They'd half kill me if they thought I was suspecting any of them for this. We've had talks about it, naturally, at break time, but they all think it's an outside raider. The hole in the roof's done that for them. But I'm not easily fooled, Mr Wain.'

'Nor I,' smiled Pluke. 'Anything else to ask him, Wayne?'

'No thanks, that's all, Mr MacArthur. For now.'

'Well, I'm always here if you want to talk to me, and I'll keep my ears and eyes open here and in the village. As I said, Mr Pluke, this sort of thing leaves a nasty taste, we're all suspected until the real culprit is traced and I believe we should do our best to recover those boxes. All of us, I mean.'

And so, with Bob MacArthur's view ringing in their minds, they left the premises. They decided not to interview any of the attendants who were on duty because they were at their posts and dealing with members of the public, although those not at work today could be seen in their homes – Pluke's favoured practice.

Once outside and heading for their car, Pluke asked, 'Well, Wayne, what did you make of Mr MacArthur?'

'A surprisingly wise man, sir, one who's clearly given a lot of positive thought to this affair. He's used his knowledge and experience to come up with a likely theory. I'm convinced now, sir, that you and he have come up with the right MO.'

'So you don't think he's guilty and trying to make us believe otherwise?'

'Like those murderers who deliberately report finding the body in the hope it will establish their innocence? No, I don't think he's that sort of person. Here we have a man who is an expert at his job, someone who knows the museum inside out, along with all its practices and daily routine, and he has produced the same theory as you.'

'I tend to believe his innocence too, Wayne, although we might decide to interview his wife, just to confirm his presence in his shed and in his bed that evening. So, shall we find one of those attendants who is not at work today?

186

I think we have time for one more interview before we finish for today.'

And so it was they found themselves talking to Emily Craggs, Miss Emily Craggs as she pointedly indicated. She lived in the ground-floor flat of a large converted house at the west end of the village; it was called Pebblewick Manor and she was No.1 Pebblewick Manor. A nice address, one befitting a lady of Miss Emily's breeding. She insisted on presenting them with tea in delicate porcelain cups adorned with red flowers and gold rims, along with some tiny home-made buns; she settled them before the fire, fussed over them as if they were schoolchildren and, when all the fussing, tea presenting and introductions were complete, she smiled.

'So, Mr Pluke, what is all this about? I do hope you are doing your very very best to catch those dreadful people, really I do not know what the world is coming to, what with this kind of dishonesty, all that street violence, the courts not doing anything about it and there being no discipline in schools . . . Now in my day when I was headmistress, we could use the cane and my word those children knew better than misbehave and if they did they knew what they would get and I never had any problems with discipline in my school and then the poor police, with all their powers taken away and the government not doing anything to help, imposing ever increasing taxes and pouring it all down a big black hole so that no one gets any benefit and then what about all those motor cars, blocking the motorways and –'

'Yes, Miss Craggs.' Pluke found himself in the dreadful position of having to rudely interrupt her flow of words and wondered how he was going to compete with her during the interview. 'I must get on . . . we have a lot to do.'

'Of course you have, Inspector Pluke, of course you have and it is dreadful of me to go on but really, I am very very concerned about the state of the world and when people

187

come into your village like this and break into somewhere like our museum to steal our treasures, then I do think the government and that Mr Blair should do something about it. They just spend all our money and what do we get in return? Nothing I tell you. Absolutely nothing, Mr Pluke.'

'Quite, Miss Craggs, quite. Now, the break-in. You are one of the voluntary attendants, I believe, and you work part time in the museum, answering queries, giving guided tours if necessary, guarding exhibits and so on.'

'Yes, I do, and I must say I love it, Mr Pluke, it gives me a real thrill to see the interest on the faces of those visitors, especially children as they look at something which is thousands of years old and which has survived into these dreadful modern times and I do like explaining to them that this piece of pottery or that piece of stonework or those bronze plates were made by people with none of our modern benefits such as machinery or computers or telephones or motor vehicles or nice warm houses or clothes. . . .'

'You were on duty last Tuesday afternoon?' Pluke managed to ask as she paused to take a sip of tea.

'Tuesday is one of my half-days at the museum, Mr Pluke, and if you are going to ask whether I was on duty in the snuff box room corridor, then I have to say no because due to my age, I am seventy-three next September you know, I cannot cope with all those stairs up to the top landing so I stay on the ground floor among my Stone Age and Bronze Age exhibits but some children do try to handle them you know and on more than one occasion I have had to stop youngsters rolling lumps of stone down the corridors, they will not leave things alone, you know, it's all the fault of these modern teachers, they have no control and there is no discipline. Now in my day –'

'So if you were not in the snuff box corridor, Miss Craggs, you would not be aware of anyone paying particu-

188

larly close attention to them? Or anyone sneaking off, trying to gain entry to the private areas of the museum?'

'Oh, well, no, I mean, no one ever tries to steal Stone Age exhibits, they are far too cumbersome to slip into one's coat pocket or shopping basket, Mr Pluke, although there is a policy, you know, of asking visitors to leave their bags and baskets in the entrance, labelled of course, but I must admit I have never had any trouble with visitors trying to steal my exhibits or slip anything into their pockets although once when I was put on farming implements a silly man tried to start the combine harvester, but it was a very old one and the engine was out of order anyway but it all shows how stupid some visitors can be, and it's all down to a lack of discipline in schools, you know, now in my day –'

'Did you see anyone being furtive in the museum, Miss Craggs?' Pluke now realized his only chance was to interrupt this voluble old lady with positive questions.

'Well, now you mention it, Mr Pluke, there was a funny man that afternoon, one of the visitors told me. She said she was looking for the Ladies and was it along that corridor because she'd seen a man go along there and if a man had gone along there then he might have been going to the Gents and if the Gents was along there then the Ladies might be as well but I said no, the toilets weren't along that way, they were near the main entrance clearly marked and she had missed the sign so I had to show her where it was –'

'The man who went along the corridor,' Pluke managed to slip his question in despite her onslaught. 'Who was it? And which corridor was it?'

'It was the one that goes into the back area, Mr Pluke, not along the public's tour route at all and certainly not leading to the toilets, but there's stairs you know and that's the back way up to the loft, not that I've ever climbed those stairs, not at my age and with my knees –'

'What did the man look like?' he almost snapped.

189

'I never saw him, Mr Pluke, I told you that. You never listen, you know, you should listen more carefully. Now when my children refused to listen to me, well, not my own children, you understand, but the children at school, then I made them stand in a corner –'

'So who did see him?'

'I have told you that as well, Mr Pluke. Really, this is becoming a very difficult interview. If you will not listen, how on earth do you expect to solve your crimes? It was a visitor, Mr Pluke, a lady looking for the toilets, that's all I know. I never saw the man, so how can I say what he looked like?'

'Did you tell anyone else?'

'No, of course not. Why should anyone else be interested in a lady looking for the toilets? I have no idea who she was, just a visitor, from somewhere out of the village. I didn't know her and I don't think she saw the man at all, no one ever goes along that corridor, it's marked "Private" in big letters and there's a rope barrier across, so I think she was making up the whole story, you know, trying to be clever or something.'

'And what time was this?'

'Just before we closed, Mr Pluke, we close the doors at quarter to five and then we give them time to get well into the museum, and then Mr Porter goes around after them and checks for people lingering and loitering, and we close the doors at five thirty, well it was just before quarter to five. But I can't see how a lady looking for the toilets can have anything to do with a man who made a hole in the roof, Mr Pluke. Really, the way these investigations is conducted is beyond me. Now in my day when one of the children had stolen something or tried to steal something then we acted immediately –'

'Yes, Miss Craggs,' said Pluke. 'Well, we must be getting along, we have a lot to do. Come along, Detective Sergeant Wain, we really do have lots to do.'

'Yes, sir,' said Wayne Wain.

190

Chapter Thirteen

Having escaped relatively unscathed from Miss Craggs, Pluke decided he and Wayne should return immediately to the museum. He wanted to see precisely where she had been standing when the toilet-seeking lady had noticed the mysterious man heading into the area which was out of bounds to the general public. He realized, of course, that the man could have been the curator or another attendant or member of staff or indeed anyone with a legitimate reason for being there. But it could likewise have been the thief or someone operating on his behalf, perhaps taking a sneak look around so that he could formulate his plans for the theft.

The old men, having drunk their fill at the inn, had returned to the seats under the lych-gate. As Pluke and Wain passed through, Ted made some incomprehensible comment which they ignored, although Pluke acknowledged his presence with a slight wave of his hand. As they entered the foyer, they saw it contained about a dozen visitors who were being entertained by the current duty attendant, a small man with grey hair. With some enthusiasm, he was telling them about the tumuli on the moors and indicating a selection of associated pottery exhibits arrayed along the main corridor to the left. That led visitors from the reception area into the heart of the museum. Mrs Collins, always alert, spotted the detectives and raised a hand in a gesture of acknowledgment and welcome.

'Hello again, Mr Pluke and Mr Wain, can I help you?' she beamed.

Pluke decided to tell her about the revelations of Miss Craggs because this might prompt Mrs Collins to recall a similar experience.

'Thank you, yes,' he smiled. 'We have just been talking to Miss Craggs at her flat. She was on duty last Tuesday afternoon, the day before the raid, and I believe she would be working here, in this very area.'

'Yes, she was, Mr Pluke. We always try to place an attendant here, as a sort of welcoming person to guide people to where they want to be and to answer any preliminary questions and tell them about the shop. Miss Craggs is very good at that, she is never lost for words.'

'I would not dispute that assessment of her,' smiled Pluke. 'Now, she tells me that last Tuesday, about four forty-five or so, around the time you halted admissions, a man was seen to walk along a corridor into an area marked "Private".' And Pluke walked the few paces to the area in question. It was a narrow corridor leading past the right-hand side of the reception desk as he faced it; it was barred with a white rope on two metal pillars and a sign on the wall saying 'Private. No admission to the public.' He had no idea what lay beyond; he had never been into this part of the building and, he learned, neither had Wayne Wain.

'Did she see the man?' asked Mrs Collins.

'No, a visitor saw him. A lady visitor. She was looking for the toilets and saw a man heading that way, into the private area. According to Miss Craggs, the lady thought the toilets must be along there because she had seen the man heading that way and I presume she was puzzled due to the lack of signs in that passage.'

'Yes, well, our only public toilets are just off reception, Mr Pluke, and well signed, I might say. We do get people coming off the street to use them.'

'There being no public conveniences in the village, I understand?' smiled Pluke.

'Quite, and we don't object. Indeed, some do enter the museum having made that little journey, and others buy things in the shop. I take their money, you see, the shop is self-service. We think we offer a service to the public.'

'I am sure it is appreciated, Mrs Collins. Now, I understand that Miss Craggs then explained the real situation to the lost lady and guided her accordingly. It goes without saying, Mrs Collins, that I am very interested in that man and would like to trace him. He seems to have vanished.'

'Well, we do have some men on the staff, so it is quite feasible that one of them might go along there. Not to the toilet though, there are no toilets through there. So what did he look like?'

'Sadly, I have no description except he was "funny". Did you see a man go along there at that time?' he asked. 'Your reception desk is next to the passage.'

'No, I must admit I didn't, Mr Pluke, but if it was at that time, it's when I leave my desk for a few moments to close the main doors. I usually pop my head out to see if anyone is on the point of coming in. Sometimes people are heading up the path from our lych-gate and I can't really turn them away at that point, so I allow them in. It only takes a few minutes. Then I close the doors. It is very likely I was doing that while Miss Craggs was attending to her last visitors of the day. If so, I would not have noticed that man, I'd have been looking out into the street. If I had seen him, and if he had been a stranger, then of course I would have halted him.'

'I am sure you would. So how long does it normally take for you to complete that chore?'

'Not long. A couple of minutes or so. More perhaps if there is a last-minute influx of people or if those old men who sit under our lych-gate decide they want a chat or to use the toilet before we close. As they sometimes do! And once the last customers are in, I have to take their entrance fees and issue tickets.'

'So you could be distracted and away from your desk for, what, two, three, four minutes?'

'I suppose so, Mr Pluke, but I must admit I have never timed myself!'

'Miss Craggs told us she was talking to her last visitors of the day,' said Pluke. 'It seems no more arrived that afternoon.'

'Probably not, I can't be sure, the days just merge with one another when we are busy. And we are getting busier, thank goodness. But even so it takes a minute or two to close the door and put the "Closed" sign up.'

'That seems to agree with her version. Now, where does that corridor lead?'

'To the former servants' staircase, Mr Pluke. When this was a private house that corridor didn't emerge into the main hall like it does now, it went into the kitchen area which is at the back of the house. The museum had alterations made to accommodate our needs, such as offices, the shop and display rooms, and so that old staircase now emerges right here.'

'Most convenient,' he agreed. 'A staircase, you say? So it is a form of short cut for the staff?'

'Yes, it is. It leads down to the cellars which are below us at this point, which we use for storage, and it also goes up to the other landings. There are back stairs to all floors by that route, Mr Pluke, not for use by the public of course.'

'Really? I had no idea this led to a staircase. Does it go right up to the loft with the water tanks?'

'Oh, yes, it means we have access to the whole building without fighting our way through crowds of visitors. Most of us tend to use that old back staircase when we want to reach somewhere quickly, or perhaps have a word with one of the attendants. I think they use it too, at change-

194

over time. I'm sure you can see how it is quite possible that one of our staff was the man in question.'

'And which men were at work at that particular time last Tuesday?'

'I have our duty rotas here, Mr Pluke.'

She lifted a clipboard from the wall of her reception area and turned to last week's rota. 'Well, obviously Mr Porter was here and so was Fred Cullingworth and Bob Mac-Arthur, and I see Mr Greaves was here too. He was upstairs, Mr Pluke, in Costumes and Furnishings, so it is not likely he would be going along that corridor just then. He would have to remain at his post until the last visitor had passed through, and that would be around that time. You could ask him, Mr Pluke, it's the gentleman there, behind you, the one talking to those people.'

'Thanks for your help, Mrs Collins. We will speak to the others in a few moments.'

'Do you think someone sneaked in with the crowds to steal our snuff boxes, Mr Pluke? But that doesn't explain the hole in the roof, does it?'

'All I can say is that we are looking at all possibilities, and the theory that someone did sneak in and conceal themselves while the museum was open is just one of those we are examining. Now, thinking along the lines that someone could have crept up that back staircase unseen, or that it might have been a legitimate visitor getting lost, did you see anyone *emerge* via that route?'

'No, I didn't, Mr Pluke. So far as I know, no one used that rear route at all while I was on duty, either to enter or to leave.'

'Well, that's emphatic enough! Now, whilst we are talking, can I ask where you were last Tuesday night?'

'Oh, yes, it was my art class, Mr Pluke, Tuesday nights in the Arts Centre at Crickledale. I never miss. I go with my friend, Mrs Edwards from Rosemary Cottage, and we usually stop at the Green Dragon for a snack and a drink on the way home. Which we did that night. Then I came

195

home, my husband will verify that. I have a good alibi, you see, Mr Pluke, not that I hope I need one! Now, if you want to talk to Mr Greaves, I should catch him before he goes home, he lives near Malton, quite a long way off.'

'Ah, yes,' and he recalled that address from the list he'd received earlier. He and Wayne waited until the grey-haired Mr Greaves had completed his mini-lecture to the visitors, and then asked if they might speak to him. As the visitors were now heading into the depth of the museum, they could talk in the entrance hall.

'Mr Greaves?' Pluke introduced himself and Wayne and explained his presence. 'Might I ask where you were working last Tuesday afternoon?'

'I was on the first floor, Inspector Pluke. In the corridor, in my usual position outside Costumes.'

'Did you come down for any reason? Did you use that corridor, it leads to the rear staircase?' and he pointed to the private route past reception.

'No, Mr Pluke. I remained at my post until Mr Porter came along to dismiss me, after the last visitor had passed through. But even then, I didn't come down that way, I used the main staircase, it was then free of visitors.'

'Thank you. And did you see anyone moving around the museum in places where they should not have been?'

'No, certainly not. I find our visitors are generally very well behaved and are not likely to go wandering off. Some do make mistakes of course, but I have no reason to think it is deliberate. They just get lost sometimes, lose their sense of direction, miss the signs and start going the wrong way.'

'If someone had trespassed along that small corridor and gone up the back stairs, would you have known? From your post on the first floor, that is.'

'If he had opened the door which emerges from that landing on to the corridor, then yes, I might have seen him. Our own staff sometimes use that route, the caretaker for example, or the curator. It's a handy short cut. But if the man had continued to climb without emerging on to the landing, Mr Pluke, then no, I would not have seen him.'

'He could have sneaked out while you were looking elsewhere, perhaps?'

'No, Mr Pluke. I'd have heard the door anyway, it's a big solid one with a loud clunk when it opens and shuts. I can state without fear of contradiction that no one emerged on to my landing via that route.'

'Thank you, Mr Greaves, that seems very positive. Now, what did you do last Tuesday after leaving work?'

'I am a part-time lecturer at night classes in Malton, Mr Pluke. I specialize in the ancient history of the moors, and I was there, with my class. From after tea, half-past six or so, until I got home around nine thirty.'

'And then what did you do?'

'I didn't go out again. I had a drink of cocoa and watched the news with my wife. I did not come here in the middle of the night to climb a ladder or break into the snuff box room, Mr Pluke, not at my age anyway, I can assure you of that!'

Pluke thanked Mr Greaves for his co-operation and then said to Wayne, in formal terms because they were with other people. 'Detective Sergeant Wain, we need to speak to Mr Porter, Mr MacArthur and Mr Cullingworth before they leave this evening, to establish whether any of them used this route last Tuesday just before the doors closed at four forty-five. And we need to explore that route ourselves. But first, we must talk to the curator. Is Mr Porter in, Mrs Collins? I know it's his busy time, but I do need to ask him just one important question.'

'I'll buzz him,' she said. Moments later, she added, 'He'll see you now, Mr Pluke. In his office. You know where it is?'

When they entered Neil Porter's office he smiled a welcome and said, 'You've just caught me, before I set out upon my closing-down routine. So how can I help you?'

Pluke explained about the mysterious 'funny' man, saying he could not expand on the word 'funny', and then asked if Porter had used that route last Tuesday.

'No, I go in the opposite direction about that time, following the visitors along their tour, it's a prescribed route. Sorry, Mr Pluke, but it wasn't me. Are you quite sure about this supposed sighting?'

'The only way I could be completely sure, Mr Porter, would be if I had seen the man myself. Which I did not. I have to rely on witnesses, some of whom might not be all that reliable, and although your Miss Craggs did not see the mystery man herself, I have good reason to believe someone else did. It could explain a lot,' and he told Porter about the increasing likelihood that someone had concealed themselves in the building prior to carrying out the raid.

'I need to talk to Mr MacArthur and Mr Cullingworth before they go home this evening. Then, with your permission, I would like to climb that rear staircase.'

'Yes, of course. If I were you, I'd catch those two first, they don't lose much time getting away from these premises at the end of their day and it's getting pretty close to knocking-off time now.'

'Wayne, you speak to Mr MacArthur while I see Mr Cullingworth, then meet me outside the reception desk.'

Ten minutes later, Pluke was again standing in the reception area having spoken to Fred Cullingworth. Fred denied having used the back staircase last Tuesday, saying he rarely ventured into the museum and when he did, it was usually to discuss something with Mr Porter in his office. In any case, he'd rarely go into the museum at that time of the evening, particularly when it was being closed for the night. When Wayne Wain returned, he told a similar story. Bob MacArthur, in his dual role of caretaker-cum-groundsman, did use the rear stair on occasions, usually to gain rapid access to one or other of the floors to effect a repair or change a light bulb or even to get out on to the roof, but on Tuesday last, he'd done no such thing.

He had used it, though, several times during the past few months although he could not give times or dates. He'd told Wayne that in any case it was highly unlikely he'd use the rear staircase at such a late stage on a working day. And, as Pluke confirmed with Mrs Collins, there was no other man, apart from Mr Greaves, on duty in the museum at that time last Tuesday. So the question remained – had a man really gone along that passage and up the rear stairs? If so, who had it been? And why? And what did funny mean? Strange behaviour? Clothing? General appearance? Or had he gone so far and turned back, a lost visitor realizing his mistake? And why had no one else either seen him or noticed his return? It was feasible, reasoned Pluke, that someone familiar with the museum, say a regular visitor or someone with a knowledge of the layout of the house, might know of that rear short cut. Following a visit to the toilet, that person could have dashed through the off-limits corridor to catch up with some colleagues on an upper floor. Or the unknown woman witness might have been completely mistaken. Even in such a small scenario, there were lots of possibilities, many uncertainties but no firm answers.

'Come along, Wayne,' said Pluke as Mrs Collins was preparing to close her reception desk. 'It's time to examine this staircase. Don't lock us in, Mrs Collins! You didn't explore this route, Wayne, on your earlier visit?'

'No, sir, I must admit I had no idea it existed. It shows how careful one should be. I just thought that corridor went into some rear storage rooms.'

They walked along the narrow corridor past the reception, through a door and into a darkened area. Wayne found a light switch and clicked it on. Ahead lay a winding stone staircase, very similar to those one might find in the tower of a medieval castle, and to their left there descended another staircase. They went down just one flight and switched on another light; it led into the basement or cellar, and this was windowless but full of objects which had either been used as exhibits or were awaiting display. They left, switched off the cellar light and began their climb. The staircase was steep with narrow steps but there was a handrail and so the puffing Pluke made his way slowly upwards until they arrived at a landing. Ahead was a stout door with a small glass window near the top.

It wasn't locked so Pluke opened it. It led on to the first-floor corridor; visitors were still moving slowly along, popping into the various display rooms or examining artefacts which lined the wide corridor.

A woman attendant stood on guard but didn't notice them. Wayne peeped out too, saw what lay outside and then closed the door to follow Pluke. The second floor had a similar landing and an identical door leading on to that corridor. Again, there was a woman attendant on duty and she was talking to some visitors; she didn't notice Pluke or Wayne. Then they moved onwards and upwards, arriving at the top. Here there was a smaller door, a simple wooden one with a metal sneck, and it opened into a corner of the upper loft. It was pitch dark but there was a switch; in moments the entire space was illuminated to reveal the water tanks, a mass of piping, electrical cables and a good deal of surplus furniture which in itself would probably be of value as exhibits. They entered by crouching through the little doorway; from the other side, it matched the panelling of the loft which would explain why Pluke had not noticed it on his earlier visit. The entire floor of the loft was boarded and although one had to stoop in places, there were areas where they could walk upright. And ahead lay the door on to the roof. Leading into the loft not far away was another staircase, the main one from the house below. Pluke went across to that roof door but it was securely locked, as indeed it should be.

'Well, Wayne, here we are. The same loft as before but entered by a different route. That staircase is virtually a secret entrance, one can easily overlook its entrance into this loft. I think this provides even more evidence that the theft was the work of someone who used this route, and who was very familiar with it. A thief could enter the museum as a paying visitor, sneak up this staircase and into this loft, conceal himself here and wait until it was safe to carry out the theft at his leisure.'

'With all the time in the world and no fear of discovery?'

'Absolutely. And with ample time to remove the tiles and make it seem like an outside raider, and then leave in a calm manner. We know he could have dealt with the alarm system – that is something else to check at reception today by the way – and then left with the stolen property.'

'Very feasible, sir, I'll grant you that.'

'But the question, Wayne, is who did it? And why?'

'Sir, with all due respect, I haven't a clue,' said Wayne Wain. 'I've been listening to you talking to these people, and we've finished up with nothing. Not a hint of a suspect. All we have is a load of theories and possibilities, with no positive evidence. I mean, sir, the thief *could* have got in through the roof, improbable though it seems. That can't be ruled out.'

'Nothing is impossible, Wayne, I'll grant you that.'

'A good cat burglar could have done it, sir, he would not need a ladder and he'd leave little or no trace of his presence on the exterior of the building. And yes, he might have had an accomplice hiding inside to guide him to the right place . . . or it might have been one of the staff . . . or the raid might have taken several days or weeks in the planning. Quite frankly, sir, I'm baffled, truly I am.'

'I am sure there is an answer, Wayne, and I am equally sure it is staring us in the face, if only we can recognize it. Now, is there any merit in having Scenes of Crime carry out a search of this back staircase? If so, what would they be likely to find?'

'They didn't examine it when they came on Wednesday, sir, because we had no idea it was there.'

'I doubt if it would have helped, knowing this existed. If

it is used quite regularly, then it might not yield any useful evidence. If there are deposits or DNA, then it might have been left by a member of staff – they use the stairs anyway so that would tell us nothing. I think we need not trouble Scenes of Crime over this one, not now. It is too late for them, I fear.'

'Sorry, sir, I should have found it and checked it last week.'

'I am not criticizing you, Wayne, I missed it too. Had it not been for that anonymous lady visitor talking to Miss Craggs, then I doubt I would have found it or checked it. What we do know, however, is that a person could have entered the museum as a paying guest, gone into the toilet, say, until Mrs Collins began her locking-up routine, and then slipped along that corridor whilst she was occupied.'

'It would take a matter of seconds, sir, while she was attending to the main door.'

'And it would also allow him enough time to make his way out of sight and into the dark recesses at the foot of this staircase. Do you agree that is feasible?'

'I do, sir, yes. Having seen all this, yes, it is very feasible. But not by a member of staff, you think? They could not risk hiding, could they? Their absence would be noted, especially at going-home time when the place is checked for lingerers.'

'Exactly right, Wayne. So it means our suspect is not a member of staff but is someone who knows his way around the inner regions of this building. Someone quick enough, both mentally and physically, to take advantage of a very short time when supervision was relaxed, and then slip unseen – almost – into that back staircase and hide until he felt it was time to commit the crime. He could commit it any time between five thirty on Tuesday evening and eight thirty next morning but I fancy he would not want to remain here all night. A clever criminal, Wayne, and one who can cope with the alarm system. So where do we go from here?'

'Back downstairs I think, sir, otherwise we might get locked in.'

'But before we leave, we have to check the workings of the security system, remember. I need to know how our anonymous suspect dealt with it.'

When they descended, Neil Porter was standing beside the reception desk along with Mrs Collins, evidently awaiting Pluke and Wayne or perhaps anxious to lock up and go home. Their routine must not be interrupted. One half of the main doors was standing open to allow the final visitors to depart, some of whom had lingered in the shop and were now carrying plastic shopping bags bearing the museum's logo. It seemed that everyone had left the premises, except for these two officials.

'Well, Mr Pluke,' queried Porter. 'What do you make of our secret staircase?'

'I think it has served our criminal very well indeed, Mr Porter, by allowing him to slip unseen into the less known regions of this museum so that he could carry out his dreadful deed.'

'You still think one of us is responsible?'

'I am veering towards the theory that someone entered lawfully, as a visitor, and took advantage of both the situation and the layout of these premises to conceal themselves until the right moment for an assault on the snuff boxes. I think that is feasible even though the question of the alarm system remains. You will be pleased to know that I am moving away from the idea that a member of your present staff is responsible.'

'You've no idea how much relief that gives me, Mr Pluke. Living with the possibility, remote as I thought it was, that one of my trusted staff could have stolen those snuff boxes was intolerable. I've not been able to concentrate on my work today . . . so that gives me some measure of relief.'

'I must stress that is only an opinion, Mr Porter. There is still the question of the theft actually benefiting the

203

museum, that's assuming your insurers will honour the claim. It is a factor which must continue to be taken into account.'

'So the finger still points at me? Or one of us?'

'How can the theft benefit the museum, Mr Porter?' demanded Mrs Collins who had not been trusted with knowledge about the state of the finances. 'I can't see how that can happen, not when we've lost such valuable treasures. Surely they're irreplaceable?'

Mrs Collins' question now confirmed in Pluke's mind that she and Porter were not colluding. But he had erred in making reference, within her hearing, to the museum's financial plight.

Pluke recovered quickly. 'Mrs Collins, if the theft is proved to be a crime rather than a loss through carelessness, and if that is done to the satisfaction of the museum's insurers once they have received an abstract of the police report, then they will pay compensation for the loss. Because of the value of the lost articles, that might be a considerable sum – and that must be of benefit to the museum in some way, even if the snuff boxes cannot be replaced. A large financial input of that kind could be of enormous benefit to the museum's long-term future.'

'Oh, I see, I never thought of it like that.'

'Thank you very much for that simple explanation, Mr Pluke.' The relief was evident on Porter's face. He didn't want the entire staff knowing of the museum's perilous state. 'Now, is there anything else you need from us before we close for today?'

'Just one more small thing, Mr Porter. The security alarm. I would like you to show me how it works, how it can be disabled and how it can be triggered off.'

'Before I show you that, and in view of your latest suggestion that the crime was committed from inside, I must tell you that once the alarm is set, it will still allow someone to move around inside the building without triggering it.'

'That fact has not escaped me, Mr Porter,' smiled Pluke.

'We must consider a more efficient system. So far as this one is concerned, I can lock myself in, set the alarm and work inside without triggering it. As indeed I have done on occasions.'

'So please show me how it works.'

As the final visitors departed with their bags of souvenirs, Porter gave Pluke a demonstration. He explained that the system depended upon sensors. These were placed at strategic sites through the museum so that they monitored and protected all entrances, however large or small. When the alarm was activated, all windows and doors must be closed. Any attempt to force or merely open a door or window, or smash a pane of glass, would break that protective beam and so activate the alarm. When this happened, sirens sounded at the museum, an alert was activated in the curator's house and in the Control Room at Crickledale Sub-Divisonal Police Station.

'The alarm is set by the last person to leave the building, Mr Pluke. That is usually me or sometimes Mrs Collins. If we have an evening event in the grounds, then it might be a volunteer or a member of staff. Even the gardener or groundsman. They've all been trained to set the alarm and to disable it. I'll show you.'

Porter led him across to the main doorway and on the left, some six feet above ground level, there was a small box containing a set of buttons. Some were marked with figures from 0 to 9, others marked with legends such as Override, Reset and Cancel, and four bore the letters A, B, C and D. At the moment, a small button was lit and showing the legend Off.

'When I leave the building with the alarm set, Mr Pluke, I am allowed thirty seconds to close and lock the main door. If it's open longer than that, the alarm will sound. The last thing before I leave, therefore, I must key in the code which sets the alarm. That is a series of four figures.

We adopted the date the museum was founded, 1952, but we didn't use such an obvious number – we made it 5192.'

'I follow. And so, once you've left, the system protects the doors and windows, sounding if anyone tries to open them unlawfully. So when you enter in the morning, how does the system cope with you opening the main door? One would expect it to sound the alarm once the door opens.'

'For that door, and that door alone, which has a secure locking system by the way, I am given thirty seconds to cancel the alarm system. I do that by pressing that same number, but adding the letter D after it, and I must do that within seconds of coming in. That disables the alarm. It remains like that during the day.'

'Quite a simple system?' said Pluke.

'Yes, but effective enough for us. Until now.'

'Highly effective, except against an intruder who has smuggled himself inside. So how did he move around without triggering it?'

'So long as he kept away from outer doors and windows, he could move around because there are no beams at other sites. None of the exhibits or exhibit rooms are individually alarmed. To disable it, all he had to do was approach this control box without breaking the beam where it crosses the door – in other words move towards it from the left – and then press in the cancellation code.'

'Which he must have known?'

'True. Then, when he left through the door – and he must have gone out via the main door – he must have pressed in the Set code. He knew how to do that and it would strengthen the idea that the intruder had come in through the roof. The alarm was set when I arrived next morning.'

'So we are saying the thief is someone who is very familiar with this alarm system, Mr Porter.'

'Unless the alarm was not set in the first place,' put in Wayne Wain.

This comment was followed by a long silence.

'It was set, I set it myself, I know I did,' said Porter, now showing signs of anxiety. 'I always set it when I leave . . . it's second nature to me.'

'I saw you,' said Mrs Collins. 'I left with you on Tuesday, Mr Porter, I had the takings, and I saw you set it, I waited and we both walked away together.'

'Good,' said Pluke. 'That settles that small matter. But one other matter arises . . . are you sure the door was locked when you arrived on Wednesday morning, Mr Porter?'

'Yes, it was. It locks automatically. You can open it from the inside without a key, it is based on the familiar Yale system, but from the outside you can't unlock it without a key. I unlocked it as usual on Wednesday morning, I swear it.' Porter was sweating now. 'It's hot in here, isn't it . . . these June days, they can get too warm for comfort,' and he wiped his forehead with a handkerchief.

'Well, thank you,' said Pluke. 'I will go away and consider what I have learned today. And if you think of any other matters which might be relevant, Mrs Collins or Mr Porter, please inform me. I shall return, probably tomorrow, for we haven't finished interviewing all your volunteers yet.'

'Well, you are always welcome, Mr Pluke,' and so Pluke and Wayne left, leaving the perspiring curator to set his alarm.

'I hope he searches the building before he leaves,' smiled Wayne. 'He's not had an easy time of it.'

'I think he will do everything in his power to show that he is in full control and above suspicion. Come along, Wayne. Let's get back to the office and do some serious thinking about what we have learned today.'

Chapter Fourteen

In the car during their drive home, Pluke announced tomorrow's intention of returning to the museum with Wayne. Wayne could interview the attendants and volunteers not yet interrogated, preferably in their own homes. Meanwhile, Pluke would have another chat with Bob MacArthur, Fred Cullingworth and perhaps Neil Porter. There were also the trustees to consider as well as past members of staff and volunteers who were no longer working at the museum, particularly any who had left involuntarily and who might bear a grudge. He asked Wayne to write up the notes he had made today, cutting out any superfluous material but being careful to include important matters and any corroborative statements.

'So what will I be looking for?' asked Wayne, driving to the limit of the speed restrictions as he always did. 'So far as I can see, sir, we've plenty of theories with little to support them, but no positive leads and no firm suspects.'

'We have a village full of suspects, Wayne,' retorted Pluke. 'And a museum full. Remember the crime must have been committed by someone who knows his or her way around the building, who knows the locking-up routine, who knows how to deal with the alarm system and who is cunning enough to set up a very convincing false trail. In my view, Wayne, that also indicates a degree of advance planning which in turn means the crime was not done on the spur of the moment. I am sure a great deal of thought went into it. There's a wealth of interesting detail

208

concealed in this crime, Wayne, every piece of which needs to be considered very carefully.'

'Not many people can claim all those skills, sir.'

'Exactly, Wayne, so it narrows the field of suspects somewhat, but don't forget family members and casual helpers. And so remember the key matter is to determine *why* the snuff boxes were stolen. At this stage it is the why, not the who, which is important. If we can determine the why, that will lead to the who.'

'Are you saying we should forget about the museum's financial state? That sounds like a very strong motive in my opinion, and it does concentrate our minds on those who are aware of it. And that's a small handful of senior officials.'

'And the trustees, don't forget. But, yes, there are rumours about the financial plight, Wayne, one of which has even reached Siena. I was told about it in a souvenir shop! Nonetheless, we must not forget or ignore it, it is an integral part of this investigation and we can't overlook the fact that outsiders have become aware of the museum's shortage of money. Unauthorized people to be sure, people who are friends or family of those who are aware of the parlous state of affairs. People visiting the museum perhaps, people living in the village. People do talk, Wayne, they overhear conversations, they read the signs . . . secrets are always difficult to keep, and there are obvious indications of current problems with cash-flow, like not filling staff vacancies. So yes, keep that in mind but not to the exclusion of other possibilities.'

'What about arresting each of those who are officially aware of the financial state? If we brought them in one by one and quizzed them in our custody suite, it might loosen a few tongues, we might learn if they've revealed that sensitive information to their family or friends, we might even learn if any of them are in personal financial trouble.'

'It's a thought, Wayne, maybe someone needs a helping

hand from the sale of a few stolen snuff boxes. It could keep the bank happy or the bailiffs at bay but I think such action would be regarded as rather heavy-handed. I don't want to antagonize the museum staff. We are not dealing with ruthless mob violence or street crime, we are dealing with a rural museum which has suffered a serious and damaging loss. We need to proceed with care, Wayne, and more than a little tenderness.'

'You're not going soft on criminals, are you, sir? I thought we had to be tough on crime and tough on the causes of crime? Surely we need to show we mean business? If the criminal is one of the staff, we should make him or her aware of our determination to root out the truth, to leave no stone unturned, even if that stone is a door stop from Neolithic times!' And Wayne chuckled at his own apt little joke. 'If we arrest one or two of them and interrogate them in the cells, it'll show we are not to be messed about, that we are taking this very seriously.'

'I disagree, Wayne. At this stage, it could be counter-productive. As I said, first we need to determine *why* the boxes were stolen. Remember they were stolen in a very strange manner, with a very devious means of trying to set up a false trail and, I might add, with some handyman skills. That is hardly the work of a conventional thief for whom time is of the essence. Most thieves rush in and rush out; this one adopted a very leisurely approach knowing time was on his side. He took the trouble to establish that false trail instead of fleeing immediately he'd obtained the goods. So why steal those very identifiable boxes in such an odd way? That is what we must be thinking about. It is what I shall be thinking about.'

'And you think the clues might lie in what we were told today?'

'It's all we have to guide us at the moment, Wayne,' smiled Pluke. 'So while you are compiling your edited version of those notes, I shall be conducting my own research and thinking my own thoughts. I will see you in the office tomorrow morning as usual.'

And so Wayne completed his journey, dropping Pluke at his home before heading back to the police station with the car, and then went home.

Tomorrow was another day.

As it was a very mild summer evening, Millicent had prepared a dinner table in the garden. It was nicely set with knives, forks and spoons, serviettes, water glasses and wine glasses, and she had prepared a meal based on Italian recipes and ingredients. She thought it would be nice to eat out of doors in the manner of the Italians and so, when Montague had discarded his voluminous coat, his panama hat and his heavy tweed jacket and removed his tie and opened his shirt collar, he swilled away the grime of the day by washing his face and hands, then settled in his favourite garden chair. Beside it stood a log, up-ended to serve as a side table, and as this was Montague's first day back at work after his memorable trip to Italy, she felt he might indulge in a glass of wine. Although this was not his usual custom, she felt he had thoroughly enjoyed Italy and rather hoped he might adopt some of that country's more pleasant practices.

'Ah,' he said when he spotted the full glass of red wine awaiting him on the upturned log. 'A celebration perhaps?'

Beside Millicent's chair was another up-ended log and it bore a glass of white wine.

'This is a celebration of your first day back at work, Montague. I saw how easily and readily you relaxed in Italy and thought you might care to make the most of this lovely summer evening along with a flavour of Italy.'

'You are a very thoughtful person, Millicent,' smiled Pluke. 'So, yes, let us enjoy this balmy evening. And did I smell Italian food in the kitchen?'

'I know how much you enjoyed those Italian meals, Montague, and so I have done Scaloppine di Vitello alla Parmigiana, which is veal cutlets with butter, mozzarella cheese, tomato sauce and grated Parmesan, Italian fashion. I popped into town to get the ingredients and found them with no trouble, and some bottles of Italian red and dry white. I got six. I might even play a little Italian music too, to accompany our meal. Softly of course, so as not to disturb the neighbours. We can hear it through the open window of the lounge, we have some Italian records.'

'Good heavens, Millicent, it's hard to believe I am sitting in my own modest garden in Crickledale with all this happening around me. How wonderful, I don't know what to say.'

'Then say nothing. You work so hard at your detecting, Montague, and there are times I think you don't relax sufficiently. It is never easy, the first day back at work, and so I thought you might enjoy this experience.'

And so, after she had turned on the music which filtered to him as a soft backcloth to this delightful reception, he settled down to an extension of his Italian holiday. When he closed his eyes in the heat of the evening, he could imagine himself back in Siena. The scents of the food wafting from the kitchen evoked memories of that wonderful city and its continuing buzz of happiness, the sound of the music reminded him of those lovely tanned Italian girls who seemed to be everywhere and the flavours of the wine transported him back to the trattoria overlooking the Piazza del Campo in Siena.

And with his eyes closed he could visualize the beautiful Gaia Fountain in the piazza with its white marble statues, pigeons and blue water. Then, if he really concentrated, he could imagine the Golden Horse Trough of Siena in position near the fountain. The Golden Horse Trough . . . it had not dominated today's activities but hadn't that gardener said something which had triggered a distant memory in Pluke's mind? As the evening sun beat down upon his face, Pluke tried to recollect Fred Cullingworth's words. Something about the family, the de Kowscott-Hawkes. Now what was it?

Then Millicent was speaking to him. He opened his eyes. 'Pardon, I was miles away . . .' He felt somewhat self-conscious at this lapse in his attention to Millicent.

'I said let me know when you are ready to start and I will bring out the antipasto . . . the starter. It is *zuppa*, Montague, *zuppa di verdura*.'

'That sounds fascinating! *Zuppa*, I remember that is the word for soup. What sort of soup is it?'

'Vegetable soup,' she said.

'Ah, yes, of course. Well, let's start in just a few minutes, my dear. I am truly enjoying this sunshine, the wine, the wonderful atmosphere you have created. It makes one feel like retiring to spend all one's days hunting lost horse troughs, Millicent, on the Continent perhaps, there must be lots of lost horse troughs in Italy, Spain and elsewhere. What bliss that would be! What heaven!'

She settled on her chair, sipped at her wine and asked, 'Now, Montague, tell me about your day.'

'There is not much to tell, if the truth was known, Millicent, I have achieved so little today.'

'Well, it can't have been easy, getting back into your stride after our holiday. And having to investigate the missing snuff boxes too, the Siena box in particular. It must have been quite mentally draining.'

'Perhaps it was but I am made of sterling stuff,' he said, sipping at the wine. 'It is a most peculiar set of circumstances,' and although he usually refrained from discussing confidential police matters with Millicent, he felt the Siena snuff box introduced a very personal element and so he found himself relating today's events. He knew she would be discreet. Perhaps it was the wine which loosened his tongue, especially that second glass, but he told her of his concerns and his strong belief that this was a very clever raid, done with a degree of forethought and cunning. She listened as the story unfolded, with Montague placing due emphasis on the peculiar hole in the roof.

'Well, I suppose it is nice that the crime, bad though it was, will bring some measure of relief to the museum, Montague,' she responded in her common-sense way. 'It is not all bad news, is it? If you don't recover the stolen goods, the museum will benefit, won't they? It might be wise not to investigate it too thoroughly, Montague.'

'But I have to recover the stolen goods, that is my duty – I must investigate crime and prosecute offenders. And that means tracing and recovering all the stolen property wherever possible.'

'But if you recover the boxes, the museum will get them back and perhaps they might not want them back, might they? Perhaps they would rather have the money. From what you have told me, that would be much more use to them.'

'That thought had occurred to me. I am extremely concerned that if the boxes were stolen for that reason, to secure an insurance pay-out, then they might all be destroyed and never found. And that would include the Siena snuff box, Millicent, the one which is so crucial to my search for the Golden Horse Trough of Siena.'

And as he spoke those words he refilled his glass and found himself pondering again precisely what the gardener, old Fred Cullingworth, had said about the family and a horse trough. Pluke had understood that an ancestor had brought the snuff box back from Italy because its design had matched a horse trough already in the family's possession in England. So was he referring to the trough which had stood near the inn, the Marble Trough? He'd said the trough had been brought from Italy – so could this be the Golden Horse Trough of Sienna? Was it really likely? The inn sign was no help because it depicted a modern version of a marble trough, probably the product of an artist's imagination rather than an historic record.

Millicent was saying, 'I don't think any of the staff

would have stolen them, do you, Montague? Not for personal gain, that is. I mean, where would they dispose of them? The minute you try to sell any of those boxes, especially in this part of the world, someone will recognize them. There's been a lot of publicity and it's the talk of Crickledale. Even old Miss Ashwell knows about the theft and if she knows, the whole district must know.'

'But a member of the staff, with a distorted sense of loyalty, might have stolen them to gain the insurance money, Millicent. They could be lost for ever. I might never set eyes on the Siena box.'

'Well, from what you tell me, it seems the museum is definitely going to benefit from the theft. You don't seem to have any idea who is responsible or where the snuff boxes might be. But forget work, Montague, this is not the police station and you are not on duty. It is our time together, our quality time at home. Our *zuppa* will be ready and I fancy a bit of Pavarotti as we eat.'

And so their relaxed Italian-style evening began, a real tonic for Montague Pluke who still found himself once more going over Fred Cullingworth's words about the snuff boxes and the trough. There *was* something else he'd said, something very important . . . The food was wonderful, the music relaxing, Millicent at her charming best, and the evening air like a tonic. Pluke found himself pouring yet another glass of red wine and chattering non-stop to Millicent.

In going over Fred's conversation in his mind, Pluke *knew* there was something else, something he had missed. It was about the Siena box and it was of great significance to this enquiry. He hoped Wayne's notes would record it because it had momentarily slipped his mind due to his deep concentration upon the details of the crime itself but it was some little phrase, something very insignificant at the time but growing vastly in importance as his enquiry had proceeded. He'd recalled it during some of those latter chats to witnesses, but it had slipped away again and he

215

couldn't recall it now. He knew it was a lead of some kind, some casually spoken comment which he must recall.

'Mr Cullingworth made reference to the Golden Horse Trough, Millicent,' he suddenly said, having returned from a dream-like haze. 'At least, that's how I understood it even if he didn't use that name.'

'Really, Montague? Tell me about it.' She was smiling at him across the table, marvelling at the new Montague, so relaxed. Italy had been good for him, and was still being good for him. And he really was enjoying that wine. How many glasses had he poured? It was a blessing she had bought six bottles, if only to get the discount. Three reds and three whites. This was becoming rather like a party.

'Well, the old gardener at the museum, who used to be gardener when it was a private house, Fred, said when he was young old Mr de Kowscott-Hawke had showed him the Siena snuff box. He said it had been copied from a horse trough long ago, which was why the Siena scene is on the front, not the lid. It's a model of a horse trough, you see, Millicent, as I thought, but he said more. Much more.'

'He is reliable, is he, this old gardener?'

'I would say so, yes, Millicent, without a doubt. Well, he said the trough had caught the eye of that de Kowscott-Hawke who travelled a lot and brought trinkets back to England. He brought it home because it matched a trough already owned by the family in England! Think of that, Millicent, my dear. Just think about that.'

'Do you mean the de Kowscott-Hawkes brought the Golden Horse Trough to England?' She was astonished at this possibility. 'Are you all right, Montague? That wine is quite strong, you know, and you are not accustomed to heavy drinking . . . '

'I am perfectly sober, thank you, Millicent, and the odd glass is not regarded as heavy drinking. But one of the old Mr de Kowscott-Hawkes brought the Siena snuff box back to England because it matched a horse trough owned by

216

the family in England, that is definitely what the gardener said. I regard it as highly significant.'

'So where is it now, Montague, this trough they brought to England?'

'He doesn't know, Millicent, that is the tragedy of those circumstances. I feel it is no coincidence the local inn is called the Marble Trough, but that is a white one and probably from an artist's imagination. If I can trace the history of the de Kowscott-Hawke family in this country, I might find evidence of the trough in one of the family's former big country houses. In fact, it might still be there . . . even if branches of the family have lived in different houses over the years. The trough, like the houses, might have survived or been moved to another site. Just think, even as we speak, the Golden Horse Trough of Siena could be in some English country garden.'

'Well, if you've not found a thief today, Montague, you might have a lead in your search for the golden trough. That is a considerable achievement even if it is not strictly police work. Now, there is a sweet to follow . . . I'll go and get it.'

And she left him to take away the dirty main course plates and fetch the sweet; she might open another bottle of that red wine too. Montague had almost emptied one bottle. Most unlike him, but he *was* enjoying himself.

But when she emerged with two dishes of *macedonia con panna* (fruit salad with cream), he was fast asleep with his head on the table and an empty wine glass at his side.

'You don't look too well, sir, if I may say so.' Next morning in Pluke's office, Wayne Wain thought his boss looked rather ghastly. 'Shouldn't you be at home?'

'A minor stomach upset, Wayne, nothing to be concerned about.' He tried to sound unaffected by his thumping head. 'Something I ate last night. But let us get on with our work. Did you manage to produce that set of notes?'

'I did, sir. I dictated my report into a tape-recording machine and it is now being typed up for us. It should be ready in half an hour or so.'

'Did anything emerge? Were you aware of any snippet of evidence hidden somewhere among your notes, something that might provide us with a useful lead for today? A little jewel of some kind?'

'No, sir, nothing. The only thing that strikes me is that the museum is going to benefit from this crime. I think that is the key factor, the reason behind the crime, sir. The why factor as you called it. And as I said yesterday evening, I think that boils down to a handful of suspects, those with knowledge of the museum's state of affairs. I found nothing else of consequence in my notes.'

'Well, I still think we should return to Pebblewick to ask more questions, Wayne. House-to-house enquiries in the village perhaps, and we need to trace those former members of staff, attendants and trustees, reinterview the gardener, caretaker and curator . . .'

'House-to-house enquiries, sir? Did I hear right? This is not a murder enquiry or a violent shotgun robbery.'

'I want to see the homes of those I've already spoken to, Wayne, and the device of conducting house-to-house enquiries is a simple means of doing that. We can be selective, of course, I am not saying we should knock on every door in the village, that would take days and days with just the two of us doing what you call leg-work.'

'So you are rather cunning yourself, sir?'

'Determined is perhaps the better word, Wayne,' chuckled Pluke, an act which reminded him of his headache. And so it was, that after coping with the routine morning mail, reading Wayne's notes of yesterday's interviews and stealing himself against the lusciousness of Mrs Plumpton in her flowing gossamer attire with its low neckline, Pluke, with Wayne at the wheel, sallied forth once again to Pebblewick.

Pluke sat at Wayne's side swathed in his almighty coat

and hat in spite of the hot summer sunshine but secure in the knowledge that the rabbit's foot was safe in his pocket and delighted that as he had walked down the garden path this morning, a seven-spot ladybird had settled on his sleeve. That was another sure sign of impending good fortune, far more valuable than a mere two-spot ladybird. Thanks to a constant blast of air from the open car window, Pluke's headache was receding as they arrived in Pebblewick just before eleven. The old men were already in position under the lych-gate preparing for a day of gaping at the visitors and Pluke found himself just in time to be beaten by a coach which was disgorging its load of visitors outside the museum.

Pluke, not wishing to join the crowd, said, 'Wayne, you have that list of museum staff and volunteers? Let's start with some of their home addresses, it'll allow time for all those people to get inside and spread out around the place before we have to go in. We're on house-to-house enquiries, remember.'

And so it was they knocked on the doors of several volunteers, attendants and trustees, some of whom were at home and some of whose husbands, wives or families were at home. They had no wish to remain long at any particular address, but merely asked simple questions about whether the householders had seen anything suspicious on Tuesday evening or in the early hours of Wednesday morning last week, or whether vehicles had been heard, suspicious characters seen or talk over criminal intentions overheard. In all cases, they drew a blank. By eleven forty-five, they had visited seven assorted houses without producing one snippet of useful information.

'Time for the museum, I feel,' said Pluke. 'You speak to the attendants or volunteers there, Wayne, and I will re-interview Messrs Porter, MacArthur and Cullingworth.'

'About what, sir? I thought we'd exhausted our enquiries with those chaps.'

'I'm interested in the history of the snuff boxes, Wayne,

219

and how they came to be here – and why. As I told you earlier, it is the why that intrigues me. That old gardener might know the answer, he seems to know a lot about the de Kowscott-Hawkes.'

'He'll think he knows a lot, sir, if he's been with them for all those years before being adopted by the museum. I should take his contributions with a slight pinch of salt, old stagers like him tend to reminisce, you know. What they don't know, they will make up, especially if they've got an interested audience.'

'I am aware of that, Wayne, thanks, but come along, it's time we completed this chore, and then I would like to visit those houses which back on to the museum grounds.'

'I visited those, sir, last week, when the crime was first reported. I went to all of them, to see if the occupants had heard anything or seen anything suspicious.'

'And they had not, I'll warrant.'

'No, sir, not a thing.'

'Did you ask whether they had seen anyone on the roof, Wayne?'

'Not specifically, no sir, not actually on the roof. I asked if they'd seen ladders or people climbing at night, seen lights, heard noises, that sort of thing.'

'But a man on the roof would not be suspicious, would he, Wayne? Especially in daylight? That caretaker regularly goes up there to fix things. The sight of a man on the roof doing something to the tiles would not be suspicious, would it? I went up there and out on to the roof without anyone becoming concerned about it.'

'But, with due respect, sir, the caretaker doesn't go up there at night.'

'Who said our crime was committed at night, Wayne? It was committed some time between five thirty one evening and eight thirty the following morning, in summer. There are not many hours of darkness on a June night in summer, Wayne, so it is possible someone saw a man on the roof

220

and did not regard it as suspicious. It wouldn't be, would it, in daylight? Would an observer merely think it was someone effecting a repair?'

'Point taken,' said Wayne. 'Yes, I agree we should ask again.'

And so they went across to the museum and passed beneath the lych-gate to run the gauntlet of the old men. Ted was there with his dog and called out, 'Not caught him yet, then?' while laughing loudly. His companions chuckled at his bravado.

'Not yet, but just give me time,' and Pluke did not smile. He and Wayne climbed the path to the main door, now standing wide open. Although Mrs Collins was busy at her desk and coping with a miniature crowd, she waved in recognition and her sign language suggested they should enter without any further ado. Pluke felt it polite, however, to appraise the curator of their presence. Accordingly, he knocked on his door. It was opened by Dorothy Chapman.

'Oh, hello, Mr Pluke. Back again, eh?' She held the door open and they could see Mr Porter speaking on the telephone.

'There are one or two small matters we need to settle, Miss Chapman, including some unfinished business from yesterday. I just wanted Mr Porter to be aware of our presence on the premises. We shall be talking to some of the attendants we did not interview yesterday, that's if we can catch them away from their customers, we don't want to interrupt the business of the museum.'

'That's no problem, Mr Pluke, just help yourself. Call if you need anything else from me.'

'I'd like further words with Mr MacArthur and Mr Cullingworth – I can interview them in the grounds.'

'Fine, I'll tell Mr Porter you are here when he's finished on the phone.'

'Right, now, Wayne, can you take the list of staff and speak to anyone here who's not been interviewed. In their break time or at some other suitable stage. I'll go and talk to Mr MacArthur and Mr Cullingworth.'

And so they went about their respective tasks. Pluke found Bob MacArthur in his shed as usual where he was planing a length of wood.

'Hello, Mr Pluke, back again, eh? This is to fix a piece of our fence at the far end of the grounds. The neighbour's got an adventurous labrador that's taken it into its head to join us, and to be honest, we can do very well without him. He likes to swim in the pond but if he wants to see the museum, he should pay like the rest have to! And not use our lawns as a toilet. So what can I do for you?'

'You were very helpful yesterday, Mr MacArthur, so I wonder if I might pick your brains again?'

'Aye, well, if I can help I will.'

'There's one or two little points to settle first, Mr Mac-Arthur. The roof. You told me you go up there fairly frequently to carry out repairs and maintenance.'

'I do, Mr Pluke, more often in winter time what with blocked drains and gutters, tiles loosened by gales, that sort of thing, but at other times an' all.'

'So the sight of a man on the roof is not all that unusual?'

'No, Mr Pluke. I've been up there with the grounds full of visitors and no one's batted an eyelid. Most of 'em never notice me anyroad.'

'And the people living around the museum? They'll be accustomed to you as well?'

'Absolutely, Mr Pluke. Mind you, if I went up there at night, they might wonder who it was and what he was doing, that's if they could see me in the dark., although if there was an emergency in the night, I'd be up there to see to it. But you can go up there, Mr Pluke, and never be seen by anyone, there's that many peaks and troughs, corners and whathaveyou.'

'So if the thief had ventured on to the roof during the hours of daylight, he would not attract much attention?'

'I don't think he would, Mr Pluke. In fact, he might not even be noticed, depending where he was. There are places he could work up there without being seen from most parts of the ground area or from the surrounding houses.'

'Thank you for confirming that.'

'Are you saying the crime was committed in the day-time, Mr Pluke?'

'It is very possible. He must have been able to see clearly in order to carry out his mischief up there,' said Pluke. 'And to stack those tiles so neatly. And if he'd had a torch up there in the darkness, I think it would have attracted attention.'

'You're right, Mr Pluke, good thinking that. Yes, I agree with you. You're not saying he got into the building during the daytime, are you? While we were all here?'

'I think he got in just before the place closed, then climbed on to the roof in daylight to remove the tiles. And who would think that was suspicious? Certainly none of the surrounding householders if it was done around clos-ing time or even if it was soon after the staff had just left. They'd think it was some last-minute repair. And, if he'd worked in the dark, he'd have needed lights, both on the roof and in the snuff box room. I've had no reports of lights being seen at night in either place, Mr MacArthur. And if there was a big hole in the roof, any light from the room below would shine up like a searchlight. And that would also attract attention.'

'So you think he got in as a visitor, hid himself until we'd nicely cleared the premises, then set about his task before it got dark? He could have left in daylight too, eh?'

'Yes, that's my theory,' said Pluke. 'I wanted to test it on you.'

'Well, I reckon you could be right. He'd be less suspi-cious in the village too, walking about among the tourists, there's usually quite a lot around in the early evening, and quite a lot of pub visitors. He could walk out of the front door as if he was a late visitor or someone with permission to be there, and who'd challenge him? Only a member of staff, and most of them would be at home having their teas.'

'Right,' said Pluke, knowing the best place to hide was among a crowd.

'A cool customer,' said MacArthur.

'A very cool customer,' agreed Pluke. 'Thanks again for that help, now I need a word with Mr Cullingworth.'

'Try his shed, Mr Pluke, he spends a lot of time in there.'

Fred Cullingworth was having a cup of coffee from a flask when Pluke arrived, and he was invited to join Fred by drinking from its lid, but he declined.

'Well, Mr Pluke, back again, eh? You've not caught our thief yet?'

'Not yet, Mr Cullingworth, er Fred, we are still making enquiries. Which is why I am here, I need to ask for your help again.'

'Well, I'll do what I can, but there's not a lot more I can tell you.'

'I am interested in the history of those snuff boxes, I think that might have something to do with their theft.'

'Really? Somebody knew them for what they were, you mean?'

'Yes, something like that, Fred. I think you know more about them than anyone else.'

'Well, I wouldn't go so far as to say that, Mr Pluke, I'm no expert on such things, not like some who can tell their date and who made them just by looking at them.'

'When we last talked, you told me they brought bad luck to the household.'

'That was the tale that went around, Mr Pluke, folks said they brought bad luck to the de Kowscott-Hawkes.'

'And did they have bad luck?'

'Well, things never seemed to go right, there was always some kind of trouble or problem and the family always said it was the luck of the de Kowscott-Hawkes, the fault of them snuff boxes.'

'You told me about one of them, the Siena box, being copied from a horse trough.'

'That's what old Mr de Kowscott-Hawke told me, Mr Pluke. One day when I was a lad, he showed them all to me, and said that one had been copied from an old horse trough, that's why it had the picture on the front, not on the lid.'

'In England, the trough was in England?'

'Oh yes, it was brought here years earlier by one of the de Kowscott-Hawke ancestors, a distant relation, he'd found it discarded in Italy, lying among some rubbish. He brought it to England, so he told me, and so when that collector saw that snuff box, he just had to have it, he thought the two must be associated.'

'And have you remembered where it was? The trough, I mean.'

'No, it could have been at Tillabeck, Mr Pluke, or it could have been here, mebbe it was that one that used to be outside here, near the pub. It makes sense, with it being called the Marble Trough, but you'll know all that. Anyway, the trough was moved for road widening, years ago it was, and I never saw it. I don't know what happened to it, it was all before my time.'

Pluke could hardly contain his excitement at this casual confirmation that the legendary Golden Horse Trough of Siena could be in England, but he told himself that he was not searching for it at this moment. He was endeavouring to find a reason why the snuff boxes had been stolen. He must be careful to separate his private work from his official duties.

'You said that old Mr de Kowscott-Hawke showed you the snuff boxes, Mr Cullingworth, er Fred. Is there any

225

reason why he should go into such detail about them with
you?'

'Aye, there was, Mr Pluke. They were a favourite of my
mother's.'

'Your mother's?' frowned Pluke.

'Yes, she used to live here, Mr Pluke.'

Chapter Fifteen

Pluke, whose overnight thinking, fortified by several glasses of wine, had produced a possible solution to this puzzle, was not in the least taken aback by Fred Cullingworth's statement. Indeed, he had almost expected it. If there was any element of surprise it was because Fred had volunteered the information without it having to be extracted from him through questioning.

'Ah,' said Pluke. 'That explains a lot.'

'It does?' puzzled the gardener.

'Yes, indeed it does,' acknowledged Pluke. 'The relationship between you and this museum, or to the former house. And the cottage, your cottage, I mean. It all means something to me now. Am I right in thinking the cottage was yours for life, or to be precise, your mother's – your family's, in fact?'

'Aye, it was, there's no secret about it, Mr Pluke. The whole village knew at the time but nobody talks about it now, it's old news. In 1952 it was a condition of the museum buying the big house that it bought my cottage as well, as part of the deal, and kept me in it for as long as I lived. I pay a rent, summat to do with the law, but it's only a few pence a year. It's been my home ever since I was a lad.'

'And might I hazard a guess as to the reason for that remarkable show of generosity by Mr de Kowscott-Hawke?'

'Well, there's no need to guess, Mr Pluke, as I think you

know, and there's no need to be shy about it, the whole village used to know, not that incomers would know these days, mind you. It's past history now but I'm not ashamed by it. They've always been good to me, the de Kowscott-Hawkes, and I've had a good life here. I've nowt to hide, I believe in being open and honest.'

'So your mother worked at the big house, for the de Kowscott-Hawkes?'

'A maid, Mr Pluke, a good worker so they told me, honest and reliable. Then I came along. Not that it was my fault, you understand.'

'And I suspect your mother was not married, and you were a love-child, as they used to say? Fathered by one of the Mr de Kowscott-Hawkes?'

'Aye, that's it, Mr Pluke. I don't mind admitting it, as I said, I've nowt to be ashamed of. Old Mr de Kowscott-Hawke it was, not that he was very old then. Bit of a young buck if you ask me, not married at the time either. There was no chance of him marrying her, such types didn't marry working class lasses then, and my mum would never press him into doing summat like that, summat he might have regretted later. And her. He didn't love her, Mr Pluke, and she didn't love him. It was a bit of a fling that backfired. But he and his family stood by my mother, gave her a permanent home and her family, me that was, and kept her on at work. Gave her a job and a home for life. And me. You'll not find his name on my birth certificate though, Mr Pluke, there was never any formal acknowledgement, but just an unwritten acceptance that he was my dad. He went off and married somebody else who never knew about all this. I'd see him sometimes, he was always kind to me as a lad.'

'Which is why you are here today, working as a gardener for the museum?'

'Aye, the family looked after me, like I said, long after he'd died. Made me secure, and my mother. They kept her on, as a maid, after I was born. In those days, she might have been sent away in disgrace, but he was a nice man, Mr Pluke, and the family was real nice as well. Real toffs.'

'I would think that makes a welcome change from most, Fred, some might have rejected your mother and left her without a penny.'

'It could have happened, Mr Pluke, in any other household. She could have been thrown out without a penny and without a home to go to. My mum used to live in, as maids did in those days, that was her room, Mr Pluke, where the snuff boxes were on show.'

'Her bedroom? Now that is a coincidence!'

'Aye, that's what I thought when they put them in there, it being her old bedroom. I was born there, would you believe? I kept her surname, she was Ada Cullingworth, Miss Ada. There were no maternity hospitals and such in those days, and then we were given that cottage, where me and Ted live now. We were a happy family even if we had no dad.'

'And your brother? He's much younger than you? With the same surname?'

'Aye, but he's not got the de Kowscott-Hawke blood, Mr Pluke. She met this other chap much later and got pregnant again, you think she'd have learned her lesson by then but she was going to marry the new chap, then he died. Nothing suspicious, he just dropped dead. He was only a young chap, a road man. He collapsed and died while at work one day, shifting a horse trough, would you believe?'

'A horse trough?'

'So they said, not the one in this village, you understand. Dicky heart, it turned out to be. So I had a sort of brother. We've lived together ever since, me and Ted. We've allus got on. He worked as a builder's labourer, doing jobs all over. He's worked here quite a lot, doing jobs on the house, and he's helped me of an evening if we'd had summat on, indoors or out. Thanks to the de Kowscott-Hawkes, we could keep the cottage when my mother died. The family bore no grudges, I never felt a burden to them. I earned my keep, like I'm doing now.'

Pluke's lack of surprise at these revelations followed his sudden recall of the phrase used by Fred in yesterday's interview. He and Pluke had been discussing the snuff boxes. Ted had told him that the outgoing Mr de Kowscott-Hawke, upon selling the house in 1952, had hated the snuff boxes, adding that he was surprised he had donated them to the museum. Then Fred had said, *'but that's what he wanted, so it was all right by me.'*

It was that phrase Pluke had been trying so hard to recall, a very short phrase but so full of meaning. In Pluke's opinion, at the time it had been spoken, it implied that Fred had had some kind of claim to the snuff boxes and it was that which had lodged itself in Pluke's mind, picking at his consciousness like the tiniest of splinters in one's finger which constantly snags one's clothing.

'Mr Cullingworth, er Fred, I really do appreciate you being so frank and honest. I am not sure whether I would have asked all those questions but certainly it has been most helpful. Now, might I return to the question of the snuff boxes?'

'Aye, that's why you're here, Mr Pluke, not to hear my life story.'

'Am I right in thinking your family had some kind of special interest in them?'

'Well, Mr de Kowscott-Hawke always wanted my mother to have them, she used to clean them and look after them and was always fascinated by the pictures on them, but he hated them, he thought they brought bad luck, Mr Pluke. He wanted my mum to have them, as a gift. No strings attached. That was Mr de Kowscott-Hawke senior, my dad's dad. My natural grandad, he'd be.'

'I understand,' said Pluke.

'Yes, but because he thought they brought bad luck, and often said so in front of mother, she wouldn't have them in the house. He tried again and again to give them to her, for birthdays and things, and she always refused. She could be quite stubborn, you know, even against her superiors. I think he knew what they were worth and it was his way of giving her summat extra, for what had happened, for me in other words, but still she'd have nothing to do with them. She'd clean them, make a good job of looking after them and all that, but she didn't want them in our house.'

'So they remained with the big house?'

'Aye. Mind you, some of his family thought they should stay, seeing they'd been part of the family history for years and years. I don't think they liked the idea of him giving them to a working girl, and on top of that they didn't all believe in that bad luck story.'

'Obviously, they regarded them as an important family heirloom?'

'They did, Mr Pluke, along with all sorts of other things in the house, paintings, furniture, porcelain and the like. But Mr de Kowscott-Hawke was just as determined as my mother, and wanted rid of them. Even though some of his family objected he found a way to do what he wanted when he sold the house; he decided to leave the snuff boxes behind. It was a clever trick, Mr Pluke, he donated them to the museum, it was his idea and the family couldn't do anything about that.'

'So that was instead of giving them to you, as your mother's natural heir?'

'Aye, well, I didn't really want them, Mr Pluke, they weren't really mine, I had no real claim. If they should have been anyone's they should have been my mother's, but she didn't want them. That doesn't mean to say I should have had them. Taking everything into account, I reckon they were better where they were, on show in this museum for everyone to see them. And they were in my mum's old room. That was nice, Mr Pluke, even if the museum people had no idea of its significance. So you see, that arrangement was all right by me, quite all right. I know they are worth a lot of money now, but what good is money to me? I've got everything I want, I'm turned eighty, Mr Pluke, unmarried with no children, so money and riches is not the slightest bit of good to me. But I wouldn't have wanted anybody to steal them.'

'So you have never tried to lay any claim on them, either through the de Kowscott-Hawkes or the museum?'

'No, Mr Pluke, never. And I never will. Not even the museum folks know about my real part in all this, I don't spread the word around. Mum's the word, I suppose,' and he grinned wickedly.

'Mum's the word,' repeated Pluke.

'Whenever I wanted reminding of her, like the anniversary of her death or her birthday, I would go up to that room and have a look at those snuff boxes, knowing she'd cared for them all those years ago. Ted would come with me most times, he was fascinated by them. Now they've gone, it's all a bit sad. I do hope you get them back, Mr Pluke. Really I do.'

'I shall do my best, Mr Cullingworth, Fred. I promise you that. So you are not too concerned about their reputation of being unlucky?'

'Well, things did happen to the family while they had them in the house, and things have happened to the museum while they've had them on show. I know it's all a bit strange and I can see how folks blamed the snuff boxes. Once they got that sort of reputation, you can't take it away, can you? Even if it's not true. But how can you say a display of snuff boxes brought bad luck? Those mishaps might have happened anyway, Mr Pluke, with or without them.'

'Would you have had them in your house?' Pluke asked.

'Now that's a leading question, and I don't rightly know the answer. I reckon if mother had accepted them, we'd have grown up with them around us and mebbe me and

Ted would have had bad luck. Who knows? But I didn't have to make that decision, did I?'

It was a politician's answer and Pluke decided not to press the old man for a straight 'yes' or 'no'.

'I'm going to ask another question which is not directly related to the snuff boxes, Fred, and not directly linked to my enquiry. I must ask it while I am here, it is too good an opportunity to miss even if it is not strictly a police matter. It is about a horse trough. It is known as the Golden Horse Trough of Siena and it is linked to the snuff boxes because one of them bears a decoration which is said to be copied from that old trough. The original trough was made some-time during the fourteenth century and was installed, so we believe, in Siena. Then it vanished. You've already told me you'd heard about a trough which was brought to England from Italy by a relation of the de Kowscott-Hawke family and I wondered if it had ever been de-scribed as the Golden Horse Trough?'

'As a lad, I often heard them talk about it, Mr Pluke, whenever they were showing the snuff boxes to visitors. They would show them that one, the one you mentioned, and always said it was copied from an old marble trough. I've heard them mention that many times but never heard it called the Golden Horse Trough even if the snuff box was coloured gold. It might have been the one at Tillabeck, it's now an hotel, Mr Pluke. When the Earl of Tillabeck died in 1788, he was last of that line and the de Kowscott-Hawkes inherited the estate. They sold everything and brought the contents here, to this house. That little foun-tain nymph in the fish pond came from there, she's on a plinth because it's deep in the centre but I've never seen anything of that trough. It all happened before I was born. I grew up thinking there was a lovely old trough made of bronze-coloured marble at Tillabeck. Maybe they left it there? It couldn't be moved very easily. You know Tilla-beck Hall?'

'I do, Fred, I do indeed. I must pay it a visit to see if the trough is still there. . . .' and his heart was pounding. Was he really living and working so close to the fabled golden trough? Had it really been spirited out of Italy at some distant date and transported to England, to this very part of England? To Pluke country? After years of searching, not only by him but also by other trough experts, had the fabulous golden trough been almost on his own doorstep the whole time? And was it made from bronze-coloured marble, not gold? Furthermore, being marble it would not deteriorate with the passage of time, it was vitually eternal, like the city of Rome itself. It was a most exciting thought.

'The local inn is called the Marble Trough, Fred,' said Pluke.

'Aye, it is, Mr Pluke. That used to belong to the Kowscott-Hawkes as well, you know. They sold it long before they sold the house to the museum though, before my time in fact.'

'I know I've mentioned the name before and its links with a real horse trough,' Pluke could hardly contain his excitement now, 'but my research into the pub's inn sign history has produced nothing to link it with a real trough.'

'As I said, Mr Pluke, it had gone before I was born and I've no idea what happened to it. I suppose it could have been the one from Italy, eh? Mebbe put there if they brought it over from Tillabeck all those years ago?'

'It doesn't bear thinking about. . . .' Pluke felt as if he was on the brink of a great discovery, then remembered he was here on police duty and in hot pursuit of the missing snuff boxes, not troughs.

Now, though, he had an idea who had stolen them. And why.

'I must thank you most warmly, Fred,' he said. 'You have been most generous with your time and I appreciate your honesty and forthrightness. I must now leave you. My colleague is interviewing other people at the moment,

234

then we shall tour the village to visit some of the houses. I want to make some house-to-house enquiries around the village before we leave today.'

'Well, you are welcome to call at my house, Mr Pluke, I expect Ted will be in. He doesn't go far, he said he had some gardening to do. If he's not on that seat under the lych-gate and not in the pub, he'll be gardening. He gets out and about and does hear things in the pub, gossip and folks chattering . . . he's worth a visit, Mr Pluke.'

'We did have a quick word with him the other day but we didn't ask him any specific questions.'

'Well, if you do see him, don't mention what I've told you about our family secret, he gets a bit touchy about that.'

'I'll be careful,' Pluke assured him and went to meet Wayne in reception.

Wayne, always able to charm the ladies, was chatting to Mrs Collins and telling her of his exploits as a famous detective when Pluke arrived. He heard Pluke's approach and turned to greet him.

'Ah, sir, you've made it.'

'I have indeed made it, Wayne. And you?'

'I have indeed, sir, everyone has been interviewed. With no luck, I might add.'

'So be it. Well, come along, we have those house-to-house enquiries to complete next. There is no time to lose, Wayne.'

And so they left the museum with a thank-you to Mrs Collins, and a parting word that they would return, perhaps today, perhaps another day. As they walked down the path, the old men on the seat bade them a cheery farewell, but Pluke noticed Ted was not among them, and neither was his dog. Making their way into the village, Wayne explained his interviews with the attendants, having managed to speak to them during their break-times, but none had been able to offer any useful information.

'So how about you, sir? Were your enquiries successful?'

'Very,' said Pluke before providing Wayne with details of the Cullingworth family history. 'I am now going to interview Ted Cullingworth, he'll be at home.'

'Fair enough, and while you're there, I'll revisit some of those houses which surround the museum grounds.'

'No, Wayne. I suspect we might not need to visit them. I would like you to accompany me to the Cullingworths' cottage.'

'You sound as you've got a suspect in mind, sir!'

'I have indeed, Wayne.'

Chapter Sixteen

'Might I ask who it is?' asked Wayne Wain, struggling to keep pace with the galloping Pluke. 'I ought to know what's going on in your mind, sir.'

'Ted Cullingworth, Wayne. He's my prime suspect.'

'That scruffy little old man with the dog?'

'The very same.'

'But he's not capable of committing a sophisticated crime like this, sir, and besides, what motive would he have for suddenly deciding to steal such an unusual collection of objects? They'll be no use to him.'

'Think about what we have learned, Wayne. We know the culprit must be someone who knows his way around the museum, who knows how to operate the alarm system and who knows the daily routine. That could be one of several suspects but we did learn that on occasions villagers have also helped during the evenings, when a large crowd has assembled. Bob MacArthur told me so. And Ted went with Fred to view the snuff boxes on family anniversaries. It seems he was fascinated by them. I believe he worked sometimes in the museum too, both as a helper and at his trade. People pop in to use the museum toilets too, Mrs Collins told us that. I suspect that amongst those making use of those toilets will be those characters who sit on the seats under the lych-gate, especially after their few pints in the pub. Ted is included in that band of merry men. And a visitor saw a funny man heading into that rear corridor.'

'I can see the sense in your argument, sir,' panted Wayne.

'With frequent visits to the museum, and perhaps after brooding for a long time about committing this crime while wanting to get his hands on the snuff boxes, I believe Ted eventually found the opportunity to carry out his wishes. He would discover that Mrs Collins leaves her desk each evening to lock up; he would know where the toilets were so that he could hide for a few minutes and his presence there would not be unusual; he knew he had enough time to dodge her while she was occupied with her chores; and I suspect he knew of that back staircase.'

'And if he had helped inside the museum, he'd know the routine for setting the alarm, probably through watching or even helping his brother, or even by watching the locking-up procedures from time to time.'

'And, Wayne, I suspect he might have been assisted by his brother, inadvertently of course, perhaps by helping Fred to lock up in the evenings. If Ted had always coveted those snuff boxes, he would have been looking out, over the weeks and months or even years, for some means of acquiring them. An obsession perhaps but one to which he was prepared to devote a lot of time in planning.'

'Always wanted them, sir? You said this was no spur of the moment crime.'

'It has all the elements, Wayne, it was too well thought out to be spontaneous.'

'But why, sir? Why would he covet something like that?'

'Ted has nothing, remember, and Fred told me not to mention Ted's family background in front of him. I can believe Ted is bound to feel rather angry about his upbringing and birth.'

'This is more than just anger, though?'

Pluke agreed, adding, 'It won't help with Fred having the house and the status of being retained, if that is the right word, first by the de Kowscott-Hawke family and

238

now by the museum while poor Ted has had to fend for himself. On top of that, Wayne, their mother could have become the owner of those snuff boxes, they could have belonged to her sons upon her death, both as a source of pride and wealth. But their mother rejected them. I think Ted has always been deeply upset about that, he sees it as a loss, a personal one too.'

'A hint of sibling rivalry, perhaps? Fred has everything, Ted has nothing.'

'I'm sure that's how Ted views things. Suppose Fred dies before Ted? And suppose the museum wants to sell the house to raise some capital? What would Ted then do? Where would he live? He's not a tenant, he has few rights, if any, in the house. So I believe he has been brooding over this, possibly for years; he's become obsessive about those treasures which, in his mind, rightly belonged to his mother, or even him and Fred. So he decided to help himself. It became his secret obsession. Wrongly so, but perhaps without any feelings of guilt.'

'But a man like him, who's not a criminal, wouldn't think of making the crime look like the work of a professional thief, surely?'

'If he has been thinking about this for a long time, Wayne, he will have been considering all kinds of ways of stealing them – and he's not stupid! I think he's rather cunning. He would know that if anyone hid on the premises and stole the snuff boxes without setting off the alarm, it would obviously point to the work of someone with inside information. I believe he will have considered other ways and he was crafty enough to perpetuate the theory about them bringing bad luck, then recently he hit upon the idea of making it look as if someone had entered through the roof.'

'Apparently copying the Lake District crime, you mean? A clever move.'

'Yes, the Cumbrian raid was mentioned in the newspapers, Fred told me he had read it. And so Ted seems to have decided to make his crime look like that one. But he took care of the tiles so they could be easily replaced, a professional wouldn't have done that, he wouldn't have had the time or inclination to be so thoughtful.'

'So how did you begin to suspect him, sir?'

'His family background was one clue, Wayne, but I became suspicious when he challenged us to find the culprit. It's very similar to murderers who think they can avoid suspicion by "finding" the body. Ted committed a crime and thinks he has been exceptionally clever by creating a diversion, the hole in the roof. He thinks he is much cleverer than us, he's trying to tell us that we will never suspect him, that we will never find the thief. I think the drink makes him talk more than he would otherwise, to say things he might regret, and of course, there is his injured finger.'

'Injured finger, sir?'

'He's got sticking plaster on one of his fingers, I noticed it when he approached us outside the inn. I think he cut it while removing the roofing felt, Wayne, he would require a very sharp knife for that and I think he nicked his finger and dropped blood on to the felt; he was alert enough to realize that if he left the felt behind, with the tiles, the police would find the blood and match it to his.'

'Which they would have done, if they'd found the felt.'

'Exactly, and people are well read these days, most are aware of that aspect of forensic science. Then there is the question of the dog hairs.'

'Dog hairs?'

'Ted has a dog, Wayne, one of those collie-type curs which are used for tending sheep on the moors. A black and white one. I am sure you will remember that some black and white dog hairs were found in the snuff box room, they were mentioned in the SOCO report.'

'Among other things?'

'Yes, among lots of other things. There was a lot of debris as one would expect, not only from the damage to the roof but also from the feet and clothing of people who have been in that room. Perhaps if we took a hair from Ted's dog, DNA analysis might possibly match it with those found in the attacked room.'

'Well worth considering, sir.'

'A valuable piece of evidence, I would hope. I think the hairs would have dropped from his clothing while he was working on cutting open the roof. Just a thought, Wayne, a little extra snippet of possible evidence, although I appreciate the hairs could have come from elsewhere.'

'So how did he work without being seen, sir? He must have used lights.'

'No, I believe he worked in the early evening, in daylight; that would account for his ability to stack the tiles so neatly on the roof and, of course, the sight of a man on the roof is not unusual during daylight hours. I have established that. He might even have avoided being seen, that's easy, you're well hidden from below. Then having stolen the snuff boxes, I think he let himself out of the main door to mingle with people outside, the area is always full of tourists and they would never be suspicious. He'd have watched them before doing so, of course, and would know that tourists would never think it odd that a man was emerging from the museum in broad daylight, especially one who looked rather like a workman. Then he joined his brother for a pint, we know they both went to the Marble Trough at nine that Tuesday evening. I think the crime was committed between five thirty and nine that evening, in broad daylight.'

'So what would he do with the snuff boxes as he was leaving the premises?'

'Put them in his pockets, perhaps he had a plastic bag, or even a bag from the museum's shop, with its name on . . . just like a visitor buying a souvenir.'

'So what will he have done with the snuff boxes since then, sir? I hope he hasn't destroyed them.'

'He won't, Wayne, not if he regards them as family

241

heirlooms. He won't have destroyed them or disposed of them. He'll have put them somewhere safe.'

'You know, sir, this is rather a sad story, isn't it? Do you think the museum would want us to prosecute him if they knew the story?'

'I doubt it. I did think that if we recover the collection intact, it should be renamed the Cullingworth Collection, I don't think the present generation of de Kowscott-Hawkes would object. I doubt if they are aware of the background anyway and after all, Ada Cullingworth looked after the boxes for years in the big house.'

'A nice idea, sir. Ah, well, here we are. The Cullingworth residence. Will he be in? He spends a lot of time at the pub.'

'I am sure he's here, Wayne,' and so Pluke hammered on the door and waited. It was a neat stone double-fronted cottage with a small lawn at the front, nicely kept with green paint on the windows, doors and garden gate. There was no reply after several attempts and so, being seasoned police officers, they went around the side of the house towards the rear door. As they followed the path, they found themselves in a spacious garden, much of it full of vegetables but there were lots of flowers too with rose bushes dominating. There was the inevitable shed, a greenhouse, several cloches and some very well-tended hedgerows around it. A gardener's garden, not a place of leisure. And at the far end, Ted was working with a hoe. His dog was lying on the lawn, snoozing.

'Hello, Mr Cullingworth,' shouted Pluke in a voice which was surprisingly loud. It roused the dog which got to its feet, barked once and then wagged its tail. Ted halted in his endeavours and stood up to face his visitors who were now approaching him, two abreast and with serious expressions on their faces.

'Mr Pluke, Mr Wain . . .' The bravado which Ted had revealed before his pals and before the public had now evaporated. The expressions on the faces of these oncoming detectives revealed the seriousness of their purpose, 'What can I do for you?'

'Mr Cullingworth,' said Pluke in his most official of tones, 'we would like to talk to you about the theft of the snuff boxes from Pebblewick Folk Museum.'

'You've not found the thief then? Like I said, you've not found him?' There was a faint echo of his former bravado, but no offer to take the officers indoors. They would have to conduct their enquiry in the garden.

'I think perhaps we have, Mr Cullingworth,' said Pluke. 'I would like you to tell me where you were last Tuesday evening between, say, four forty-five and nine o'clock.'

'Me and Fred went to the pub, for our Tuesday pint.'

'That was at nine o'clock,' Wayne said. 'We are interested in the time before nine, from the time the museum closes its doors.'

'Well, I don't rightly know, Mr Pluke. Out and about, mebbe here doing a bit of gardening, mebbe pottering about the village chatting, sitting on the seat . . . I can't remember.'

The dog had now come to Wayne and was sniffing at his trouser legs; Wayne patted the friendly animal and hairs flew all over. Wayne stooped and made a show of picking one or two from the ground. It was partly due to the summer moult. Ted watched him.

'They get all over, dog hairs,' said Wayne, pointedly pulling a plastic envelope from his pocket. He opened it and popped the hairs inside, watched by Ted, then sealed it. 'We found some dog hairs in the snuff box room, Ted, they could have come from anywhere, any visitor in fact, or they could have fallen from your clothing. DNA, that new scientific method, will tell us a lot about these hairs along with the ones we found in the museum.'

'I have been there, you know, helping out sometimes and sometimes to look at the snuff boxes with our Fred, I must have dropped them then.'

'When?' asked Wayne.

'Ages ago, before Mr Porter came . . .'

'And did you have this dog at that time, Mr Culling-worth?' asked Pluke. 'Or another dog? Now, before you answer that and before we continue, did you go to the toilet inside the museum's reception area last Tuesday? Just before it closed.'

'I might have done, I often go there, there's no public toilets in the village, visitors often use the museum's when it's open, the bosses don't mind.' His eyes were now revealing something of the desperation in his mind. He knew these policemen suspected him but he did not know how much they knew or how much evidence they possessed.

Pluke said, 'We would like to search your house and garden, Mr Cullingworth. You can give us permission in which case we will not require a search warrant, or we can arrest you on suspicion which gives us the right to search your premises for evidence, or we can obtain a search warrant from the magistrates which will take a while in which case we shall remain here, on the premises, until the warrant has been issued.'

Ted looked at them with his sad eyes and then he said, 'You'd better come with me, Mr Pluke, Mr Wain.'

With the dog at their heels, they followed the old man through the back door and into the house.

It was plainly furnished but very tidy and clean, and Ted led them upstairs. He opened the door of his bedroom; it was very bare – there was a single bed which had been made up, a single wardrobe, a chest of drawers and a clip rug on the floorboards. Without a command, the dog remained downstairs. Ted stooped and eased a suitcase from under the bed, lifted it on to the covers, pressed the catches and opened it. Inside was an old sweater but when he eased back the folds, there were the snuff boxes among the wool, all wrapped in tissue paper and protected from harm. They were inside one of the museum's own plastic shopping bags.

244

'They're all there, Mr Pluke.' The old man's eyes were moist. 'Does Fred have to know about this? Does anybody? They are mine, you know, by rights. I don't believe in all that bad luck rubbish, I'm not doing this to protect the museum, I know they've had a bad run but I couldn't let 'em sell these to raise cash, they should have been my mother's . . .'

'It is for the court to decide,' said Pluke in his most formal voice. 'We shall present all the facts and the important issue so far as you are concerned will be whether or not you acted dishonestly. I shall find a good solicitor for you, Mr Cullingworth, I think you deserve one. Now, I must inform you that I am arresting you on suspicion of committing criminal damage, burglary and theft. You do not have to say anything. But it may harm your defence if you do not mention when questioned something which you later rely on in court. Anything you do say may be given in evidence. Take him to Crickledale Police Station, Detective Sergeant Wain. I will remain here a while, I need to speak to Mr Porter.'

'Are you going to tell our Fred?' sniffed Ted.

'I feel obliged to,' said Pluke.

'Aye, well, I deserve what's coming to me. Thinking back, it was a daft thing to do. I must have had too much to drink, to think I'd get away with a thing like that. I've looked at 'em every night in that case, wondering what made me do it . . .'

'Come along, Ted,' said Wayne. 'We'll process you, then fetch you home. You won't be locked up tonight.'

'Jess'll be all right, will she?'

'She'll be fine, Mr Pluke will ask Fred to see to her.'

'Aye, right, thanks.'

And so they left, with Wayne taking the key to the cottage after making it secure. Now alone, Pluke walked back to the museum carrying the suitcase full of snuff boxes. He could not allow them to be returned to their display just yet for they would be required as evidence in court and perhaps subjected to a scientific examination. But at least Mr Porter would know they were safe.

'Coming to stay overnight, are you, Mr Pluke?' smiled Mrs Collins when she spotted the suitcase as Pluke walked in.

'I can think of worse places to spend my time, Mrs Collins.' He tried to be as jocular as possible. 'But is Mr Porter in?'

'He is, yes, just go to his office. I'll buzz him.' He did not reveal the answer to her evident curiosity. That was for Mr Porter.

'Ah, Mr Pluke, we meet again,' smiled Porter, eyeing the case.

Pluke placed it on his desk, opened the lid with something of a flourish and turned back the woollen jumper to reveal the contents. 'Your snuff boxes, I believe, Mr Porter. I shall need to have them examined scientifically for any possible evidence and then, when they are unwrapped, I shall need you to identify each one positively as the museum's property.'

'But Mr Pluke! How on earth . . . where were they? This is wonderful . . .'

Pluke explained how and where he had recovered them, giving brief details of the brothers' background while stressing its confidential nature. He also provided Ted's explanation for his uncharacteristic behaviour. Porter listened in silence.

'I wouldn't want to prosecute him, Mr Pluke, not under these circumstances. It seems such a sad story, I had no idea of their mother's role in all this.'

'The full process of law must go ahead, Mr Porter, but I shall find a very good solicitor for Mr Cullingworth and his punishment, when it comes, will not be severe. A conditional discharge, perhaps, or probation. He's an old man but he's not a criminal. Clearly he is devoted to those snuff boxes. Perhaps, in honour of his mother, you could rename them the Cullingworth Collection, or even call the room the Ada Cullingworth Room? With the donor family's agreement, of course.'

'I'll do my best. Once we get the room repaired, a new display cabinet and our exhibits back from you, we will proceed. Now, has Fred been told?'

'No, that's my next task. But I have a favour to ask, one which might involve Fred. I know police officers are not supposed to seek favours but this one is not for me, it may be something which will benefit the museum either directly or indirectly.'

'I shall be pleased to help in any way I can, Mr Pluke. All you have to do is ask.'

Chapter Seventeen

'I would like to know exactly what that nymph in your fish pond is standing upon,' said Pluke. 'Clearly, she is too small to be standing on her own two feet in such deep water.'

'Well, that is an odd request, but come with me, we'll have words with Fred.'

And so they left the museum, with Pluke clutching the precious suitcase. They found Fred in his shed as visitors toured the grounds.

'Fred,' said Pluke, 'I have some good news for you and some bad news, and an odd request.'

'Oh, well, is this where I say I'll hear the bad news first?'

'I have just arrested your brother, half-brother to be precise, for stealing the snuff boxes. He is currently on his way to Crickledale Police Station with Detective Sergeant Wain. He has admitted the crime. And the good news is that we have recovered the snuff boxes, they are in this suitcase.'

'Well, I'll be damned! What a stupid thing to do . . . Why did he go and do a daft thing like that?'

'He thinks your mother should be the real owner, Fred, and that he has a claim of right to the snuff boxes. I shall do my best to ensure he is fairly treated by the legal processes, he will be home this evening after processing and I have taken the liberty of explaining to Mr Porter some of your family background. I am sure you would like to provide him with further details, he will need it so he can do his best for Ted.'

'Aye, well, yes. The silly blighter . . . yes, I'd be happy to explain, Mr Porter, it's summat you should know about.'

'All right, Ted. I'll arrange a time when we can meet without interruption,' and Porter then offered to help Fred in dealing with Ted's dilemma. 'Now,' he said eventually when Fred had accepted the situation, 'Mr Pluke has a request for you.'

'I'll help in any way I can, Mr Pluke, especially as you've got our snuff boxes back.'

'This request is not for my personal benefit, you understand, Fred, but I would like to know what that nymph in the fish pond is standing upon. I know the water is quite deep – it must be, to accommodate the goldfish over all these years – and I know there is a plinth of sorts. I am curious as to exactly what it is.'

'You're right, Mr Pluke, the water would have been up to her head or even higher if she'd been allowed to stand on the bottom, but she's on a big block of stone or concrete or summat. I can't rightly say what it is because it's covered with slime and muck and stuff that grows underwater. It's been there years and years, Mr Pluke, put there long before I came on the scene. The lady with the fountain was installed when it was a private house, by the de Kowscott-Hawkes a long time ago, they brought her from Tillabeck Hall and stood her on that plinth. So far as I know, it's never been shifted since and the pond's never been drained so I've never had a good look at it. I couldn't put a date to all this, except it was a mighty long time ago. To be honest, you can't see what's under the nymph because of all the muck clinging to it, it would have to be scraped off.'

'So how can I get a good look at it, Fred?'

'Well, when we want to clear the weeds, dredge the bottom or clear the outlets, we use a pair of fisherman's waders. The water comes up to your chest in some places,

249

Mr Pluke, and I reckon it's deeper in others, but if you wanted to use those waders to take a closer look, then I'm sure there would be no objection.'

'Of course not!' echoed Mr Porter.

'I cannot do it now, I am on police duty, but perhaps another day, when I am off duty?'

And so it was that the following Sunday evening, when Ted was back at home wondering what would happen at his court appearance, when the snuff boxes had been formally examined by SOCO and placed in the exhibits box for the case against Ted, and when the visitors had departed, Montague Pluke, now in his role as trough expert *par excellence*, waded into the fish pond. Millicent, Mr Porter, Fred Cullingworth and Bob MacArthur stood by to observe events. The museum officials wanted to see what on earth this odd detective wanted in their fish pond; Millicent was merely his chauffeur but she was equally fascinated by her husband's endeavour for he had kept his purpose a secret, even from her. He was not clad in fisherman's waders, however; he was naked except for a pair of striped bathing trunks and a pair of flip-flops, and was equipped with a mask and breathing tube to enable him to look at things with his head underwater. Without his famous coat, hat and spats, Montague Pluke was an even stranger sight in this outfit, looking something like a cartoon snorkeller or a plucked chicken.

Oblivious to his impact upon the others but bravely shivering for the furtherance of trough history, he entered the cold pond, caught his breath as the water flooded his vulnerable parts, and waded towards the nymph on her plinth. He was equipped with a wallpaper scraper and a brush with stiff bristles, although he had no desire to damage the object of his interest. He wanted to clear away a little of the mess in which the plinth would be coated to see what lay beneath and, in the meantime, he placed those tools for safekeeping in the arms of the nymph.

The observers then saw him bend down and slightly

stroke the plinth; it was entirely beneath the surface and he reached down with his hands, feeling it for height, width and breadth, manually removing slivers of green slime and sliding his hands down the sides, feeling for irregularities or some clue as to its shape or size or from what it was made. He ducked his head and sometimes his entire body under the water on several occasions, startling the fish and frightening the birds in the nearby bushes. He made bubbles as he worked, and then he gently scraped with the scraper, brushed with the brush and came up for air after further duckings beneath the surface.

Then there was some kind of explosion because the onlookers saw Montague Pluke shoot out of the water with his arms and legs waving, rather like an octopus which had been stung in all parts by a swarm of bees; he was dripping with green ooze and he was shouting something which sounded very like Eureka, and then he flopped back into the pond, thrashed about as he shouted with joy, and then calmed down.

'It's here,' he shouted at them as he wrapped his arms around the naked nymph. 'This is the Golden Horse Trough of Siena, it's here . . . can you believe it?'

'Montague . . .' was all Millicent could think of saying. 'Montague, how wonderful!'

'It's upside down,' he was shouting at them. 'The nymph is standing on its base . . . it's covered with slime and filth but I can see the outline of the Palio horses, the Virgin Mary, the Piazza del Campo, and the inscription . . . I can't believe it, I just cannot believe it.'

Having examined it again, just to make sure he wasn't dreaming, he calmed a little over the next few minutes, then waded out to join them, smelling like an overflowing sewer and looking like something fairly gruesome from the bottom of the sea. But his ecstasy was complete . . .

And so it was that Montague Pluke crowned his lifelong career in troughs by rediscovering the mysterious and legendary Golden Horse Trough of Siena. In a North Yorkshire fish pond of all places. In spite of denials by the Siena authorities, he had known it existed . . . and here it was! It was quite, quite amazing. Truly astonishing. Mr Porter, supported by Bob MacArthur and Fred Cullingworth, assured Pluke that the museum would recover it from the pond. They knew a volunteer who had the necessary equipment and expertise, and it would not cost anything. They would replace the nymph's plinth with some other form of underwater support; this operation would enable them to service the nymph too, and her pipes.

When recovered, the trough could rest at the side of the pond until a decision about its future. If it could be cleaned and restored, it would become an attraction in its own right, at least until the Siena authorities decided what to do with it.

Pluke said he would contact them without delay about their wishes for the disposal of the trough; after all, he considered it to be their property. There was a bathroom in the rear of the museum, a relic of its private house days, and so Pluke was able to clean himself and dress in his usual gear before being driven home by Millicent. Mr Porter said he would ring Pluke once the trough had been removed from the pond, and Pluke said he would contact Porter with the decision of the Siena authorities.

At home, Millicent celebrated with two sherries and Montague, still relaxed after his holiday, opened another of her bottles of red wine and drank a toast to the trough, saying he must write to Siena without delay. That night, he addressed his letter to the Record Office in the Piccolomini Palace, announcing his rediscovery of the famous trough and offering confirmation with photographs when the trough had been removed from the water and cleaned. He posted it by air mail and waited.

On the Friday evening following, Neil Porter rang to say the trough had been expertly removed from the pond and now stood on an elevated site overlooking it; while removing it, his men had found a pair of marble

252

rests at the bottom of the pond. Clearly they belonged to the trough because there were two indentations in the base which fitted them precisely. It was now standing on those, cleaned to reveal a glowing golden-coloured marble trough, and on its face was the bas-relief scene from the Palio. He invited Pluke and Millicent to come and see it, and wondered if Montague might agree to a photograph?

He gave his consent and so it was arranged that he and Millicent, in a private capacity during his off-duty time, would visit the museum tomorrow morning, Saturday, for a formal photograph beside the trough, a permanent reminder of his role in its rediscovery. But, he said, he had not yet heard from Siena.

On Saturday morning, before the Plukes left for Pebble-wick, a letter arrived from Italy. It was from the Records Office in the Piccolomini Palace of Siena and said, in English:

Dear Mr Pluke,
We are in receipt of your letter about the rediscovery of the trough in England but have to inform you that the Golden Horse Trough of Siena (l'abbeveratoio del cavallo di Siena) does not exist, and has never existed. It is pure legend. The trough in question is clearly no concern of ours, nor does it belong to this city. I thank you for your interest.

And it bore an illegible signature.

'Why do they not acknowledge it?' asked Millicent. 'You'd think that after six hundred years, they would be glad to have it back.'

'I have a theory,' said Pluke. 'It was installed just before the Black Death and people, as well as horses, would drink from its waters. I think the authorities blamed the water for the spread of the plague and so disposed of the trough. Later, of course, it was shown that it was not the water but rats and fleas which were the source of the plague. Imagine the embarrassment of the authorities, having disposed of such a prestigious trough for such a false and ill-considered reason . . . so I think they have denied its existence ever since. They dare not admit they wrongly disposed of it, so they deny its existence. Over the years, who can dispute it? It has been wiped from their history, all that is left is an unsupported legend. It was discarded and left for an enterprising English gentleman to find and take back to England. Not an easy job, I am sure, but if such determined people could bring Cleopatra's Needle here, others could cope with a marble horse trough. That is just a theory of course, we may never know the real answer. But come along, Millicent, it's time to drive me out to the museum. Am I smart enough to have my photograph taken?'

There was a little ceremony at the trough, now gleaming in its wonderful golden marble, and Pluke had his photograph taken for the museum's records. And then, in his little thank-you speech, he said:

'Mr Porter, I have heard from Siena. As ever, they deny the existence of this trough and want nothing to do with it. I suggest you keep it here, perhaps linked to the water supply which serves the pond, and then it will fulfil its original purpose. Instead of serving Palio horses, it could serve Tally-ho horses!' and he laughed at his little joke.

'Mr Pluke, how generous! I would have thought it was yours by right, that you should have custody of it.'

'No, it belongs here, Mr Porter, it is part of this establishment and will become an asset for the museum, I am sure. It will help you recover from your visitor downturn for once the news gets around the horse trough fraternity, they will flock to see this, the most famous horse trough in the world. And I don't think it will bring any more curses or bad luck.'

'You mean the bad luck, the curse or whatever you call it, came from this, not the snuff boxes?'

'If indeed there is such a thing as that curse then, yes it

could emanate from this trough. If so, it was because this wonderful and historic piece of construction was so ignominiously dumped into that pond, after being equally ignominiously cast aside from its original purpose in Italy. I am so grateful it was rescued all those years ago by some relation of the de Kowscott-Hawkes and brought to Tillabeck Hall, and then here. I suspect it once stood in the village, outside the inn which was also owned by the family, hence the inn's name, although I accept that trough may have been a replica or even a poor copy, but when it was eventually brought to this house, unwanted it would seem, it found a secondary use as a plinth for the nymph, hidden in the pond. I have no idea why that was done. Perhaps someone was searching for it, and it was concealed from view in case of theft? Who knows. At the time of my research, of course, I had no cause even to think the marble trough in the inn's name was in any way linked to the famous Siena trough – that is grounds for further research. Now, it has all come to light in a most satisfactory manner, and once the trough is established with its new water supply, and perhaps with horses coming into your grounds to enjoy its waters, I think all thought of curses and bad luck will evaporate. Just to be sure, of course, you could always place a horseshoe nearby – with the points upwards!'

'We shall make a plaque in your honour, Mr Pluke. We shall have a formal launch day once the installation processes are complete. I shall invite the press and we shall make the most of our new folklore asset, even if it is from overseas. Perhaps you will unveil it for us?'

'That will be my great pleasure,' said Montague Pluke.

On their way home in the car, Montague said, 'I must inform Father O'Flynn and Mr Green, Millicent. I feel sure they will be interested and I am sure Mr Green will be able to sell his miniature plastic troughs at this museum. You know, if I had not gone to Siena this would never have happened, the trough could have remained hidden for

255

ever. What a piece of luck!' and he thought of his rabbit's foot.

'Or if I hadn't bought the little plastic trough that Mr Green had made from the snuff box in the museum . . .' and Millicent smiled in her contentment.